PRAISE FOR SIGNA

"In many ways, *Signal to Noise* is a coming-of-age tale, but it's also the tale of what comes after—and what happens when forces beyond our control, magical or otherwise, are better left that way."

NPR

"Haunting and beautifully nuanced, *Signal to Noise* is a magical first novel."

The Guardian

"The book is this rich, elaborate symphony of awesome that defies simple definitions."

Kirkus

"Vibrantly new... one of the most important fantasy debuts of the year."

Locus

"Plenty of books use magic to talk about coming-of-age stories and the secrets that people bury... but few of them are as sad, or as evocative, as Silvia Moreno-Garcia's new novel *Signal to Noise*."

io9

"If you like well drawn characters, cool tunes and lashings and lashings of nostalgia, then you should check this out."

Starburst Magazine

This charming literary fantasy will resonate for readers of all ages."

Barnes & Noble Sci-Fi and Fantasy Blog

"Numerous '80s musical references make this unusual story a welcome blast from the past."

Publisher's Weekly

"*Signal to Noise* is a perfect young adult crossover novel, full of appeal, diverse characters & setting, wonderful writing— and magic."

School Library Journal

"Refreshing, lively and unique, Moreno-Garcia's debut novel is a triumph."

RT Book Reviews

Signal to Noise

This edition published 2022 by Solaris
First published 2015 by Solaris
an imprint of Rebellion Publishing Ltd,
Riverside House, Osney Mead,
Oxford, OX2 0ES, UK

www.solarisbooks.com

ISBN: 978-1-78618-644-7

10 9 8 7 6 5 4 3 2 1

A CIP catalogue record for this book is available from the
British Library.

Designed & typeset by Rebellion Publishing

Printed in the United Kingdom

Signal to Noise

SILVIA MORENO-GARCIA

SOLARIS

Mexico City, 2009

MECHE FOLDED THE magazine and finally decided to look out the window. The Federal District lay below, a great beast with no beginning and no end, towers and buildings rising and dotting the valley. The roads were twisted snakes criss-crossing its surface, the cars tiny ants racing to their anthill. Twenty million people all gathered together—smashed against each other in the subway, crammed into the buses—with the Angel of Independence saluting them from above its pedestal.

It was eighteen years since she'd seen the city. Twenty since she'd last seen her father.

Now he was dead.

He had been pickling his liver for three decades and smoking since he turned twelve, but she'd thought him immortal.

Meche rubbed the bridge of her nose.

She didn't even have a black dress. She knew her dad would have said to wear whatever the hell she wanted: dead is dead. But her mother would expect black. The whole nine days of mourning. The meals they'd feed the guests. The nightly prayers.

If it had been up to Meche she would have cremated

him and tossed his ashes in the Gulf of California, like he wanted. But her mother had insisted on the casket, the funeral, the prayers to follow.

She collected her bags and pulled the luggage, trying to find the familiar face among the sea of strangers.

"Meche!"

Her cousin Jimena stepped forward, giving her a big hug and a kiss on each cheek. Jimena's hair was dyed a fake-looking red. She wore a lot more makeup than Meche remembered. Jimena's lipstick was so dark it looked purple and Meche could feel the greasy traces of it on her face.

"Girl, how was your trip?"

"Alright," Meche said, rubbing off the smudges of lipstick with her hand. "I thought my mom was picking me up."

"She's too busy. Your dad didn't make any arrangements."

"Ah."

That sounded like him. Inconsiderate until the end. He was probably chuckling from beyond the grave thinking of how, even in death, he could screw everyone over. Because that was her father.

Jimena's car was very small and there were plush toys sitting on the back seat of it. A Garfield was stuck on a window, grinning. It had been there since the 80s.

Jimena turned the key and the car sputtered into life. Meche could not see a CD player. Just the old cassette deck.

"I heard you're working with computers now," Jimena said. "Do you build them?"

Her cousin switched on the radio and ear-cringing

pop music filled the car. Clearly Jimena's taste had not improved with time.

"Programming."

"Well, you sure had the brains for it. We were all drinking beer on the weekends and you were doing your math homework. You were such a nerd."

"I remember."

"Do you make much money? You must if you can fly your mom over to Oslo for Christmas every year."

"The benefits of being a nerd," Meche said with a shrug.

"Do you remember what you used to wear? Oh, my God. I remember that dress you had on at Tita's party."

"I remember you were hot," Meche shot back.

Jimena did not seem to catch the pointed use of the past tense and smiled, very proud of herself. "Yes. Absolutely. Hey, do you remember..."

Meche looked at the little kid juggling balls while the traffic light glowed crimson. The yellow and red balls flew up and down in the air. He took a bow, then walked by the cars, cap in hand. Meche rolled down the window and gave him a bill.

Jimena frowned.

"You shouldn't do that," Jimena told her.

"What?"

"Give money to the street kids."

She shouldn't be in Mexico City either, breathing the sticky, grey air of the city and filling her lungs with pollution, but she was.

Jimena took out a pack of cigarettes, pulled one out and lit it.

Meche disliked smoke and smokers. They reminded her of her father. It had never mattered that he made his living through his voice and that cigarettes could—would—one day ruin it. He never quit. He chain-smoked and he even did it inside the radio studio, even though it was forbidden.

"Do you want one?"

"No," Meche said sternly. She rolled the window down.

It wasn't any better with the window rolled down, but it was a symbolic gesture. She pulled out her music player and picked a playlist, pressing the earbuds into place.

"I'm going to close my eyes," she told Jimena.

She did and pumped the volume up, listening to Nina Simone. Don't Let Me Be Misunderstood. The Animals covered it and Santa Esmeralda made it famous, but Nina sang it like it was nobody's business. Powerful blues and a voice that just punched you in the gut.

She let Nina sing to her, watching the city fly by. The old neighbourhood began revealing itself. Buildings had come down. The pharmacy had been replaced by condos. The bakery was gone, in its place a bank. The park seemed intact, still shitty and desolate, with its concrete benches and its sad trees. The teenagers used to make out there, by the bushes, but not Meche.

The cantina remained and she turned her head to stare at the men standing by the entrance, almost expecting her father to be there, waving back to her after drinking a dozen reposados.

Jimena touched her shoulder and Meche took out the earbuds.

"I said you'll never believe who I saw the other day."

Meche did not know and frankly did not care, but she understood she should bite her tongue and try to be congenial.

"Who?" she asked.

"Okay. Tall. Dark hair. He used to play with you when you were a kid."

"I have no idea."

"You're not even trying!"

Meche was not in the mood for trying. The drawers of her memory were shut tight, and with good reason. She had hated the neighbourhood and everyone living in it. If she'd had a can of gasoline when she was about fifteen, she would have organized the biggest bonfire and laughed like Nero while it burned.

She had promised herself nothing would drag her back to that ugly web of streets and peeling paint, stray dogs and factory workers leaning against the walls of the corner store, back to the circle of hell from which she had escaped.

"I'll give you another clue," Jimena said. "He used to draw on his shoes with markers."

Meche had grown to become a person of a certain composure. Things took place inside her head and heart, but she did not let people take a peek, preferring to show them only the smallest ripples of herself. Jimena's words, however, had the capacity to make her forget about her cool exterior and she turned her head whip-quick, staring at Jimena with wide eyes.

"Sebastián?"

"That's the one," Jimena said chuckling.

"I figured he moved."

God, she didn't want to see him again. If he was living with his mother she would probably run into him.

"He did. But his mom's been sick and he's come back; been looking over her."

"She still lives in the area?"

"Same apartment."

Three blocks from Meche. Past the tortilleria. Fourth floor. Blue curtains with sunflowers. Knock three times. That was the code.

"He has a fancy car. He got hot," Jimena said.

Meche laughed.

"No, really. He was such a dweeb. Who would have thought?"

He had never been ugly, but Jimena wouldn't have noticed back then. His skin had been too dark, his hair too black, for Jimena to fancy him. Like all the girls in the neighbourhood, Meche included, Jimena would have gone for the blond, hazel-eyed Constantino.

"I was the dweeb," Meche muttered. "He was the freak."

"I always figured you two would end up together," Jimena said.

"In a parallel universe where I didn't want to rip out his asshole, maybe."

"I never got that. You guys were sewn together at the hip and one day you just stopped talking."

"Childhood friendships don't last."

Jimena laughed loudly, her painted mouth open wide.

"He used to have that stupid motorcycle and you guys used to ride it all around the block. Oh, my God, it was so old! It used to make so much noise! It was falling apart and you'd jump on it together and think you were so cool!"

They had been cool. Sebastián had been gangly and greasy-haired, Meche as developed as an eleven-year old boy with pimples dotting her face. They'd both dressed in atrocious clothes and the company they kept—sickly, chubby little Daniela, with the stash of Twinkies and Chocotorros under her bed—didn't help.

But they *had* been cool. For a little while. When magic was real.

And she had cared the world for him.

And he'd said, once, "Let's run away." On the old motorcycle, of all things. Like it would even make it to the outskirts of the city, never mind to the highway. "Let's just run away from this fucking place, this fucking city, this fucking everything."

And Meche, staring at the maps on his wall.

The map of France and the map of Spain. The Arctic circle.

Because they were going to take over the world.

Together.

Fucking Sebastián. Fucking, fucking Sebastián.

Daniela, too.

No, childhood friendships will never last. No friendship will ever last.

"You know, I don't remember that," Meche said, lying with a flat voice. "I don't remember any of that."

"Really?"

"I remember you looked like a marshmallow in your quinceañera dress."

"Oh, well. It was a while back."

Meche put her earbuds back in and pressed play, hoping that was the last bit of chatter she would have to endure. She tried to stare ahead and focus on Nina's voice, but despite her attempt not to look, she craned her head and glanced at Sebastián's building as they drove past it.

She wanted to know if the curtains were blue.

They were green.

This made her feel relieved. Like the building was saying, "Hey Meche, it's not 1988. You are here. In the present. Relax."

There was movement by the curtain and, for a moment, Meche thought Sebastián was about to pop up, in the window, and she'd be looking straight at him. The prospect of seeing him there, framed by the old window, caused her to panic, as though it wasn't just some guy she'd known as a teenager, but the damn shark from *Jaws*.

Nobody looked out the window and Meche let out her breath slowly.

Three blocks later Jimena parked the car. Meche pulled her luggage from the trunk while Jimena looked for the keys to the building, which were sitting somewhere in the abysmal depths of her huge purse. After a small eternity, Jimena pulled out her key chain and pushed the heavy front door open.

Meche dragged her bags into the hallway, stopping to glance at the statue of the Virgin of Guadalupe sitting on its niche with the plastic flowers and the bare light bulb.

The long, dark hallway led towards a wide staircase. Meche rested a hand on the bannister. This building looked the same. The changes that had dotted the neighbourhood had not reached inside. Stepping up would mean stepping into a replica of her past. She was afraid of bumping into the ghost of her dad and slipping into bitter memories.

But hadn't she done that already?

Jimena went past her, up the steps and turned to look at her.

"What?"

"Nothing," Meche said, hauling her suitcase.

What the hell. She was here.

Mexico City, 1988

MECHE DID NOT do sports. She resented the uniform they had to wear each Tuesday and Thursday: short white shorts and white shirt. As though they were trapped in the 1950s. Had no one heard of pants and sweatshirts in the intervening decades? Besides, she had no desire to chase after a ball, like an eager puppy.

As a result, Meche tried to spend as much time as she could evading gym class. When she was forced to participate in some group activity, she stood at the back, listened to her Walkman. Her classmates knew not to pass her the ball. A tacit understanding—Meche was invisible—took place.

When the students gathered in the central patio of the school and put up the nets Meche grabbed a cassette and began listening to Serú Girán singing Canción de Alicia en el País, about the dictatorship in Argentina. She had reached the part where the walruses have vanished when a ball hit her smack in the face.

Meche pressed her hands against her nose and heard the unmistakable, loud laughter of Teófilo spreading across the play yard.

Squinting, feeling her face tingling with pain, Meche stared at the boy.

Meche had a lot of little hates nestled in her heart, but she reserved the biggest for Teófilo, the bully of the class. He was tall, fat and liked to slap the asses of all the girls in his class. When he tried to slap Meche's ass, she told him to go to hell and he had made it his mission that fall to get back at her.

One day she found her Math book had been defaced with a big red marker. The pages had been marked with UGLY WHORE. Someone stole her sweater and dumped it in a puddle. She earned herself a new nickname: Unibrow. Meche had no proof this was the work of Teófilo, but she knew. The evidence was in his smug grin.

She knew perfectly well that Teófilo had done this on purpose and she knew perfectly well there was nothing she could do to get back at him.

"Are you alright?" Daniela asked.

Meche nodded. "Yeah."

Meche wiped her mouth with the back of her hand. She tasted copper and rage.

MECHE SLAMMED THE door to her room and fell back on the bed, the cool compress pressed against her face. She tried for serenity because there was no benefit in reliving the whole episode. But her stomach was an ugly black pit which had to be filled with something.

She filled it with music.

Meche put her dad's copy of The Doors' debut album on the portable record player. The cymbals clanged and Break on Through bounced against the walls as she stared at the ceiling thinking about Teófilo. Thinking how much she hated him. Thinking how much she wished she could hurt him.

But really, what could she do?

Meche could not appeal to a higher power. She could not seek assistance from the teachers or her parents or the other kids.

Meche didn't have anything except the record sleeves strewn around her bed as she pictured that big bully.

Teófilo had to be stopped.

In a corner of her room, the thumb-tacked poster of Jim Morrison agreed.

So she played the record and she tried to believe. Tried to hold on to that slim thread of hope that something was going to happen soon. Something good. Because, damn it, something *had* to happen.

Jim Morrison yelled "break on through" and she pictured Teófilo breaking, shattering like a piece of glass. She imagined her foot slamming on his arm and the arm crumbling like a sugar cookie.

When the song finished playing she got up, moved the tone-arm and began playing it again. She turned the volume up and the room vibrated. She felt very tired all of a sudden, as though this great weight had descended upon her, crushing her chest. Meche closed her eyes.

MONDAY. HOMEWORK DONE. Heavy textbooks stuffed inside the backpack. White socks—which looked yellow—on. Meche kissed her grandma goodbye—her mother had already left for the pharmacy, her dad was sleeping after a late night of drinking—and headed to school.

She took a short cut instead of her usual route because she did not feel like talking to Sebastián. She did not feel like talking to anyone. There was still a bitterness in her stomach and she felt like nursing her wounds alone, to the tune of her cassettes. She was tired and irritated, dark circles around her eyes a quiet testimony to her unpleasant weekend.

So she walked to school by herself, feet shuffling slowly towards their destination.

Around eleven, she encountered Teófilo on the school's main staircase. She was coming down and he was going up.

He didn't see her. He was busy chatting with his friends. Meche felt like slamming his head against the wall and beating him senseless. She gripped her Walkman and flipped the cassette.

And then, just then, Teófilo slipped. There was no reason why he should slip: no obstacle, nothing at all. But his feet stumbled, as if hitting an invisible barrier. It was just as she had been picturing it all weekend: he simply tumbled down the stairs. Bam! Slipped, fell at a weird angle and suddenly he was splayed on the floor, whining like a baby. A big asshole like that, just bawling his eyes out.

She watched him, crumpled at the bottom of the stairs, his notebooks lying all around him on the floor, and realized he had broken his arm.

His friends tried to help him up.

Meche stomped over one of the open notebooks, leaving her footprint upon Teófilo's homework.

She chuckled. A few minutes later as she was walking to

Arts and Crafts, she realized it had not been a coincidence. It couldn't be a coincidence.

It was the record's fault. It was a spell, like in grandma's tales. It was the moment she'd been waiting for.

MECHE RUSHED DOWN the hallway, her notebook pressed against her chest. She went into the bathroom and leaned close to a mirror, staring at her reflection, trying to see if there was a visible change. Did magic change you?

The mirror was old and had a thin crack near the bottom. It reflected the pea-green sink which matched the tiles. It revealed a teenager, long hair neatly pulled back in a ponytail and smeared in place with a generous amount of lemon juice and hair gel. It showed her slightly rumpled navy school uniform with the gold buttons. It did not, however, provide proof of any great psychic or magical powers.

She had not sprouted an extra finger or changed her eye colour. She was Meche. The same Meche who had walked the one dozen blocks between home and school that morning, plaid skirt hitting her below the knee, an egg torta tucked in her knapsack for lunch, three yellow pencils and a blue pen tucked in a pencil case.

Meche stared at her reflection for a long time, ignoring the bell which indicated a change of classes.

Three girls walked into the bathroom, chatting and giggling together. Isadora Galván and her two hierophants. They gave her a weird look, like it was some bizarre occurrence to run into her even though they were all in the same grade. School girls went to the bathroom in packs. Meche only had Daniela and Sebastián, and she couldn't giggle outside the stalls while Sebastián peed, so her pack was immediately nonexistent.

Which reminded her that she needed to find Daniela.

She walked out and headed to the second floor, trying to poke her head through the window and see if Daniela was in Typing.

Daniela was sitting at the other end of the room. The machines went ding-ding clang-clang as the girls bent over the keys. Old Miss Viridiana sat half-asleep behind her desk, her hands folded over her tummy.

Meche waved to her. Daniela did not see her.

"Dani. Psst."

Daniela was busy looking at what she was typing.

Meche ripped a piece of paper from her notebook, balled it up and tossed it at Daniela. It hit her on the head. Daniela turned around.

"Hey," Meche said.

Daniela moved towards the window, glancing at Miss Viridiana to make sure she was still half-asleep.

"Why aren't you in class?" she asked.

"Teófilo broke his arm."

"How?"

"He fell down the stairs."

"Is he with the nurse? Is he alright?"

"Who cares?" Meche said. "I think I discovered something cool."

"What?"

"Magic."

Real magic, the kind grandmother talked about. Her father did not believe grandma's wild tales of shape-changing witches and amulets which could heal the sick. Meche, however, was fascinated by this stuff.

"Are you and Sebastián talking about weird stuff again?" Daniela asked, wrinkling her nose. The other kids thought Daniela was odd, but then everyone thought Meche was even weirder. That little shit, David Sanz, called her a Satanist because she once wore an Iron Maiden t-shirt to a kermesse.

"No. This doesn't have anything to do with that."

"I don't like it when you talk about that devil-worshipper."

"Oh, my god, Aleister Crowley was not a devil-worshipper."

"Mercedes Vega."

Shit. Meche turned, trying to don her most innocent expression.

Principal Estrada was a thin, unpleasant woman. She dyed her hair blonde and wore a grey, buttoned up sweater every day of the week. She enjoyed patrolling the hallways, ordering the girls who had folded their skirt in order to show more leg to pull the skirts down, ordering others to wipe the lipstick from their faces, telling the boys to tuck their shirts and cut their hair. When she couldn't catch you committing an infraction, she'd make one up. Like, "Don't stare at me so oddly, Vega," or, "Why are you walking funny, Vega?"

Sebastián called her Frankenstrada behind her back and she did kind of have a resemblance to Boris Karloff, what with the square-shaped head and the general stiffness.

Estrada glared at Meche, her thin eyebrows arched with contempt.

"What class are you supposed to be in?"

"Arts and Crafts."

"And why aren't you in Arts and Crafts?"

"I had to pee."

"What, do you have the bladder of a two-year-old? You were hanging out by the bathrooms an hour ago."

Meche did not understand how Estrada knew the comings and goings of all students but she did. And, indeed, Meche had been hanging out by the bathrooms just an hour ago.

"Get yourself to your classroom this instant."

"Yes, Miss Estrada," she muttered.

It was not like anything exciting was going to happen in Arts and Crafts. They were supposedly making papier-mâché sculptures that week—alebrijes, bizarre creatures from Mexican folklore, part bird, part lizard and part whatever you wanted—but Professor Ortega liked to drone on about Art and quickly lost his train of thought, which meant they did precious few crafts. At least it wasn't Home Economy.

Meche went down the stairs, crossing the patio. Like any decent Mexican school, Queen Victoria had an interior square where the students could gather for recess. Most of the classrooms were located on the north side of this square in a structure that resembled a big box of Kleenex with holes, which some idiot with a desire to create prisons had built in the 70s. To the east there were the great metal double-doors which allowed access to the school and Don Fermín—the school guard who made sure nobody left the premises—sleeping on his stool. There was really very little need for Fermín. If any students wanted to escape the school they could follow the wall towards the west side and climb it at an angle hidden by a clump of trees, which passed as their version of nature among the cement.

Also to the west was another, smaller gate which connected the junior high and high school to the primary school.

To the south was what had once been the original Queen Victoria in the 1940s: a great, old Mexican house, three stories high. It had housed an all-girls contingent before mixed education became fashionable among the middle class. Now it was where the school's offices sat. This was also where the Arts and English classes took place.

Meche trotted up the stairs and slipped in the back, sitting next to Sebastián. He was drawing a skull on his desk, carefully decorating the teeth with his black marker. The teacher had begun to talk about form and meaning, which meant they could whisper in peace for at least another fifteen minutes.

"I thought you weren't coming."

"Did I miss something?"

"No," Sebastián said, snorting.

"I had a close encounter with Frankenstrada," Meche said. "She thinks I shouldn't pee."

"How are you supposed to do that?"

"I don't know. Carry a bottle around with me and go in there?"

"She told me I have to cut my hair again this morning or she'll cut it for me."

Sebastián had a pseudo-punk aesthetic going and he liked to style his black hair with an obscene amount of hairspray.

It was still pretty tame compared to what real, hardcore punks did with their hair, but then again the Queen Victoria didn't smile too kindly on any of that stuff so you really couldn't try a mohawk. Plus, punk was a bit lame.

Rich Mexican kids who could visit the USA and England imported this wild aesthetic, but it was all show and no substance. Sure, some good bands had emerged from that primordial ooze, like Atoxxxico and Ritmo Peligroso, but Meche was pretty tired of the studded belts and bracelets, patches, and junk which supposedly went with being punk. It wasn't cool.

The only reason why Meche could stomach Sebastián was because he was pseudo-punk. He knew, or cared, little about punk music or punk culture in general. But he liked sci-fi and horror movies and had watched *Mad Max* obsessively, to the point of using a couple of old car tires to build himself what he termed a "rubber exo-skeleton" on top of his leather jacket. For him it was the aesthetic thrill of the whole thing.

"You should get a tattoo and really piss her off," she said.

"Sure. Then I'll get kicked out by my mom."

Meche leaned her chin against the back of her hand and looked at Sebastián's skull with its wide grin.

"Hey, can you come to my place after school? I want to show you something."

"It's meatball dinner."

"So go home later and have the meatballs."

"They'll be cold. Plus, my brother will eat them all if I don't show up." Sebastián paused. "What's your grandma making for dinner?"

"I dunno. Green beans with egg."

"Gross."

"Come on, what are you going to do all afternoon by yourself? Homework?"

"Read and draw," he muttered.

"Come on over. Dani's coming."

Meche had not even told Daniela she was invited, but she assumed Daniela would tag along. Dani was as different from Sebastián as night was from day, always dressed in pink, her Barbies still lined up on her shelves, an Easy-Bake oven in her room—even though the three of them were fifteen—and a predilection for soap operas. She liked listening to Lucerito, which made Meche want to barf, and thought Luis Miguel was the hottest man in the world, which was a double-barf. As far as Meche was concerned the only way she would listen to Ahora te Puedes Marchar was if someone tied her hands and feet with duct tape, then pushed a rag into her mouth to drown her screams.

But hey, Daniela was a good listener and of the three friends she was the one with the most money, which meant a chance to have free tickets to the movie theatre and loads of pop courtesy of her father, the accountant of a small furniture store.

"Mmm," said Sebastián. "You're not going to play boleros, are you? That shit's so *old*."

Meche punched him on the arm and he turned to stare at her with his usual stiff, offended face.

"You're talking about Agustin Lara, you idiot. One of the greatest Mexican songwriters of all time."

"You know, I really do want to have meatballs. Why don't you come over to my place?"

"My mom doesn't like me going over to your place."

Meche's mom had this over-developed fear of teenage pregnancies, courtesy of too many articles in too many ladies' magazines. It was a bit hard to get pregnant when Meche had never even been kissed, let alone had a boyfriend, but Meche's mother considered every boy in a twenty-block radius to be a danger to her daughter. As if anyone would try and date her.

"Fine," Sebastián said. "I'll come."

Meche tried to grab the marker Sebastián was using, but he slapped her hand away and hunched over, busy with his drawing. She sighed, unrolled the headphones and pressed play on the Walkman.

The tape rolled and Black Sabbath sang about children of tomorrow and revolution while she tapped her fingers against the desk, waiting for the bell to ring.

"So what you're saying essentially is that you've gone nuts."

Sebastián lay on the floor of Meche's room, drawing in his notebook. He had traded the skulls for stars and was busy creating a night sky.

"Why is it so nuts to believe in magic? My grandmother says there are witches and in the countryside you can see them fly at nights in the shape of balls of fire."

"Your grandma is a really good cook, but no offence, I wouldn't take her stories at face value."

"Why not?" Meche asked, sitting down in front of Sebastián. "You're the one who told me about spiritism and mediums and shit in the nineteenth century."

"I believe in ghosts," ventured Daniela, raising her hand weakly.

"See?" Meche said. "She believes."

"Okay. So how about we play Teenage Idol. Do I get to become Emanuel tomorrow and sing at a bunch of concerts?" Sebastián asked.

"Why don't we find out?"

"You're serious."

Meche stared at Sebastián. He ripped out the page from his notebook, balled it and threw it in her wastebasket.

"Why shouldn't music have power? My dad says it's the most powerful thing in the world. Nietzsche says that without music, life would be a mistake."

"Don't quote me Nietzsche. I showed you Nietzsche," Sebastián said in an offended tone.

"Why can't music be magic? Aren't spells just words you repeat? And what are songs? Lyrics that play over and over again. The words are like a formula."

All around Meche's room posters of band members and enlarged album covers looked down at them. Freddie Mercury leaned back on stage, Pedro Infante played the guitar. In a corner the Beatles were ready to ride the Yellow Submarine. Stacks of records were piled along Meche's floor, cassettes poked out from a couple of boxes.

"Okay, how about backmasking?" said Meche. "Doesn't Aleister Crowley suggest that adepts should listen to records reversed?"

"Yes," said Sebastián. "But that doesn't..."

"And all these people flipping out because they think Led Zeppelin's Stairway to Heaven has a Satanic message?"

"So we should play records backwards? Do a Satanic ceremony?"

"Guys, I just want to remind you I have to be home by seven," Daniela said. "I'm also not allowed to do any Satanic stuff."

Sebastián and Meche looked at their friend. Daniela blinked and went back to working on the personality test culled from a teen magazine she was completing.

"Not a Satanic ceremony. You're always talking about this stuff. Crowley? Rasputin had to be killed three times?"

"Because I like to read lots of weird shit. But I don't want to go around brewing poisons and stuff. People already think I'm odd, I don't want to give them any extra ammunition," Sebastián muttered.

Sebastián began drawing on the side of his tennis shoes. More stars in black marker.

Meche wanted to hit them both on the back of the head. They didn't get it! She expected it from Daniela because Daniela got about 10 percent of what went on in the world, but Sebastián? Sebastián loved this stuff. They had become friends four years before because Meche had been listening to Alan Parsons Project's *Tales of Mystery and Imagination* and she didn't get the references. So she decided to ask the only person in her class who might have the answer. At first Sebastián had been offended she didn't know Edgar Allan Poe, but she had been equally offended he didn't know Alan Parsons Project because they sang Games People Play from *The Turn of a Friendly Card* which, in her opinion, was a very nice concept album. Not the best, but nice. The best was an easy pick.

Most people would probably say the concept album of all time was *The Dark Side Of The Moon*, but Meche preferred The Kinks' *Arthur (Or the Decline and Fall of the British Empire)*. Her parents had met thanks to that album.

"Aren't you curious to see if it works?" Meche asked.

Sebastián capped his marker and stuffed it back in his pocket.

"It'll never work," he said with finality. "I have to go. I have a couple of hours bagging groceries tonight. Later."

Meche scowled as Sebastián stepped out of her room. Great. The big ninny was not going to play ball. Daniela, looking pained, patted Meche on the knee.

"Cheer up. Why don't we go to my house and bake cupcakes?"

"It better not be in the Easy-Bake oven. The stuff you make in the Easy-Bake oven tastes like ass," Meche muttered.

Daniela's mother didn't like it when her daughter was in the kitchen, afraid she'd burn or cut herself, therefore Daniela was restricted to playing with toys much too young for her. Sometimes the girls escaped the restrictions and cooked in Meche's apartment. She was hoping Daniela would suggest they do exactly that, but Daniela chuckled.

"My mom wants me home early. It's the Easy-Bake and whatever snacks we can find in my kitchen, or nothing."

"Your mother is going to cut bits of celery and make us eat that," Meche muttered. "Why did she have to get into macrobiotics?"

"Race you the store and we can split a bag of chips and she'll never know," Daniela said.

"Deal."

MECHE COPIED THE linear equations neatly into her notebook. She was good at math.

Daniela wasn't. Sebastián sucked even more.

Most students thought math was boring, but math was the foundation for so many things, including music. Music of the stars and all, and hadn't Kepler...

Meche held her pencil, suspended over the page. She looked at the book again, at the black letters and numbers against the white pages.

Equations. Letters are not letters in equations. They stand for numbers and if you balance them right, you'll find the right number. What if it was the same for music? Songs stand for something, don't they? They have a symbolic value. So if you were to somehow balance them... ugh, she was getting herself all into knots.

She heard the door opening and looked up. Her father shuffled in, taking off his coat and putting it on a peg.

"Hey, Meche," he said, patting her head as he walked by. "Doing homework?"

"Math," she said.

"What did you eat today?"

"Grandma made green beans. Should I heat them up?"

"Don't bother. I'll have some cookies."

He sat down, poured himself a glass of milk and opened a box of animal crackers. Meche's dad and her mom had married young and sometimes he still looked like half a kid himself when he sat hunched over a glass of milk, his shoulder-length hair pulled back.

He was the coolest adult Meche knew. She wanted to be like him when she grew up.

"Does mom have another late shift at the pharmacy?" her dad asked.

"All week," Meche said, shrugging.

"I don't remember her telling me."

"She did."

"Your grandmother in bed yet?"

"An hour ago."

Her dad ate a cracker and lit a cigarette, nodding absentmindedly.

"What did you play today?"

"Oh, let me see," he said. "Miguel Bosé. A bit of Sabina. A bit of everything."

Ever since Meche had been born her dad had worked as a DJ. He had originally intended to study veterinary medicine but had never cared for the career, which he had been more or less forced into by his family. He eventually dropped it altogether and went to work at a record store, where he'd met Meche's mom. The radio station was where he was most comfortable. The microphone was his natural prop. Without it he seemed unreal.

He cut a cracker in half and dipped it in the milk.

"Do you believe in magic?"

"What's your grandma been telling you?" he asked. "I hope you're not believing any of her kooky stories about putting saints upside down so you can get a boyfriend."

"No. I mean like serious magic."

"Nothing serious about magic. Just superstitions."

"What about music?"

"What about it?"

"I don't know," Meche muttered, looking at her equations.

"Cracker?"

Meche nodded, taking a cracker shaped like a lion.

Her dad closed the box and took the glass to the kitchen, leaving it in the sink. Then he grabbed his jacket.

"I'm going out."

He didn't have to say he'd be at the bar. Weekdays it was at the bar. Weekends it was the pool hall. Sometimes, when he stayed out too late, her mom had her go pull him out. Meche felt humiliated when this happened.

Her mother was out tonight, so maybe Meche wouldn't have to put on the sweater and head there. It wasn't far. It was just… annoying.

She wished he'd come home early. Otherwise her parents might fight. Again.

"Be careful," she said.

"Yup. Finish your homework, alright? Don't skim on the reading. You can't read, you can't do shit. No matter how good you are at adding numbers."

"I'm going to work with computers, dad," she reminded him.

She had decided this two years before when her parents finally bought her a Commodore 64. She had learned how to program little games on it and thought she could make a go at it as a real career when she grew up.

"You still need to read."

"Yes, captain."

"Arrr. Don't stay up late."

Meche raised her hand, saluting her dad. She watched him put on his old leather jacket and step out.

She dropped her hand and chewed on her pencil, starring at the numbers.

IT WAS A rainy morning. Meche jumped and tiptoed around puddles to the rhythm of Soda Stereo. She shook her head and snapped her fingers.

A hand grasped her shoulder and she frowned, turning around. Sebastián Soto, lanky and dour, just like every morning of the week, stood with an umbrella under his arm. He was the tallest kid in her class and when he stood like that, grimly looking down at her, Meche had to agree with the kids that teased him: he did resemble Lurch from afar.

"Hey," he said. "I was thinking about what you said yesterday."

"And?"

"I don't know. Maybe we should give it a try."

"For real? When?"

"How about now?"

"School day."

"So?"

"Oh my God, you just want to skip the chemistry test."

"Maybe. But do you really want to go to school?"

"Nope."

Sebastián rocked back and forth on his shoes, which, against school regulations, he had painted with faint traces of whiteout spelling out THE RAVEN. Meche pulled up her left sock, with the broken elastic.

"Daniela will be pissed if we skip out without inviting her."

"Yeah, but her mom drives her to school. Tough luck. I'm heading to the factory. Are you coming?"

"I studied for the test."

"Why bother when you can cheat?"

Meche rolled her eyes and held on to the straps of her backpack. On the one hand she was annoyed at Sebastián for trying to miss the test. On the other hand this might be a good chance to convince him about the music and spells. He was halfway there already. She could tell. He had the same expression as he did when they had done that Ouija session. Daniela had freaked out because she had recently seen a movie about demon-possessed people, and she swore she'd never speak to them again because they were morbid and freaky, but she came back to roost with them all the same. What else could she do? It was not like any of them had much of a social circle.

"Fine," Meche said.

Sebastián led the way, purposely sinking into the puddles and splashing her.

Wanker.

Meche put her headphones on again and the cassette player told her about a voyeur staring through the window.

She followed Sebastián until they reached the abandoned pantyhose factory. Most of the windows were covered with wooden boards, but Sebastián ducked and went in through a large opening, obviously knowing what to do.

Meche leaned down.

She had never liked the pantyhose factory. The little kids enjoyed playing tag there and the older ones came to drink beer and make out, but it had always seemed so sad and grey.

She shoved her backpack in and then crawled in herself, emerging into one of the cavernous factory rooms. It was dark and she was glad when Sebastián took out a flashlight, even if he did shine it in her face.

"Let's go up," he said, handing her the flashlight.

They rushed up the stairs, their feet clattering upon the metal and making the building echo with their footsteps.

They went into a large room with scattered furniture: a table, some chairs piled in a corner. Someone—probably not the original factory workers—had dragged a lumpy, red couch into the middle of the room.

There were more windows on the second floor and fewer of these were boarded, so there was significantly more light, even though dirt had accumulated upon the panes, blurring the view. Meche walked up to the circular window on the east wall and wiped it with the sleeves of her too-large sweater, which she had inherited from her older cousin Jimena.

The neighbourhood looked different when seen like this, so diffused.

"You've been coming here a lot?" she asked.

"Not often."

Sebastián tossed his umbrella on the floor and threw himself on the couch, propping his feet up.

"So now you believe me about the magic?"

"I think you are cr-aaaa-zy," he said. "But what the hell. Life can't get any crappier, can it?"

"Was your dad home last night?" Meche asked, frowning.

Sebastián's dad wasn't living with them, but he came around periodically to collect money and beat the kids. For old time's sake.

"It's got nothing to do with him," Sebastián said, meaning it probably had everything to do with him.

She shoved his feet away and sat on the couch. Sebastián had the backpack pressed against his chest and was staring at the ceiling.

"What's it got to do with?" she asked.

"I don't know. I just wish it was all different. You know?"

"Yeah."

Meche scratched her leg and sat quietly, thinking about all the things she would change if she could. She'd get rid of the pimples. She'd get nice, new clothes. Not Jimena's hand-me-downs. Her mother would yell less. She'd go out on a date with Constantino.

"How do we do it?"

"I don't know," Meche said. "I haven't thought about it too much. I mean, we need a turntable and lots of records, I guess. We have to figure out the formula."

"So you're saying you have no idea?" he asked flatly.

"I have some idea," Meche said, feeling offended. "It's just going to take some experimenting. I need to do more research. I wonder if there are any books I can use at the school library..."

"Aha."

"We need to convince Daniela. I figure we need three people."

"Why three?"

"Because it's the first lucky prime number."

Sebastián looked at her blankly, as though she had just spoken in Dutch. She sighed.

"Stuff always comes in threes. Like there are three notes in a triad, which is your basic chord. Or the holy trinity."

"'Double, double toil and trouble; Fire burn, and caldron bubble'," he said.

"What?" Meche asked. She had no idea what he was talking about.

"Macbeth's witches," Sebastián said, frowning. "Hey, I'm not a girl. Does that matter?"

"I don't think it does. You can be a warlock, can't you?"

"I suppose. We don't have to wear capes, do we? I don't think I'd look good in one."

She felt like telling him that, yeah, they most definitely had to use capes and pointy hats, and then watching what face he made at that, but Meche decided to spare him the unnecessary cruelty.

"No."

"Good. Do you have any food? I didn't eat breakfast."

He never ate breakfast. He also tended to eat Meche or Daniela's lunch. Meche's, usually, because Daniela was less generous with her food allocations. Meche figured that if half a cheese and ham sandwich was what it took to convince Sebastián to join her cause, it would be a small price.

She took out her battered tin lunchbox and scooped the sandwich, giving him half. Sebastián munched on it and grabbed her thermos without even asking for permission, taking a big gulp.

"What are Macbeth witches?" she asked, punching one of the lumpy cushions and putting it behind her head.

"I really can't believe you are like half-illiterate."

"I'm not half-illiterate."

"You are clueless when it comes to books. Rodríguez is so going to fail you in Spanish and World Literature."

"You are going to fail all the sciences, so who's talking?"

"Blah blah," he said, opening and closing his left hand. "That's what remedials were made for."

"What are Macbeth witches?"

"*Macbeth* is a play by Shakespeare," Sebastián said, grabbing the sandwich crumbs that were left and stuffing them into his mouth. "It's about this guy who meets with these three witches and they prophesize that he'll be king. So he begins to think about it all the time and then ends up killing the guy in charge and becomes king. It's a tragedy."

"It doesn't sound too tragic to become king."

"Obviously things don't go as planned. You should read that book I gave you."

Meche had read some of the books Sebastián had given her. Correction. Probably some of the *only* books she read were the ones he gave her, but she hadn't read this particular one because she was still a little pissed off that he'd only given her a book for her birthday instead of the album she had wanted. Getting Shakespeare's sonnets and complete works for your fifteenth birthday was like getting a sweater from your mom for Christmas: bullshit.

"I'm working on it," she said. "Slowly working on it."

"Illiterate."

"Ass," she said tossing her backpack at his face.

Sebastián dodged it and shrugged. "Better an ass than to be illiterate."

"I can't hear you," Meche said, sliding to the floor and pressing the play button on her Walkman.

"What are you listening to?" Sebastián said, sliding down next to her.

Meche pulled out her extra pair of headphone and plugged it into one of the jacks. Sebastián put on the headphones. Meche pressed the rewind button. They tilted their head backs and Soda Stereo began to sing Persiana Americana from the very beginning.

MECHE TIPTOED INTO the apartment, trying to sneak into her bedroom. She was half an hour early and needed to hide for a bit. Grandmother Dolores was in the kitchen, humming. She spent most of her time there, looking after a boiling pot or frying onions and chillis, always on her feet and always ready to make a meal. She'd been a maid for many years before old age made her unemployable. Cooking had been her favourite task during that time.

"Meche, did you skip school today?"

Meche stopped in her tracks and cursed inwardly. Mama Dolores had an internal lie detector, so there was no sense in trying to fool her.

"Yeah."

"You shouldn't miss classes. Come, sit down. You can peel some potatoes. I'm making picadillo the way your mom likes it."

"What's the point? Mom and dad both eat outside."

"Well, maybe one day your mother will come home early."

Meche walked into the kitchen, dumping her backpack on one of the two plastic chairs and sitting at the table. She grabbed a peeler and began slicing the skins off the potatoes.

Mama Dolores turned on the little radio sitting next to the narrow kitchen windows and Pedro Infante began singing Amorcito Corazón while the old woman hummed and poured some oil into a frying pan. She swished the onions to the tune of the love song.

"Mama Dolores, can you tell me something and tell me the truth?"

"What, baby?"

"Were there really witches in your town?"

"Of course there were. They'd fly off at nights in the shape of great balls of fire, nestling in the trees and cackling."

"And they did magic and it worked?"

"It did. They cast all sorts of spells."

"If they were so powerful why didn't they leave the town and become billionaires?"

"Oh, magic is more complex than that. You have to give as much as you take. There's a price to everything."

"What about music? Could there be magic in music?"

"There's magic everywhere, if you look carefully," her grandmother said. "The trouble is wanting it enough, and holding on to it."

Meche slanted the peeler, slowly stripping the potato.

"What if magic..."

"You must be careful. Magic will break your heart, Meche," Mama Dolores said very seriously.

Meche frowned.

MECHE'S MOTHER, NATALIA, was good looking. When angered, however, she resembled the Medusa in one of Meche's story books. Except she still had to grow some snakes on her head. Any day now, Meche thought those would begin to sprout.

"Okay, Meche," Natalia said, from behind the pharmacy counter. "How come I got a call from school today to ask if you were sick?"

"I don't know," Meche said. "I'm just here because I need money for the tortillas and grandma doesn't have any."

"I left money on top of the refrigerator."

"It's not there."

"Your goddamn father," her mother muttered. "Did he take it?"

"I don't know."

Meche rested her chin against the glass counter and shrugged. If she had known it was going to be such a big deal to get the pesos she needed, she would have borrowed them from someone. This was Spanish Inquisition stuff.

"Wait three minutes," her mother said as she headed to the back of the pharmacy.

Meche eyed the arcade machine sitting in a corner, right by the little children's coin-operated horse and the scale that would tell you your weight and fortune. She could play a game. Or just get the hell out of the pharmacy before her mother started asking too many questions.

"Here," her mother said, coming out from behind the counter and opening her change purse, handing her two bills. "Buy the tortillas and give the rest of the money to your grandmother."

"Alright."

"Meche, if I find out that you and Sebastián Soto are skipping classes, I'm going to beat you black and blue."

"I wasn't skipping nothing," Meche said, though she was impressed by her mother's psychic skills.

VICENTE VEGA STILL had most of his hair, only a small— though increasing—gut, and a great quantity of his charm. He had, however, misplaced his common sense and his optimism as he stumbled through the streets of Mexico City. Thirty-eight—not too old, not really young—he went through life like a zombie navigating a closed course, from home to the radio cabin and from the cabin to the cantina.

On Mondays he had the seafood soup. Tuesdays the stuffed chilli. Wednesdays he fought with his wife. The weekends were for playing pool and dominoes. He drank every day.

He remembered being young once, being happy. He remembered marrying a pretty young woman he had adored and somehow stumbling into a cold, distant stranger in bed one morning. He had been his parents' pride and joy, now a sore disappointment, their eyes turned to his younger brother who had done as he was told and—his mother reminded him every time he spoke to her—had made something of himself. His brother was a licenciado and he had a big house and two nice cars, wearing good suits which threatened to explode as he moved his corpulent form around the office. At heart, his brother was still the same tricky, devious bastard he'd always been, but he played in bigger leagues now. He had set his sights squarely on the Mexican dream: lots of money and lots of women.

Vicente, always unable to understand these simplistic desires, never one to lust after lots of money or numerous broads, had looked for that elusive something else in life. Meaning. Answers that were not printed in triplicate or faxed to the office. Beauty. But life, being the bitch that she was, had denied Vicente what he asked for, had rewarded him only with ugliness and pessimism, had sunk his dreams low.

Music. He loved music. Playing it, writing songs. He'd quit veterinary school and gone to work at the record shop and then he had got the part-time stint as a DJ because—and here he could quote more than a few people—he had the most amazing voice. But that golden voice was false gold and when the demands of parenthood, of making money and getting by intruded on the band, he quit the musician bit and went full-on onto radio.

He thought this would make Natalia happy. Natalia, however, was never happy, accumulating little hates and grudges, cataloguing them by date and carefully filing them so she could pull them out later and toss them in his face.

Only Meche loved him.

She'd been born like him, Meche. Not just the looks— the shape of the eyes, the firm mouth—but his temper and his proclivities.

If he hadn't had Meche, Vicente might have gone to live at the bar forever, installed himself in a corner and drunk himself under the table. If he shuffled his feet home every night and stumbled out of bed in the mornings, it was because of his daughter.

Vicente went up the steps, trudging back into the apartment. After hanging his jacket he went towards the stereo, running his hands over the turntable. He carefully selected a record, plugged in his headphones and sat on the floor, listening to The Beatles playing in the dark as he smoked a cigarette.

He was almost done with one side of the recording when the door opened and the clatter of heels announced the presence of his wife. She turned on the lights and glanced at him.

She didn't say anything. Her heels just moved away, towards the bedroom, with a soft sort of indifference which mirrored his own.

Mexico City, 2009

THE APARTMENT HAD shrunk or had been bigger in her memory. She walked in slowly, feeling like an intruder even though she had grown up here. At some point her mother had taken down the old wallpaper and now the interior was painted in soft, institutional beiges.

Meche looked at the photos sitting all around: Natalia as a baby, Natalia as a child, Natalia at the beach. Photos of her mother's second husband, Lorenzo. Almost like an afterthought, Natalia and Meche, her teenaged face staring at the camera.

"Mercedes," her mother said as she drifted into the living room and gave her a hug. "Little Meche."

"Hey, mom," she muttered.

"How was your flight?"

"Good. Fine."

"I have had the most awful time getting tamales," her mother said, wrapping an arm around her shoulders.

"Tamales?"

"For the novena," Jimena said helpfully.

"I really wished we didn't have to do a novena," Meche said.

"There's no way around it," her mother said. "God

knows your father can use all the prayers he can get."

"Dad didn't believe in this stuff."

"I talked to the baker and we are going to have canapés for the first night," Jimena said. "He agreed to a discount, seeing as it was us."

"Good," Natalia said, patting her niece's hand. "Meche, you are going to have to go through your father's things."

Meche had barely entered the apartment and had just sat down. She looked up at her mother, surprised.

"What?"

"Well, I certainly won't have the time. I would ask Lorenzo, but it doesn't seem right to have him going through your father's clothes. And you know how he was. It's probably a mess. But some of the records are bound to be valuable."

Valuable.

"Maybe you can play some at the party," her mother said. "I have no idea what we are going to do for music."

"You want me to go to dad's apartment and see if he had records that are worth any money?"

"Ay, don't take it like that," Jimena said. "You want a coffee?"

Norwegians drank a lot of coffee; strong and black. Meche had never taken to this custom, but she had developed a tea addiction after her year in London.

"No."

"You might as well sort it out and take whatever you want," her mother said. "Whatever he had, he left it all to you. Nothing for me."

There was a pointed bitterness to her words. Meche's

father had failed her so many times and Meche got that—because dumping your family one fine day will certainly create a few grudges. And yet… the asshole was gone. No need to auction off his goods. As far as Meche was concerned, she thought they should stuff all his possessions in cardboard boxes and give them to charity. She wasn't going to go on eBay and see if someone paid a dollar for a dusty LP. But if her mother insisted, Meche would make an effort.

"I told Meche Sebastián Soto is hanging around the neighbourhood," Jimena said. "You sure you don't want a coffee?"

"Nope."

"Yes, that nice boy."

"You never liked him," Meche said.

Meche's mother chuckled and sat next to her, patting her leg. Her hair was a burnished brown. It matched the furniture. Jimena slipped out, probably to the kitchen for that coffee she yearned for.

"I did like him."

Sebastián's new car sure must be something to cause such a tremendous change of opinion in the women in Meche's family.

"Where's Lorenzo?" she asked.

"Trying to fix the paperwork and arrange the burial," her mother said, lifting her hands in the air.

"Maybe I'll go to father's apartment tomorrow," Meche muttered. "Before the funeral."

At least in her father's apartment she'd be alone. She didn't think she could stomach her mother and her cousin at this time.

*   *   *

VICENTE VEGA'S APARTMENT was smack in downtown Mexico City, in an old building which must have been quite something two hundred years before, but which was now nothing more than a tired ruin, perched at the end of an alley, waiting in the shadows. It was cold and damp as Meche walked up the stairs and when she actually opened the door to the apartment and stepped in she realized the apartment itself was even colder.

She locked the door and looked around. The first thing she noticed was a tiny kitchen that had no right to call itself a kitchen, dirty dishes piled high. She started by washing them because it was too depressing to stare at the dregs inside coffee cups and the stains of old spaghetti. Once she was done, she stood in the living room, which also served as the dining room, looking at the piles of old LPs her father had accumulated. They were sitting on shelves, but also spilled onto the floor, peeking from beneath the sofas, drowning the side table, resting upon the battered TV set.

She went to the room which served as an office, but really was nothing more than another space used to pile boxes with records, mountains of sleeves and vinyl. In a corner, forlorn, sat her father's typewriter. When his music career failed, he had tried—and never succeeded in— writing a compendium of the history of Latin American rock-and-roll. Now that she thought about it, her father had never succeeded at anything, except maybe in finding the bottom of a bottle of tequila.

She stepped into his bedroom and discovered the same

chaotic mass of records, though her father, perhaps in an effort to escape the clutter that reigned in the other parts of the apartment, had cleared a section of the wall and pinned up a large poster depicting palm trees and a sunset. The thick curtains also had a lively pattern of palm trees, this time with flamingos, so kitsch it made her wonder if it was really her father who had rented this apartment.

She remembered when she had been younger and her dad had told her he planned to spend the end of his days on a beach, watching the waves come in.

He never made it to the seaside, though he did spend several years in Guadalajara before returning to Mexico City.

His kidneys had failed him. That's what had done him in. Not the booze. The liver put up a good fight. It was the kidneys which gave up. Her mother had told her he was on dialysis, but Meche hadn't phoned him.

Meche took a look in the bathroom. The medicine cabinet was cluttered with pills and expired medications. His glasses sat on the water tank of the toilet.

She walked back to the bedroom, sat on the sagging bed and wondered what it would be like to wake every morning to the old picture of the beach, feet shuffling upon the cold floor. Dying and knowing you were dying.

On the floor, by the bed, half-hidden under a sweater, was the portable turntable. Meche moved the sweater away and looked at it, hesitantly.

Was it the same one? It seemed to be the same walnut case. The one Meche used to have in her room could play full-size LPs, so chances were it *was* the same one.

Meche grabbed it, put it on her knees and found the sticker on the side. The little heart which Daniela had left there.

That was it. But it just looked so… ordinary and worn now. No magic to it.

Would it still work?

She reached towards a stack of records on the bedside table and picked the first one off the top. The Beach Boys.

The needle went down. Good Vibrations began to play. She flipped the record sleeve around, looking at the image of the five young men. It had been released in 1966. That would have made her father… what… sixteen when it came out?

Meche opened the bedside drawer and found a stack of unpaid bills. There were some loose pages, stained with coffee smudges: notes for his glorious book. A matchbook. Tucked beneath the matchbook, like a postscript, a postcard from Puerto Vallarta. Meche looked at the remittance address but it had never been sent. It was an old Puerto Vallarta, Puerto Vallarta from the seventies, just left there to moulder in the drawer.

She closed the drawer and The Beach Boys finished their song, the needle lifted from the record and the apartment was silent.

Meche sighed and started going through the records, making three piles: throw away, sell and keep. She placed each record in the right pile, trying to maintain the keep pile as low as she could.

The silence was depressing. She could see why her father had kept the turntable by the bed, to liven his nights and mornings. She looked for another Beach Boys record, maybe *Summer Days (And Summer Nights!!)*, but it was not to be found. She settled on *Hotel California* by The Eagles—which was not quite the same thing at all—and pulled apart the curtains to see what the view was like.

But there was no view. The windows showed the grey façade of another building. She dropped the curtains and the flamingos returned, masking the greyness, cheerfully frolicking in a land of palm trees.

She remembered that she was now almost the same age her father had been when he had left them.

Mexico City, 1988

IT'S NOT THAT Meche hated school, because she didn't. She just hated the people at school, all them crawling around with their petty thoughts and their annoying habits. A few were outright assholes, like Teófilo. Others merely bumped into you on the stairs, giggled when you walked by, talked under their breath.

There were some—few and far between—who made it worth attending. Daniela and Sebastián, of course. But also Constantino. Especially Constantino Domínguez. She looked at him across the courtyard as she sat with her friends, eating her sandwich.

Sebastián had once dubbed Constantino the King of the Clones because his friends were always intent on copying his mannerisms and clothes. Sebastián also called him Floro Tinoco on account of the comic book character from *La Familia Burron*, swearing that Constantino was equally stupid and also built like a tractor. Meche only knew what all the other fifteen-year-old girls knew: Constantino had dirty-blond hair and hazel eyes, and when he smiled, he showed off perfectly straight, white teeth.

Today Constantino was standing next to Isadora Galván, a very common occurrence. They were not an item anymore, but hung out together in the way that the beautiful and popular will gravitate to each other. You could regularly find them in the Pit—which was an empty lot two blocks from school where the smokers liked to gather—and at other high school landmarks.

Isadora was certainly pretty, in a way which Meche could never expect to achieve. She had reddish-brown hair and it curled just the right amount around her shoulders. Her skin was very pale and this alone had earned her the lead in more than one school play while Meche and Daniela had to carry heavy props and scenery backstage.

Meche would have given anything to be like Isadora for a single day.

Maybe she could. If the magic worked.

"I think we should do the spell tonight," she told Daniela and Sebastián.

They didn't answer. Sebastián was also looking at Isadora, his eyes fixed on her long legs and her very short skirt. That kind of skirt looked sloppy and unflattering when Meche wore it, but on Isadora it was positively lovely. She supposed Isadora could wear a garbage bag and look amazing.

Daniela, for her part, was busy writing in her diary. Well, writing was an exaggeration. She just drew lots of little hearts with arrows going through them.

Meche snatched the diary away and hit Sebastián on the back of the head with it.

The boy looked at her, irritated.

"What?"

"I said we should do the spell tonight."

"I can't go out tonight," Daniela said.

"Who are you kidding, you can never go out," Meche muttered.

"No, I mean it."

"Then we'll go to your place."

"Okay," Daniel said demurely. "Can I have my notebook back, please?"

Meche looked at the diary and tapped her finger against the page.

"This is what we need," she told Sebastián.

"My diary?" Daniela asked.

"No, dummy. A place where we write down what we do. A grimoire."

"What's a gri-moy-re?" Daniela asked.

"You should pay more attention when we watch horror movies," Meche admonished her. "It's a recipe book for witches. We've got to have one. If we're going to do this right."

"There's really no point in explaining it to her right now when she's so distracted," Sebastián said. "We'll do it later."

Daniela pouted, but Sebastián was right. Daniela was always going off on a tangent, dreaming away, getting distracted. Sometimes it seemed the only thing Daniela's brain was able to retain was the cheesy dialogue from those romance novels she borrowed from her sister. Then again school sucked and it was no wonder Daniela didn't exactly feel like living in the moment. Before Meche and Daniela had become friends, the other kids used to steal Daniela's lunch money. One of the benefits of banding together was that they were less likely to be extorted.

Sebastián extended a hand towards Meche's juice box. She frowned, but gave it to him in the end. Sebastián was constantly broke, this despite his attempts to earn a few extra pesos by bagging groceries at the supermarket, a job, which, by the way, he was getting too old for: everyone preferred very young baggers and he was reaching the end of his career as a bag boy.

Sebastián sipped the juice, his eyes fixed on Isadora again. Isadora, probably feeling the weight of his gaze, turned her head and looked in their direction.

Sebastián immediately dropped his head, staring at the juice box between his hands. Meche smirked and jabbed him on the ribs.

LITERATURE WAS LIKE having needles pushed under her eyelids. Meche could not understand or even remotely pay attention to what was happening on the blackboard; she rested her head against the desk and tried to add numbers in her head, repeat lyrics of songs. She wondered what she would eat that afternoon.

Daniela, however, was in love with the teacher and she sat all perky and straight next to Meche, with a docile smile on her face, nodding periodically while Rodríguez—the youngest of the faculty, but no prize pie in the looks department—strolled by, babbling on about Cervantes. Windmills. Some Spanish asshole who was nuts and a fat guy on a donkey.

"What are we going to wish for?" Sebastián asked.

He wasn't taking notes either, but he didn't have to take notes. Sebastián knew all this stuff. He liked it. Hell, he had read *Moby Dick* which was as thick as a damned brick. You could maim someone with that book.

"I'm not sure," Meche said. "Something big. What do you want to wish for?"

"I'm making a list."

"God, won't he shut up," Meche whispered.

"Then he couldn't listen to himself."

Meche smirked.

"What is amusing you today, Mercedes?"

She hated it when people called her by her full name. She'd told Rodríguez this, but he refused to ever use her nickname. Meche did not reply, staring down at her book and pretending she was reading.

"No, really. I'm interested. Because you two lovebirds have been whispering for about half an hour."

The class erupted into laughter at the word 'lovebirds,' making Meche blush with mortification.

"Maybe Sebastián Soto is not such a fag," someone yelled from the back of the room.

Rodríguez let them chuckle, then gave her a twisted smile. "Extra homework for you. Stay at the end of class."

"Can hardly wait," she whispered.

MECHE GRABBED HER backpack and shuffled to the front of the class, stopping before Rodríguez's desk. She could see Daniela standing outside the door, waiting for her.

The teacher raised his eyes and nodded at her.

"You were disruptive today. Again."

"Sorry, Mr. Rodríguez."

"You know, I can't really tell if you do it on purpose, Mercedes," he said, lacing his hands together, trying to look stern although his incipient moustache made him more comical than scary. "Is it just the sugar from all those cereals coursing through your body?"

"My brain is stuck from shooting glue," she said.

Rodríguez did not get the Ramones reference. He just raised an eyebrow at her.

"It's a song," she explained, fearing he'd take it seriously and call the principal.

"That's your problem, Mercedes. Your head is filled with songs. If you spent less time watching music videos and more time doing your readings, you wouldn't be failing my class."

He shuffled a stack of papers and put them in a folder. "You need to do some extra work."

"Professor..."

"No, you do," he said. "I can help you if you need it. I tutor after school."

"I've got a tutor," she said, thinking of Sebastián. He knew books. He could help her.

"I think you could benefit from my..."

"Yeah, where's the assignment?" she asked, pissed off and just wanting to get out of the classroom.

He handed her a piece of paper. Meche stuffed it in her sweater pocket and walked out. Daniela peeked her head inside and saw her heading towards the door. She smiled at the teacher then looked at Meche.

"What did he say?"

*   *   *

THE NEIGHBOURHOOD WHERE they lived was cut by a large avenue, dividing it into two starkly different halves. To the west, the buildings and houses became progressively nicer, the cars newer, the people better dressed. To the east there were no houses. Just numerous apartment buildings sandwiched together. These turned uglier, rattier and more dangerous the more you moved in that direction. In the east side people built tin-houses in the alleys and streets. Gang members could dismantle a car in five minutes flat and beat you for your lunch money.

Sebastián was the one who lived closest to the east, just a mere two blocks from the large avenue and the division between lower middle-class and outright poverty. Meche was situated three blocks further to the west. Although three blocks might not seem like much, it gave her a surer social footing at school.

Daniela lived closest to the west, not in an apartment, but in a house with a high wall covered with a purple bougainvillea. Her father was an accountant for a furniture chain and his wealth manifested conspicuously—without taste—all through this house in the form of Tiffany-style lamps, shiny tables and a plaster replica of the Venus de Milo greeting you when you entered the home. Daniela's house, like her father, was big and ostentatious. The jolly, obese man had a wife as round as he was and three daughters, all quiet and polite, educated in archaic manners and ways right out of the 1940s. Daniela's father believed in the sanctity of virginity and the role of the woman as wife and mother. He thought men who wore earrings were fags and those with long hair hippies or anarchists. He was, however, unable to manifest any ill-will towards them, or towards almost anyone, convinced that God would sort them out in his due time.

He was a harmless, dull fellow of few ideas and few complaints, who liked nothing more than to drink a few beers, eat large portions of spicy birria and coddle his daughters. None of the three was more coddled than Daniela, the youngest daughter and also the one with lupus—twin conditions which ensured she was guarded as carefully as a princess in a fairy tale.

Daniela was picked up and dropped off at school even though she was located closer to the Queen Victoria than her two friends. She was not to play sports of any kind for if she suffered the most minor bruise, her skin would turn an ugly shade of purple and there was always the danger of a scrape turning into a mountain of turmoil. She was not permitted any boyfriends, though this was not an issue because in addition to her childish ways— no doubt rooted in the babying imposed on her by her parents—Daniela was a moon-faced, limpid girl. Her greatest assets were her breasts which had started swelling at the tender age of eleven, turning into two rather large embarrassments, causing Daniela to walk everywhere looking a little hunched.

In fact, Daniela and Meche made quite a pair when they were side by side. Meche, thin and flat as a board, pimpled, dark of complexion and intentions, standing always very straight. Daniela, dwarfing Meche with her greater height, chubby and pale, shy and slumped, with short frizzy hair of a vaguely reddish hue which she had inherited from a Scottish ancestor who had stumbled into Mexico some eighty years before.

Daniela liked watching soap operas and reading romance novels. She painted her room pink and kept all her Barbies on shelves. Having spent so many days in hospitals meant she'd missed a chunk of her childhood and wanted to recoup those lost days, extending her girlhood. Meche, on the other hand, was an old soul, a vintage wine that was quickly turning into vinegar. She was, in short, the polar opposite of Meche and loved her friend precisely because of this.

Besides, complain as she might, Meche didn't mind Daniela's little quirks. The other kids joked and said Daniela was contagious because of her lupus or they thought she was stupid because she liked Candy Candy comic books. Meche made barbed comments, but if anyone ever dared treat Daniela poorly, she'd smack them and tell them to go to hell.

Sometimes, though, Daniela had to admit Meche scared her. Early on in their friendship she had been warned by some of the other girls at school that Meche was odd, different, perhaps slightly crazy. However, beggars can't be choosers and Daniela did not have many friends. Plus, Meche's energy attracted Daniela, even if this same intensity made her step quietly back at times.

Meche had a way of roping you in with her words, of convincing you to do the unthinkable. One minute you were firmly telling yourself that you would never play with a Ouija board, the next you were gathered in the bathroom, the board sitting on top of the toilet lid, while Meche urged you on before the principal came and busted you all.

Daniela, never one to put up much resistance, constantly

fell under the sway of Meche's stronger personality, always the handmaiden to the queen.

Like that day.

She had told Meche there would be no spell casting in her home, but Meche informed Daniela that they couldn't do it in her apartment because her mother was around and they couldn't do it in Sebastián's apartment because he shared a room with his brother, and Daniela was the one who had an empty house on Thursdays because her mother and her sisters went grocery shopping that day during the afternoon. It all made perfect sense, see? Before Daniela knew it she had said "yes."

Meche arrived with Sebastián, placed the portable record player on the floor, flipped the case open, and was riffling through the records she had brought inside a tattered, nylon market bag.

Daniela wrung her hands, hoping her mother and siblings would not burst in any time soon and that this whole witchcraft thing did not involve anything gross. Once, when she was little, Daniela's mother had taken her to an old healer for a limpia. The woman had rubbed an egg and a lemon all over her body, then made her drink this bitter brew, telling her it would heal her. It hadn't. Daniela still had lupus and her mother still would not let her play sports for fear of lacerations.

"What are you doing?" Daniela asked eventually, because standing there and staring at her two friends was starting to bore her.

"We are picking spell music," Meche said.

"What spell are we doing?"

"Something about success."

"Okay, why don't we use the Iggy Pop song?" Sebastián asked, holding up a record.

"Too obvious," Meche said.

"What? We get points for being cryptic?" Sebastián said.

"You don't just go out there and blurt it out," Meche replied.

"Why not?"

"Because it would be too easy."

"Easy is good."

"My mother will be back soon," Daniela muttered.

Sebastián and Meche turned towards her, eyebrows arched, with that look that meant, *Daniela, you don't get it*. It was a very common look.

"Fine," Sebastián said. "David Bowie. We play Fame and call it even."

"That's about two degrees less lame," Meche said.

"David Bowie is lame?"

"No, using that song is lame. There's like zero effort."

"Oh, okay. So let's go with this guy we've never heard of," Sebastián said, holding up another record, "because that's not lame."

"Without Robert Johnson you wouldn't have Elvis, no Beatles, no…"

"The lyrics you showed me don't say a single thing about success."

"They don't have to. He's standing at the crossroads because he's about to sell his soul to the devil."

"I don't want to do any devil songs," Daniela said. "I don't want to give birth to a baby with hooves who throws his mom down a staircase."

"That's like a fucked up version of *Rosemary's Baby* crossed with *The Omen*," Meche said.

"No devil songs."

"Daniela, wouldn't you prefer to play a David Bowie song?" Sebastián asked.

Meche's eyes said 'absolutely not,' but Daniela could not side with her this time. She bobbed her head.

"Yes," she said.

"That is not fair," Meche said.

"There's three of us and we just out-voted you," Sebastián said, smugly sliding the record from its sleeve.

He lifted the needle. There was the faint scratch against the vinyl and then the song began to play.

"Okay, now we hold hands and dance around it," Meche said.

"Really," Sebastián replied dryly.

"Yes. That's what witches do. They dance around the fire. Only we don't have a fire, so we'll dance around the record player."

Sebastián rolled his eyes. Meche pinched his arm. They joined hands, clumsily turning around, like children playing Doña Blanca, only they weren't little kids and this was not a game at recess.

"Ugh, your palms are sweaty," Sebastián said, drawing away from Daniela.

"Don't break the circle," Meche told him.

"How about I spin in my place?" he asked, wiping his hands against his trousers.

"Seriously," Meche muttered, but she didn't ask them to hold hands again.

They did spin. They whirled. At first, it seemed silly and

Daniela thought she was going to get dizzy and throw up. But the more they did it, the longer the seconds stretched, the more it seemed to make sense. Daniela felt very warm, like there was fire blooming from the pit of her stomach, stretching up her chest and stinging her mouth. Their fingers brushed as they turned.

She watched as Meche spun. Her friend's gaze was fixed on a distant point, her body turning but her eyes always returning to that distant something. Sebastián, similarly, seemed to have locked his eyes on something. Daniela closed her eyes and licked her lips; her cheeks burned.

She didn't feel dizzy from the movement. Not really. But there was something dizzying, hypnotic about the music, and she was reminded of a documentary they'd shown at school in which some monks were dancing, their skirts flaring around them.

Fame, fame, fame.

Daniela's head lolled to the side and she snapped her eyes open. Something seemed to lift from them, quickly leaving the room, cooling her skin. She blinked. She shivered, suddenly afraid because she had almost touched *something* that didn't seem like another of Meche's games.

Meche lifted the needle and they stood around the player in silence, nobody daring to be the first one to speak.

Finally, Sebastián found his voice.

"Did it work?" he asked. "Do you feel different?"

Daniela flexed her hands. Meche moved towards the white, wooden vanity with the pink necklaces strewn around its surface. She leaned forward, a hand against the mirror.

"Not really," she said.

"Me neither," Daniela added.

"But something happened," Meche said.

Neither Sebastián nor Daniela answered her. Daniela stared at her hands, at the ugly, bitten nails. She could not stop chewing them. Sometimes she even hurt herself and this alarmed her mother greatly because every little scrape could become a life or death matter.

Daniela heard the front door opening, her mother and her sisters' voices heralding their arrival. Whatever uncertain power still remained in the room now definitely dissipated with the intrusion of the women.

Meche began gathering her records, putting them back in her bag.

"A SIX PAGE essay on Cervantes and his connection with modern realist literature," she told him as they walked home.

She was wearing a heavy, green jacket which made her look like a bag lady. He'd told her that one time and Meche had punched him, but it was true. It was a formless sack. Meche resembled a very large, very green jellyfish from behind. She drowned in that jacket, but then again she seemed to drown in all her clothes. Only the fingertips peeking out from the sleeves, the neck erased by folds of clothing. Beneath the jacket she tended to wear oversized t-shirts with names like Iron Maiden, Queen and The Who emblazoned on them.

"He must be very mad at you."

"It's a scam. He wanted me to take this tutoring session with him. All he wants is to make extra money."

"You could use some tutoring."

"Not with Rodríguez. He is such a dick."

Sebastián was carrying the portable record player, Meche had the bag. They walked down the narrow streets, side by side. It seemed to Sebastián they were always walking, going from or to school, going to the market together, stopping at the store to buy a soft drink. Except, that was, when he took the motorcycle out for a spin.

The motorcycle had belonged to his older brother, but his brother had given up on it. He'd called it a piece of crap and left it to rot. Sebastián tried to get it going again, and it sputtered to life now and then, though it was an unreliable creature. He liked riding it, when he could, because he thought the leather jacket he had found at the tianguis—used, Sebastián could never buy new stuff—coupled with the sunglasses made him look more masculine.

The boys called him Sebastián Soto el Joto and Sebastián Soto el Gran Puto, and sometimes, to be creative and not rhyme, Sebastián el Mariquita. No matter what the nickname was, the crude conclusion was always the same: he was gay. Sebastián was straight, but accuracy did not have much say when it came to these things. Marking him as effeminate was just a way to toss him into the pile of the undesirables, to mock his everything, to serve as an excuse for their rudeness.

He remembered one time when Constantino caught him looking at Isadora and snapped, "What are you looking at, faggot?" Sebastián had wanted to beat the crap out of him, to paint the pavement red with the guy's blood.

Sebastián wondered if the magic would fix this. If he might grow more muscled, leaving his scrawniness behind. Maybe Isadora would look at him if he looked tougher, if he had nicer clothes, new sneakers. Sneakers that weren't painted with a black marker.

They stopped by the bakery and stared at the confectionery for the Day of the Dead: the little candy skulls glittering in the twilight, the sugar looking like tiny diamonds. He liked this time of year. The end of October, the appearance of the orange and yellow flowers, the papel picado and the colourful skeletons which heralded the arrival of the festival, and with it, the beginning of the cold months of the year.

"Is your grandma going to bake bread for the Day of the Dead?" he asked.

"Yeah. Next week."

"Can I come and eat some?"

"Sure."

Meche entered the shop and bought two pieces of sweet bread. Sebastián didn't have any money. One more reason why he walked everywhere. She gave him one of the breads and they sat on the steps of a nearby building, eating and watching the few people go by as it got dark and the street lights bloomed into life.

"Do you think it'll all be different in the morning?" he asked.

"You still don't believe me?" she asked.

He licked some cream which was spilling from the bread onto his hand and shrugged, not wanting to look too excited by the whole idea. Not wanting this too badly, although he did.

"I'm not sure."

"Fine."

"Hey, don't get mad."

"I'm not mad."

He sat back, his head against the door of the building. Meche, in turn, rested her head against his shoulder. For others, it might have been an intimate gesture. Maybe it was, but not in the way most people might think. Meche and Sebastián were used to each other, comfortable in their proximity. They folded and kept their dreams in the same drawer, spun fantasies side by side, lived in the easy harmony of youth which did not know the need for tall walls and sturdy defenses.

Sebastián popped the last bit of bread into his mouth and chewed it slowly. The sweet potato seller pushed his cart in front of them, the hiss of steam announcing his arrival, his voice slicing the night.

"Camotes! I sell camotes!"

The man paused and glanced in their direction, but his small, black eyes did not seem to see them. They skipped over Sebastián and Meche as he moved away, the wheels of the cart turning, the steam rising towards the night sky.

Though he was not particularly musical, Sebastián thought of a song. Duncan Dhu, singing En Algún Lugar, and for a reason he did not understand he had this image of Meche stepping onto a plane. He put an arm around Meche's shoulders, holding her tight.

MECHE WOKE UP the next morning with the giddy excitement of a child heading to open her Christmas presents. She brushed her teeth, combed her hair, rolled up the sleeves of her sweater and put on her shoes. Then she bounced towards school, eager to meet up with Sebastián.

He was waiting for her at the street corner and they walked together, as they usually did, quiet and filled with hope.

Hope began to disintegrate around noon when it became obvious that nothing had changed for them. They were still the same losers as the day before, still sitting in the same corner of the schoolyard, still looking forlorn at the more popular, more beautiful, more-everything kids. When the bell signalling the end of the day rang, Meche could barely contain herself. Jaw locked tightly, she hurried back home.

"Hey," she heard Sebastián say, but didn't slow down to let him catch up with her and she dashed home, hands tight around the straps of her backpack.

They had failed.

She stomped up the steps towards her apartment, rushing into her bedroom and tossing the backpack on the floor. Meche put on a record and listened to Frank Sinatra promising to fly her to the moon. Tears threatened to leak from her eyes so she rubbed them. She hated crying. Hated feeling weak.

Meche sniffled and cleaned her nose with the back of her hand.

She had seriously thought it would work. She had pinned her heart on a stupid record, like a modern-day Jack showing off his beans.

Of course it would never work.

They would always be the same.

Life would always be this dull shade.

Meche turned her head and looked out the window, at the fragment of mocking grey sky. Birds sometimes dropped dead in Mexico City. That's how polluted the city was. Because of the overwhelming smog, you couldn't even hope for a glimpse of its snow-capped volcanoes.

Meche draped a blanket around her shoulders and went to sleep. She did not bother changing out of her uniform and into her regular clothes.

When she woke up it was dark and there was the smell of food wafting into her room. Meche walked towards the kitchen and found her grandmother busy, humming over a pot. She smiled at Meche.

"I'm making chicken soup today," she said. "It has the potatoes and carrots all nicely chopped, the way you like them."

"Thank you," she muttered.

Meche's grandmother filled a chipped bowl with soup and Meche began to eat. The warm food soothed her belly and she slowly started feeling better. Her grandmother poured her a glass of lemonade. Meche sipped it, holding the glass with both hands.

"Are you getting sick, Meche?"

She shook her head.

"Okay."

Grandmother was quiet. She didn't push or ask questions. But her silences pulled the truth out of you anyway, made you speak despite the desire to remain silent. So Meche spoke, her hands sliding against the cool glass.

"Mama Dolores, what did you mean when you said magic will break your heart?"

"You're still going on about that?" she asked, placing a bunch of tortillas wrapped in a warm cloth by Meche's plate.

Meche peeled open the wrapping and pulled out a tortilla, dipping it in the broth.

"Maybe."

"Magic gets you what you want, but it doesn't solve your problems."

"That doesn't make any sense."

"It does," Mama Dolores pulled out a chair, sitting next to Meche. "There was a man in my town who wanted to get married but he could not find himself a bride. He went to a witch and asked her for a charm. Something that would get him a wife."

"Did it work?"

"It did. He was married within a month's time."

"Then it did solve his problems."

Mama Dolores cut a lemon in half and carefully sprinkled a bit of sugar on it.

"No. Because one year later she ran away with another man."

"That's a bad story."

"Blame the magic, not the story."

Mama Dolores bit into her lemon.

"But you also told me witches fly through the night, they turn into animals, they put curses on you—"

"True. They do all that."

"But then?"

"Nothing, that. But a man may turn into a coyote as many times as he wants and may steal chickens from the farm, but the chickens won't be his and they will still be stolen. And the coyote will still be nothing but a large, ugly dog."

Meche sighed, staring into the contents of her bowl of soup. She didn't understand what her grandmother meant.

"If I was a witch—"

"Ugh, it's pouring outside. You could not believe the rain," Meche's mother said, shaking her umbrella out as she entered.

Even soaked and with her mascara running, she looked very beautiful. Meche's mother had once held aspirations to become an actress, make it big in the movies or maybe a soap. Natalia certainly had the looks. She only lacked the talent. She had given up on her dreams several years before and had gone to work at a department store. Now it was the pharmacy, where she worked as a cashier and part-time model: her photos adorned some of the flyers advertising the pharmacy. This was not as much an achievement as a form of charity because the owner of the pharmacy, Don Fernando, was Natalia's godfather.

"What did you make?" Natalia asked.

"Chicken soup," Meche's grandmother said.

"Did you take off the skin from my piece of chicken? You know I can't eat chicken with the skin on."

"Yes, yes."

"I don't want a lot of rice in my bowl. No potatoes either."

"You have to have one potato."

"It's too starchy. Is it warm? I have to go back to the drugstore for the rest of my shift. Leona is sick again this week."

Natalia sat across from Meche. Meche looked at her mother, waiting for her to say something to her. Eventually, possibly because Meche just kept staring at her, Natalia spoke.

"How was school?"

"Alright."

"Do you have a lot of homework?"

"Some."

There was a systematic indifference to Natalia's voice. It was a chore doing this, playing the mother-daughter bond. Meche saw her fret in discomfort. Normally she would have simply stepped away, back to her room, and let her mother eat in peace. She did not feel charitable that evening, so she stayed put.

"I saw you walking with that boy yesterday."

"Sebastián?"

"Yes."

Meche did not remember if they had gone by the drugstore. Possibly. Their path had zigzagged through the whole neighbourhood as they chased stars which could not be seen in the night sky, hearts filled with promise. A promise which now lay squashed beneath the soles of their feet.

"You say his name like you don't know him," Meche muttered.

"Meche, he's here all the time. Or you're somewhere with him. You act like you are Siamese twins. It's not healthy."

"Daniela is also with us."

"Yes, that girl is also not a good role model. She's odd. Plus, I don't want you catching something from her."

She liked Daniela because she was odd. Meche appreciated her friend's honest enthusiasm for all things saccharine. Daniela was always herself, with no qualms about it. It was almost a super power.

"You can't catch lupus."

"Well, I don't know about that."

"It's not scientifically possible," Meche said.

"Never mind. Meche, running around the block with a boy was OK when you were a little girl. You're fifteen now."

"And?"

Mama Dolores held up the cloth with the tortillas, but Natalia shook her head.

"I don't eat tortillas, you know that."

Mama Dolores set the tortillas down. Meche grabbed the saltshaker and began salting her broth. Her mother shook her head.

"Salt will bloat you."

"It needs salt."

"Too much salt is not good for you."

Meche kept slowly salting her soup, even though she knew now it would be *too* salty. She felt like making a point.

"What I'm trying to say—and perhaps I'm failing to express myself clearly here, Meche—is that it doesn't look right to be with a boy so much."

"It doesn't look right to whom?"

"Well, Catalina Coronado was telling me she saw you going into the abandoned factory with him the other morning."

Of course. Catalina Coronado. The neighbourhood

gossip, with her sharp, hawk-eyed gaze and her forked tongue. Ready to spill bad news at a moment's notice and spit venom in your face. She had probably relished the opportunity to tattle on Meche.

"When did she tell you that?"

"She was at the drugstore today, buying cough drops, and she told me she happened to see you. Meche, you do know what teenagers do in that factory, don't you?"

They had sex, drank booze, and smoked dope. Meche, feigning stupidity, stared at her mother.

"No, please tell me what they do."

Natalia did not reply. She stirred her soup with her spoon, carefully inspecting each chunk of vegetable, each scrap of chicken.

"Please, tell me," Meche insisted.

"You are not a child."

"No, I'm not. I don't understand why that means I can't hang out with Sebastián like I always do. Because Catalina Coronado doesn't like him?"

"Sebastián's brother just got his girlfriend pregnant and I do not want a similar surprise, alright?"

Meche did not know that. How had her mother found out? She supposed that was one of the benefits of working at the drugstore, all the little crumbs of information that fell into your lap. But it didn't matter. His brother had nothing to do with her.

"He's my best friend," Meche said. "Grandma, can I finish my food later? I think I am coming down with a cold."

Meche drifted towards the doorway. She glanced back at her mother. Natalia rolled out a magazine, already busy looking at the '10 Beauty Tips of the Week' and the 'Most Flattering Skirts of the Season.' Meche returned to her room and the company of her records.

SEBASTIÁN TRIED TO catch up with Meche. She lost him at an intersection, disappearing behind a row of food stands. He did not understand what was wrong with her, why she had not waited for him.

He gave up on finding his friend and continued on his way home, observing the sky and wondering if it would start raining before he got to his apartment. Too late he noticed Isadora and her friends hanging out near a little corner store, drinking beer, and immediately felt the desire to dash in the opposite direction. However, they had already seen him, and completely turning around would be too conspicuous. He forced himself to keep on walking, eyes straight ahead.

He already knew what was coming.

The boys immediately perked up when they saw him, the girls looked at him curiously.

"Look! It's the faggot! What ya'up to, faggot?" one of them asked.

Sebastián wished he had a Walkman like Meche. Then he might have put on the headphones and completely ignored their taunts, protected by the music. He did not have a Walkman, so he had to listen to the insults.

"Do you thinks he fucks men or he lets them fuck him up the ass?"

"I think he lets them fuck him."

"He's going to get butt cancer."

Sebastián jammed his hands into his trousers, his chin up, shoulders tense. He was taller than the whole lot, but there were four boys and he was alone. He wouldn't put it past them to try and hit him. They hadn't done it before, limiting themselves to tossing garbage in his direction—empty bottles of Frutsi, and on one memorable occasion a whole hotdog—but you never knew. They might feel adventurous that afternoon.

"He's so gay."

Sebastián walked by, his eyes flitting over Isadora. For a brief moment, Isadora looked back at him, seeming a little pained. Like she was sorry he had to endure this treatment. Then she looked away and he looked away too. Before he reached the corner, Sebastián felt something hit him in the back. The raucous laughter of the boys was now joined by a chorus of giggling girls. Was Isadora laughing, too? He did not dare to look back. He turned the corner.

When Sebastián arrived home, the whole apartment was pitch black. He flicked on the lights and wandered into the kitchen, looking for something to eat. His mother did not have the time nor the inclination to cook and his brother, Romualdo—who was supposed to cook for himself and Sebastián—had barely done so when he was in high school. Now that he was in university, he did not bother.

Sebastián cut a piece of cheese and rolled it into a slice of ham. He ate standing up in the kitchen, glancing at the dirty dishes piling up in the sink. Those were also his brother's responsibility, while Sebastián was in charge of the laundry. Unlike most Mexican families who could pay a maid— they came cheap in this country—no matter how lowly their social class, Sebastián's mother could not afford any help. Sebastián and Romualdo were supposed to divide all the chores equally, solving this issue, but Romualdo, full of misplaced machismo, refused to do "girls'" chores. Washing dishes was beneath him. In a few days, their mother would scream at Romualdo and force him to scrub the pots but until then they would sit there, ignored.

The cat meowed at Sebastián and he checked its dish. He filled it with cat food, then cleaned the water dish and filled it too. This was supposed to also be his brother's responsibility, but if it were not for Sebastián the cat would starve.

Sebastián went to his bedroom. It was a small apartment and a small bedroom, and he had to share it with Romualdo. His brother's side of the room was plastered with posters of women, some in bikinis, some completely naked; stacks of magazines full of girlie pictures, bare flesh spread all over the bed. Sebastián's side was papered with maps and pictures of Europe, many of which had come from his grandfather, who had lived in Barcelona until his late teens. Europe. That's where Sebastián was going to go one day, to write great stories in a Parisian café. Or, perhaps, he'd venture to Italy, where he could order an espresso and pretend he was in a Fellini movie, which grandpa had loved. He didn't have girlie magazines. Instead, Sebastián's books were all neatly sitting on a shelf. *The Ambassadors*, *One Hundred Years of Solitude*, *Hopscotch*.

He supposed that's why the boys at school said he was gay. Because he didn't have big-tittie posters. Because he spent all his spare time reading. Because he drew stars on his tennis shoes with a black marker. Sebastián would have loved to have been normal. He realized his predilection for novels instead of soccer had distanced him from his father, even before the old man and his mother divorced, but he could not help it.

Or maybe his father hated him because he was a measured, quiet little bag boy, packing groceries three afternoons a week, saying "yes miss" and "no miss", his sneakers squeaking over the floor as he moved to put the plastic bags in the shopping cart. He certainly knew that the boys and girls at school made fun of him because of that, giggling whenever they were in the checkout line with their parents; lofty because they didn't have to scramble for a few pesos, stretch their hands like urchins, make their money from tips in dirty change. He was a cerillo, a nothing, a thin kid wearing a black vest and a tie as he packed and packed groceries and dreamed of Europe.

Sebastián lay on his bed and stretched his arms, staring at the ceiling, the acid memory of the taunts the boys had yelled at him still fresh, still ringing in his ears. He felt his muscles relaxing in the pleasant darkness, his eyelids fluttering close to sleep.

Romualdo walked in and turned on the light. He was tall, just like Sebastián, but his brother seemed better proportioned, better looking, better prepared overall. He gave Sebastián an indifferent glance.

"I need to phone Margarita, asshole."

That was his girlfriend. She was pretty and nice enough, but Sebastián didn't like it when she came around because

Romualdo kicked him out of the bedroom so he could have sex with her. Sebastián then had to wander around the block or take a ride on the motorcycle, and sometimes he really didn't want to go out but there was no reasoning with Romualdo.

Or, just like now, Romualdo would phone Margarita and that also meant Sebastián needed to step out because he wanted privacy. Funny how Romualdo had the right to privacy, but Sebastián didn't have the right to anything.

"Phone her."

"Go to the living room."

Sebastián grabbed his backpack and shuffled out of the room. Romualdo closed the door.

Sebastián tried to read, then gave up and turned on the television. He rested his chin against the arm of the couch and watched a Timbiriche music video. They were singing Tu Y Yo Somos Uno Mismo. The lyrics and the images were incredibly corny: a man and a woman running together on the beach, a tear slipping down the woman's cheek, the kiss and the catchy, pop tune. Meche would have hated it.

But Sebastián wanted it. He wanted that corny, fabricated music video universe in which a couple could pop up from under the waves, water dripping from their bodies, embracing each other.

He had nothing of that. Just the book in his lap, the ratty couch and the cat which now drifted next to him, rubbing against his leg.

He supposed he never would, now that Meche's spell had failed.

Sebastián turned off the TV set.

Mexico City, 2009

IT WASN'T THAT Meche hated Lorenzo. She just had never taken to him. After her parents' divorce, her mother's swift remarriage had left her a little breathless and Meche had never felt quite at home after he moved in. It wasn't anything that he did or said, but she knew she was an intruder whenever she visited. Two brief Christmas vacations in Mexico City had convinced Meche there was no reason for her to ever set foot in that apartment again. The third Christmas, when she asked if her mother could fly to Monterrey instead, Lorenzo happily paid for the plane ticket. After graduation, when she secured a job in Europe, Lorenzo had also been instrumental in soothing any fears of distances and dangers. Meche knew that, as far as Lorenzo was concerned, the less he saw of Natalia's taciturn daughter, the better.

"Did you make much progress today?" Lorenzo asked, trying to make polite conversation.

"My father had a lot of things," she said. "It's hard going through all of it."

"How many records did he have?" Jimena asked, grabbing another piece of sweet bread from the centre basket.

"Thousands."

"Is that all he had?"

The question was crass, but then again so was Jimena with her bright red nails and her bright red smile. Since when had she become so cozy with her mother? Meche supposed it was to be expected. Natalia had a tendency to replace people. First her father, now Meche. She didn't blame her on the part about Vicente. Natalia had taken too long to divorce him. It should have happened years before.

Meche shook her head.

"He didn't collect CDs, only vinyl."

Meche knew Jimena had not been wondering about records. She was asking if he had anything valuable. Meche doubted he did, but discussing the amount of pesos they might make from the sale of her father's collection was very inappropriate.

"What will you do with them?"

"Ship some back to Oslo," Meche said, shrugging. "Throw away the rest. I can't carry too many things but I could buy a suitcase and pack it with the ones I want to keep. I might also take the typewriter and his manuscript."

"The manuscript," Natalia said, as she shook her head. "He was always going to finish it next summer."

Her mother smiled, gently, and for once in a long time Meche thought she glimpsed a certain tenderness towards the old man. She sounded almost fond of him.

"Ay, we need to serve the coffee. Where's my head?" Natalia asked, blinking and heading towards the kitchen. "Everyone is having coffee, right?"

"I'd like tea with milk, please," Meche said.

In Norway Meche drank her tea from a glass, with lots of milk, a custom acquired after living in London. An unusual gesture now in Mexico where she might be expected to ask for atole or coffee.

"We're out of milk," Lorenzo told her.

"I can go buy some."

"I'll go," Lorenzo said.

"No. I'll just head to the corner store."

Jimena and Lorenzo looked at her, doubtful. Meche chuckled.

She knew they were worried about her. She had not cried during the funeral. She just stood under her umbrella, eyeing the casket with scepticism, thinking that Vicente Vega would have been shocked and outraged by the whole spectacle. He certainly would have said a few words about the cross sitting atop him, considering he had been a staunch atheist.

"It's still in the same place, right?"

"Sure," Lorenzo said.

"Then I'll be right back."

Stepping out into the street was a blessing. The apartment felt stuffy and her family were very noisy. Of course, Meche was accustomed to living by herself, not having cousins and aunts rolling in and out of an apartment in preparation for her father's prayers, which began that night with a late mass and finger foods after going to church. Nine nights of prayer, to ensure the dead man's soul would reach his final destination. Nine whole nights she had to remain here. Meche had already tried talking about the necessity of flying back to Europe, but her mother had blocked any plans of an early flight.

Meche walked into the corner store, which was not really at the corner but that was what everyone called them in Mexico. It wasn't really a proper store either, but the first floor of someone's house, arranged to store foods and beverages, with the owners living on the top. In her time, the owner had been Don Chemo, the surly old man who always looked carefully at the kids, making sure they didn't steal candy.

The little store looked exactly as it had when she was a teenager. She was sure that even some of the ads on the walls behind the counter were the same, though the attendant behind the counter had changed. He did, however, bear an uncanny resemblance to Don Chemo. Meche wondered if this could be his grandson who would have been an annoying little kindergartener the last time she'd seen him.

Meche found the milk and riffled through the store, looking at the candy and chips. They had the regular tamarind Pelón Pelo Rico and a sour lime flavour she had never seen before, peanuts dipped in chilli, and chocolate Carlos V.

Meche took out a bill and placed it on the counter. Don Chemo's grandson—he had to be, he had the same disposition—gave her her change and slowly placed the things she had bought in a plastic bag.

As soon as Meche stepped out it began to rain. A light drizzle which made her smile.

She loved the rain.

Meche reached into her pocket and turned on her iPod, picking a song from the playlist. For the sake of nostalgia she settled on Miguel Bosé. Nena, which was from '86.

The writing of the handsome Bosé and a blonde woman in white all along the floor had sent her mother into a bizarre state of agitation the first time it aired on TV. Natalia had quickly changed the channel and railed against music videos, which exposed youth to so many nasty images.

But Meche liked Nena. There was something real about it. Not like some of the other videos which contaminated the airwaves. Certainly better than the chirpings of Thalía or—dear God— Lucerito. When Bosé sang about an impossible woman with an insatiable mouth and they fought—and rolled around the floor—it seemed gritty and true. A fucked up relationship, but fascinating all the same.

Meche raised her head. The street was empty except for someone standing on the other side, holding an umbrella.

Meche looked down at her iPod again, pumping up the volume so she could hear nothing but the deep voice of Bosé.

When she looked up again the person with the umbrella was still in the same place.

It was a guy in a business suit and a long, black raincoat; a matching umbrella with a nice wooden handle.

He was staring at her.

It took longer than it should have for Meche to recognize him. But then she saw the resemblance. The very tall, thin frame—though now it was not cadaveric, he was lean without seeming unhealthily skinny—was the first thing to trigger her memory. Then the other pieces were all pulled together. Very black hair, cropped short in a fashionable style. A stern mouth which had grown sterner. A carefully trimmed goatee which had never been there before. The dark, dark eyes which resembled a pair of pebbles.

Sebastián Soto, in the flesh.

He looked so different. Only the eyes had remained the same.

She wondered what she must look like now, her long hair—it had reached her waist—cut short in a boyish style, the thick eyebrows plucked, her clothes actually fitting her.

He looked at her and Meche wanted to laugh. Not a good laugh. A bitter, angry laugh. She had been so fearful of meeting Sebastián again and she had found him, smack across the street.

Meche held the plastic bag with her purchases in one hand and jammed the other hand in the pocket of her jeans, tilting her head a little, daring him to cross the street and say hello.

He just looked at her, though by now she was sure he had identified her, and stood his ground. His gaze did not waver but he did not make any effort to move her way, wave hello or open his mouth.

Like two duelists at noon, about to draw their guns, they stood on their respective sides of the street. Finally he snapped, looking away from her and continuing along the path he had been following, keeping to his side. Meche also turned away, walking in the opposite direction.

The rain did not seem pleasant anymore. The dirty puddles reflected the street lights and the trash strewn on the ground was beginning to clog the drain. Later, the whole street would ooze and the water level would rise.

Mexico City was sinking. A city slowly descending into the muck from where it had come. The Spaniards had drained its Venice-like canals and filled them with earth, creating shaky foundations for their churches. Centuries later, their descendants paid for their folly with constant inundations which threatened to turn the whole metropolis into the lake it had been when the Aztecs made their way there. A fetid sea of sewage swamped the sidewalks every year.

In Mexico City everything returns. The rains and the past and everything in between.

Meche, upset by her encounter with Sebastián, gave in and went by the house owned by Daniela's parents. They were happy to supply their daughter's number.

Mexico City, 1988

IT WAS ANOTHER one of those days; it was always one of those days with Natalia. She flogged him with her tongue, excoriated him for real and imaginary flaws, drew blood. This time the fight had been over cigarettes. They were a needless expense. He should quit smoking. Not because of his health, no. Natalia could care less if he died of cancer. Her concern was the money. They could save so many pesos if he would only stop smoking.

"You could stop doing your nails," he countered. "They're more expensive than my half pack a day."

"I do my nails because of my job."

"What job? You work at the pharmacy."

"It's customer service."

"It's bullshit. You do your nails because you want to, so don't come telling me it's because of some demanding job."

"I could get an audition."

"But you won't," he said.

She slapped him. He left afterwards, didn't even try the chicken soup that was supposed to be his dinner, and went to eat at the cantina instead.

There he nursed his glass and his feelings, hunched over

a table. Eventually some of the regulars arrived and he joined a game of dominoes, trying to find meaning in the black-and-white pieces, like a man trying to read the Tarot cards.

Where had he gone wrong? Where had his road forked towards defeat? Somehow, at some point, he had become a loser. Maybe he'd always been one but had been unable to recognize it in his youth.

Vicente smoked his cheap cigarettes. Cigarettes which were staining his once pristine teeth, turning them an ugly yellow. But did it matter? He had been a decent looking chap but that was gone. He had the same face, but it was lined with discomfort and misery. It was not the face of a music idol.

As for Natalia... Natalia had changed. Each year her eyes narrowed more, fixed more sternly on his shoulders. Each year, he knew she found the leather jackets shabbier, the long hair more off-putting, the little tricks he did to charm people—like recite the year when any song had come on the air—more stale. Each year she measured him and found him more and more wanting.

How different from when they had first met at the record store, when Natalia had wandered in looking for a present for the boyfriend she had at the time. Her taste in music did not run very deep and Vicente had spent a good hour chatting to her about this and that band, the benefits of a certain record over another, finally settling on *Arthur (Or the Decline and Fall of the British Empire)* as his recommendation for a birthday present. When he gave Natalia her change he wrote his number on the back of a bill.

"Let's go out sometime," he said.

"I told you I have a boyfriend," she said.

"It's not going to last."

It didn't and one month later she was back at the store, trying to exchange the record for another one, although, truth be told, she just wanted to see him.

He had charm aplenty in those days. He wrote letters to Natalia every day and quickly won her heart. Maybe he still had charm, but Natalia had ceased to be impressed by it. She didn't want him to compose songs for her and she certainly didn't want to read his eternal compendium on Latin American music.

Vicente smoked and drank. Around midnight Meche popped in. She'd been sent to get him from the cantina since she was ten years old. Vicente knew the routine, he said goodbye to his friends, put out his cigarette and nodded to his daughter, following her outside.

She was stuffed into her oversized green jacket, carrying her Walkman.

"What are you listening to?" he asked. He always asked her. It made her happy when he asked.

"Dylan. All Along the Watchtower."

"Depressing."

"Well, you know," Meche muttered, kicking a can of soda down the sidewalk. "Happiness is in short supply."

She passed it to him and Vicente kicked it for a little bit, then passed it to her and paused to light a cigarette. Meche looked at him with eyes that were his own. Large and sad and painted with the same seeds of misery he carried in his own gut.

"Then you steal it."

Meche frowned, confused. "What do you mean?"

"If happiness doesn't come to you, then you take it. Any way you can," he said.

He thought of the ocean. He had wanted to live by the beach but Natalia had been opposed to that. What would they do there? His fantasies of building a hut, of combing the sand for treasure, of running barefoot with nothing but a single change of clothes and a guitar, pounding on the typewriter by candlelight, did not impress her.

Maybe he could still do it. Maybe he could have his ocean and the sound of the waves heavy in his ears as he went to sleep.

Steal it if you can't get it...

"Yeah," Meche said, nodding.

MECHE NEVER LIKED dragging her father back home. She thought her mother sent her to punish him, to humiliate him. It seemed petty to her. Especially that night. She had told her mother she did not feel like going out, too busy nursing her disappointment, but her mother had shoved Meche into her jacket and pushed her out the door.

Her father had to go to work the next day, her mother said. She'd better bring him before it got too late.

Later, as Meche and her dad sat in the kitchen, dipping animal crackers in a glass of milk, she thought about what he'd said about happiness.

Steal it if you must.

Meche was willing. But that bitch, happiness, wasn't being very cooperative.

Why had the spell failed?

She looked at the box of crackers with its colourful picture of a lion tamer and a lion jumping through a hoop.

She sighed, wishing magic was more like something she could understand. More like math.

Equations, she could get. Computer languages, she could get.

Mysticism, apparently, not.

Meche paused, the lion-shaped cracker hovering before her mouth.

Wait.

When you type a computer command, you don't just type *any* random phrase. You have to be specific.

If you are, the desired result occurs.

"Holy mother," Meche whispered.

She ate her cracker.

SEBASTIÁN AND DANIELA looked around the room, carefully inspecting their surroundings. It had taken Meche a couple of days to fix it up, but the place no longer looked like an abandoned factory room: it looked frankly awesome. She had swept the floor and put up posters of several bands. Cut-outs from magazines and record sleeves were fashioned into large collages. There were all the big names: The Beatles, Elvis Presley, Pedro Infante, Toña la Negra. Newer, younger ones too.

She had cleaned the old couch as best she could. She brought blankets so they could sit on the floor. There was also a little coffee table with candles on top: the factory had no electricity.

Meche sat in the centre of the room, by the portable record player, smiling.

"What do you think?" she asked.

"It's nice," Sebastián said.

"We are not supposed to be here," Daniela reminded them.

"I bought a lock," Meche said, showing it to them, "so we can close up and others can't get in when we're not here."

"Um... why?" Daniela asked.

"Because this is going to be our base of operations. You see, I didn't get it. Not last time. We need the right environment. You know, just like with a computer program. Plus, we went too big. We need to focus on something smaller. We have to be specific."

"Oh, not the spell thing again," Daniela said.

"Yes, the spell thing again," Meche said. "I've got a notebook that is going to be our grimoire and I've got the records. Now we focus, we are specific and we experiment until we get it right."

They didn't say anything. Daniela just looked down at her pink and white tennis shoes. Sebastián slid his hands into his pockets.

"What do you say?"

"I'm up for it," Sebastián said.

Daniela seemed surprised by that. She bobbed her head, imitating Sebastián. "Sure."

"Okay, we have to focus on one thing," Meche said. "A single thing. What do you want to do? Something we can fix?"

"My motorcycle is busted again," Sebastián said with a shrug.

"Motorcycle," Meche said, "that's good. Now, let's find the right music."

She knelt on the floor, going through the piles of records she had dragged to the factory. Her friends also sat down. They began looking into her cardboard boxes, pulling records out.

"Subete a Mi Moto," Daniela said, holding up the Menudo record.

"Don't be too obvious," Meche said.

"Flans!" Daniela said excitedly.

"No."

"Lucerito!"

"It's not phone-in-the radio-station-for-your-favourite-song."

"Aw, but I like Lucerito."

Meche rolled her eyes. Of course Daniela would like Lucerito, the most saccharine, inane teenager singer on the market. And Flans... why not stab each other in the ears now?

"Cindy Lauper?" Daniela asked hopefully.

Meche was willing to grant her that, but what Cindy Lauper song were they supposed to use?

"Duncan Dhu," Sebastián said.

Meche looked up at him as he offered her the record.

"En Algún Lugar," he whispered.

Meche grabbed the record and felt a tiny, electric charge running up her arm. Like static electricity. It almost... felt warm. As though it had been resting on top of a stove. *Weird.*

Meche lowered it carefully, holding the needle between her fingers. Sebastián stared at her.

She let the needle drop.

The record hissed, like steam escaping a kettle.

The guitar split the silence, and then the beat began.

The three of them stood up.

This time they did not spin around. Instead they joined hands and stepped close around the portable record player, their heads almost touching as they looked down at the record, seeing it turn.

Meche did not feel anything. Not at first. Just Daniela's sweaty hands, Sebastián's steady grip.

And then it was... something she couldn't identify. Just this warmth, the same warmth which had permeated the vinyl now stretching up her fingers, making her arms tingle. Her body felt a bit numb yet there was this odd current churning through her blood, swimming up her veins.

It felt like the time she had sipped clandestine tequila. That had stung her mouth and this stung her body. Not very pleasant, but also not painful.

The beat rose and fell and the singers spoke of running away, of a rider who does not turn his head, leaving with the wind, the hoofs of his horse sinking into a dusty road.

Meche could see the road, painted red, lonely, and the rider reaching the bend of the road, the evening sun staining the sky red.

Meche tasted dust. She closed her eyes and opened them again.

She was standing by the road and when the rider swept by, she extended her hand and he pulled her onto his horse. They were galloping towards the horizon.

Meche opened her mouth; heat that had been accumulating inside escaped. It rose like a golden streamer, drifting like smoke, touching the ceiling. Golden tendrils also escaped from Sebastián and Daniela, coiling together.

The three of them looked up, amazed.

"What is that?" Daniela asked.

"Magic," Meche whispered.

The golden streamers coalesced into a ball and the ball grew larger, then began to collapse and dissolve, bits of it floating away until there was nothing left.

"Is that it?" Sebastián asked, sounding disappointed.

As if punctuating his words, several dirty glass panels shattered. Daniela yelped. Meche laughed.

"Let's see if it worked!" she yelled and rushed out of the room, leaving the record spinning.

They stomped downstairs and made it to the street, heading straight for Sebastián's building. When they reached it they were all out of breath. Meche slid down against the doors to his building while Sebastián fumbled for his keys. He kept the motorcycle inside, on the first floor, beneath the stairs.

"Go check it out," she said.

He nodded, turned the key and stepped inside. Meche, too exhausted to move, just waited. Daniela half-collapsed next to her, her hair in her eyes.

Sebastián walked the motorcycle out. Meche straightened up, carefully watching him as he straddled it and placed the key in the ignition.

The motorcycle coughed, sputtered and did not move.

Meche bit her lip.

Sebastián tried again and this time it worked. The old,

banged-up machine roared into life. Meche jumped, clapping.

Sebastián was beaming. Daniela seemed in shock.

"Fucking yes!" Meche said jumping up and down.

"Get on," Sebastián said.

Meche turned to look at Daniela and Daniela nodded. "Go ahead. I want to rest."

Meche hurried towards him, quickly throwing her leg over. She scooted close to Sebastián, holding on to his jacket.

He twisted the grip, applied the throttle, and they sped away, turning the corner. She leaned forward along with him and they zoomed past the corner store, then the pharmacy, the small video store, the tortilleria.

At some point her hair band snapped and Meche's hair streamed freely down her shoulders. She laughed.

"It works!" she yelled.

"Of course it works!" he yelled back.

At the stoplight, she squeezed Sebastián tight and stared at the cars as they crossed the junction in front of them. Catalina Coronado looked at them, with a disapproving glare, as she crossed the street. Meche chuckled.

She didn't care if Catalina told her mother she had been riding around on Sebastián's bike. They had power. Real power.

Things were never going to be the same again.

Mexico City, 2009

MECHE SAT IN the restaurant, looking at her cup of tea, absently folding and refolding her napkin.

"Baby, baby what are you going to do when you grow up?" asked Miguel Mateos in her ear, singing like it was the 80s again and he was pushing the cause of "rock in your language"—Spanish-language music to compete with the imports introduced by MTV.

"Meche, is that you?"

Meche looked up and tugged out the earbuds.

Daniela was pleasantly plump. She had traded her pink sneakers and pink shirts for black shoes in a ballerina style and a white peasant shirt. She looked warm and sweet, just like the Daniela she had known.

"Yeah," Meche said extending her hand.

Daniela hugged her, planting a kiss on her cheek. A typical Mexican greeting, though it startled Meche a bit, unused to such a personal hello.

"It's so good to see you," Daniela said, pulling out a chair.

"Do you want something?" Meche asked.

"Just a latte."

Meche motioned to the server and the woman took their order.

Daniela looked at Meche expectantly, a big smile on her face.

"So, is Norway cold? What am I saying, of course it's cold."

"It's fine," Meche said. "I've been there for four years now."

"Where were you before that?"

"Spain. The United Kingdom. Wherever there's work. You'd be surprised. Software development is actually quite big in Romania."

"Well, that's awesome."

Daniela's smile faltered a little.

"I heard your dad passed away."

"Who told you?"

"Sebastián."

"How would he know?"

"When something happens in the neighbourhood people know. He knows."

"So you still talk to him?"

"Oh, maybe once a year," Daniela said with a shrug. "He's been living in Tijuana for a long time now so we don't see much of each other. He only moved back this spring."

"I saw him yesterday," Meche said, taking a sip of tea.

"Yeah? What did he say?"

"Nothing. I just saw him standing across the street."

"You didn't say hi?"

"He didn't say hi either."

Daniela's coffee arrived. She opened two little packets of sugar and poured them in.

"Are you still angry at him?"

"What do you think?"

"You always could hold a grudge."

"Bingo," Meche said winking and pointing a finger at Daniela.

Daniela sighed, resting her elbows on the table, holding her cup carefully.

"I guess you've forgiven me?"

"You were not the major issue," Meche said, "although you played your part."

"Meche, we couldn't keep on forever. Casting spells, playing with people..."

"Why not?"

"It wasn't right."

"That's not why we stopped, though."

"Maybe it was a bit of why we stopped. A lot. Because you—"

Meche shook her head, tossing her tea bag onto a napkin and folding it all into a ball.

"We stopped because Sebastián broke the circle and convinced you to abandon it, to boot. He betrayed me. Fucked my life."

"He didn't..."

"He didn't?"

"Meche, Sebastián adored you."

Meche leaned back, an unpleasant smirk on her face. Adored her? Right. He had a funny way of showing it. A funny way of being her best friend.

"Look, I guessed you were still on good terms with him. That's why I wanted to talk to you. I don't want him showing for my father's novena. I know it may seem the polite thing to do, but I don't want him in my mother's apartment. I'm pretty sure Jimena invited him, but I'm against it. He should stay away."

"Meche, that's not right."

"It is what it is."

"Are you going to tell me to stay out of your apartment too?"

Meche shrugged, her face cold. She didn't care if Daniela came, but she wasn't going to encourage it either.

"That's mean, Meche," Daniela said. "We both knew your dad."

"Well, he's dead. He won't miss you."

Daniela chuckled, looking down at her hands.

"Here I thought you were trying to reconnect."

"I'm a bitch like that. See, I wouldn't want someone hexing me or my mom. Old habits."

"We wouldn't hex you."

"Liar," Meche whispered. "Just tell him to stay out of the apartment."

"I brought something for you," Daniela said, reaching for her large purse and pulling out a fat manila envelope. "Don't worry. It's not hexed."

She set the envelope in the middle of the table. Meche glanced at it but made no attempt to look inside.

"You know, Meche, I always thought you were the smartest of us. You were always so sharp. But now I realize you've always been half-blind, and not nearly as sharp as you think."

"What do you mean?" Meche asked.

"You need to let it go. My regards to your mother."

Daniela slipped away. Meche drank her tea slowly, taking her time. When she was done she opened the envelope and looked inside. It was Meche's notebook. Her old grimoire. There were also lots of photographs. Daniela's quinceañera party and Daniela looking like a bottle of Pepto-Bismol in her gigantic dress. Meche leaning against a wall, headphones on, staring at the camera as if she was daring someone to take a snapshot. Ah, Constantino and Isadora's group. Sebastián's motorcycle. And...

... Sebastián and Meche. It was a series of photos taken inside a booth. They were making faces in the first two frames, their tongues sticking out. By the third one they had settled down and were looking at the camera with a smile. The fourth one showed them looking at each other. In that last bit of black-and-white film, their expressions were inscrutable.

Meche stuffed the photos back inside the envelope.

Mexico City, 1988

SHE RECOGNIZED THE notes of power in the air. She could see them the same way one can see a spider's web when a shaft of light hits it at the right angle.

Meche's web of power.

Dolores clicked her needles together and smiled, remembering her own days of spells.

She didn't think about magic very much anymore. That was part of her childhood, when Dolores and her sisters stitched spells with their needles. Spells to make the clouds release a gentle drizzle upon their heads. Spells to catch the eye of the boys in town. All those spells which were now gone, erased the same way a slate is erased with a warm cloth. But the memory of the feeling, of the magic... ah, that was still there.

Where had she put her old thimble? It had been made of porcelain and carefully painted by her eldest sister. Dolores hadn't looked at her object of power in ages. She wondered whether it still had any strength in it.

She'd forgotten the words they used to say, how it was done. Dolores squinted, trying to remember the specifics, but they slipped out of focus. Magic was not formulas, anyway. It was feeling. Something to be discovered, to unspool... yes that was the trick.

"Grandma! I'm home!" Meche yelled, and she heard the front door bang shut, then the quick patter of feet across the hallway.

It was no more than a few seconds before a record started playing.

Dolores smiled and kept knitting.

HE WAS WATCHING his classmates across the schoolyard, eating their lunch. Isadora was leaning down to talk to Constantino and he was laughing.

Now that the Day of the Dead had passed, November marked the real festivity of the season: Isadora's birthday party. Each year she threw a birthday bash and each year Sebastián did not attend. It was not that he was not invited: everybody was. He never dared to show up.

He kept thinking about attending, wearing brand new sneakers, his hair combed back, looking like a rock star.

"What are we going to wish for next?" Daniela asked.

"Isadora's birthday party," Sebastián said before Meche could open her mouth.

The girls blinked and looked at each other, then back at him.

"We should go, at least for a little bit. Go in style. Make them notice us."

Daniela shrugged. Meche sipped her bottle of apple juice and began peeling its label off with careful fingers.

"It's not a bad idea," Meche said. "All the cool kids will be there."

"We could be just as cool as them. Couldn't we?" Daniela asked.

"If I had Constantino's money I'm sure I could look cool too," Sebastián replied.

"So are we wishing for money?" Daniela asked.

"Yeah," Sebastián said. "Enough dough to buy new outfits. What do you say, Meche? You girls could get your hair done. Makeup. The whole nine yards."

"Makeup is not going to cover my pimples," Meche said.

"So we wish away the pimples," Sebastián said.

Daniela giggled. "Can I wish for a different eye colour? Just for the weekend?"

"Sure," Sebastián said.

"We can't be wishing too much, too often," Meche warned them.

"Why not?" Daniela asked.

"'Cause I felt tired after what we did. Didn't you feel it? I slept like a rock."

"Me too," Daniela said "Why would it work like that?"

"I dunno."

Sebastián watched as Isadora moved away from her group, heading towards the school's little general store. Sebastián had no business near the store: he could not afford the drinks or sandwiches they sold there.

But he had the wild desire to talk to Isadora, to open his mouth and regale her with a sentence for once in his life. He was still high from the motorcycle trip with Meche and he felt this day he might actually do it.

"Okay, no wishing too often, got it," Sebastián said hastily. "I'll be back."

He walked quickly, moving in the same direction Isadora

had gone. He stood behind her in line, with nothing more than one peso in his pocket. When she glanced at him, Sebastián nodded and smiled.

She gave him this weird look, like she was a little surprised to see him standing behind her, but did not speak to him.

Sebastián waited in line, his hands deep in his pockets, trying to keep calm.

"So... umm... your birthday's this Saturday, right?"

"Yes," Isadora said.

"What kind of presents are you hoping for?"

"I don't know. I like jewellery."

Constantino's father owned a jewellery store. For a moment Sebastián saw his opportunities dwindle, but then he remembered he could buy anything they wanted. They had magic now. He could look for a nice, golden bracelet for Isadora. Or a little chain. Something pretty, which she might wear often.

"Cool."

"Are you going to come?" she asked.

"Maybe," he said.

"Your friends too?" She lifted her chin, looking in Meche and Daniela's direction.

Sebastián nodded. "All right. I'll see you then."

The line moved, Isadora bought a soft drink and stepped aside. Sebastián looked at the candy and junk food for sale, trying to figure out what he could buy.

WHEN HE WALKED by the Pit that afternoon, Sebastián saw Isadora, Constantino and some other students standing there, smoking and chatting.

Isadora held her cigarette with two fingers and she smiled, just a tiny smile.

He felt like waving and smiling back, but Constantino turned his head and saw him. Sebastián continued on his way, eyes fixed straight ahead.

"You know what it's like? It's like reverse engineering."

"What's reverse engineering?" Sebastián asked.

"Umm... it's when you lack the software specifications so you poke around the program interface trying to find the solution. That's what we are doing with magic."

Meche grabbed another record, looking at it critically. They had tried four different albums and none of them had produced the same magic effect as last time. Meche had been sure all they had to do was focus and be specific, but apparently that was not enough.

"I don't understand," Sebastián said.

"Okay, like the TU-4."

"The what?"

"During World War II the Russians didn't have a strategic bomber like the US and they wanted one. But they couldn't figure out how to build it. Then a few B-29 bombers had to make emergency landings in Russia and the Russians looked at them, figured how they were made and made their own bombers. It's like... like building a puzzle without the instructions. Figuring it backwards. Something like that."

"You mean it's like taking a stab in the dark," Sebastián said.

"An *educated* stab."

"How'd you learn about World War II?"

"That time they punished me and I had to spend a whole month during recess in the library. I had to read the encyclopedia and write a report on Russia during World War II."

"Who'd know," he said with a smirk.

"What?"

"You can read."

Meche punched his arm and Sebastián chuckled.

"I still don't understand what we are doing," Daniela said, holding up a bunch of record sleeves in her hands.

"We don't know either," Sebastián said.

"Oh."

Daniela blinked, then looked at her records. They had been at this for more than an hour and he sensed that soon enough Daniela would ask to go home. If they were going to figure how to cast a spell a second time around, they had to do it quick.

"Okay, let's try Money's Too Tight To Mention," Sebastián said. He was out of other ideas.

They crowded around the portable record player, holding hands tight, just like last time. The little beat began and then the chorus kicked in. But nothing happened. The room remained cold and still.

"Ugh," Meche said, falling back against the floor. "What's wrong? We've done obvious songs, not so obvious songs…"

"We can try Material Girl again," Sebastián suggested.

That had been the first song they'd attempted to use. A second try might not amount to anything, but Sebastián did not know what else to pick. Meche rubbed her hands against her eyes.

"Okay," Daniela said, sounding chipper. "Let me find it one more time."

Sebastián sat down next to Meche, bumping his sneaker against hers.

"Hey, we have time to get it right," he said. "We'll wish for the money, wish for the—"

"I so wanted to get a decent dress that's not like two sizes too big," Meche muttered. "And maybe get rid of the pimples... somehow."

"They're not *that* bad," he said, trying to be kind, though they were bad. Meche often had pimples all around her mouth and smack in the middle of her forehead. She tried to hide them with her bangs, but it didn't help. "Just fucking hormones."

"Gee, Doctor Soto, you think?"

"Don't be annoying."

Meche bumped his shoe back and turned to look at him, frowning. She looked very solemn, but a grin was about to break through, shattering her sour expression.

"Ouch!"

Sebastián raised his head. "What's up, Dani?"

"It's hot!"

"What's hot?" Meche muttered, taking a long pause after each word.

"The record."

That was about the weirdest thing he'd ever heard.

"Records are not hot," Sebastián said.

"Wait," Meche said, sitting up at once. "Hot?"

"Yeah."

"Which one?"

Daniela looked at the floor, at a record sleeve next to her foot. Meche scrambled forward and lifted it very carefully.

"Dead or Alive."

"You Spin Me Round (Like a Record)," Meche said. "Sebastián, touch it."

"Alright," he said.

He didn't expect it to really burn him, but as soon as he touched it Sebastián felt like he was handling a potato that had been pulled out of a boiling pot of water. He thrust it back into Meche's hands and she set it down on the floor.

"What's that?" Sebastián asked.

"I don't know," Meche muttered.

She knelt down, took the record out of the sleeve. Her fingers hovered above the shiny, black vinyl surface, very carefully.

"It's very warm. It's like… there's electricity here."

"There can't be."

Meche pressed her index finger against the record and a little blue spark actually shot up. She laughed. Daniela pressed both hands against her mouth. Sebastián just raised an eyebrow.

"You know what this means, right?" she told them. "It's not just any record. Some of them have power and some of them don't. Look, feel it."

Sebastián and Daniela both knelt down. He carefully touched the edge of the record. Another blue spark shot up.

"You think?" Sebastián asked.

"Look for other records which feel warm," Meche said.

Daniela began to go through one of the cardboard boxes. Sebastián grabbed another box, his fingers dancing over the sleeves, pulling some out, leaving others in its place. Nothing, nothing… and then bingo. A sleeve that itched his palm. He pulled out a single. It felt like a warm tortilla, just wrapped in a cloth.

"Hey," he said. "This one's the same."

"What is it?"

"Billy Idol," Sebastián said. "Dancing With Myself. Touch it."

Meche extended her hand, carefully setting it against the sleeve. She nodded very slightly.

"I feel it."

"It's… is it beating? Can you feel it?"

It was very weird. A sensation similar to the one you might get if you pressed your palm against your chest, over your heart. A little thumping.

Meche frowned. "I don't feel the beating."

"This is the one, Meche," Sebastián said. "The one for our money spell."

"Are you sure?"

"Oh, yeah."

"Then put it on. Daniela, are you ready?"

"Yes."

They gathered close to the record player, hands joined. The music began and Sebastián slowly moved his foot. Just a little bit, heel lifting and falling. Lifting and falling. Meche and Daniela's feet followed his lead, raising and falling and then Billy screamed and he grabbed Daniela and they began to dance.

Daniela was a terrible dancer but she moved quite easily

now, and despite her ridiculous pink dress she could have danced in Billy Idol's music video. Sebastián felt a jolt of electricity when their palms touched and they laughed, jumped back and forward.

He turned around and grabbed Meche's hand. He spun her, one, two, three times. Her long skirt, reaching beneath the knee, flared up, showing her legs for an instant, her knee-high stockings with the loose elastic pooling down by her ankles.

He spun her again and Meche stepped forward, her palms pressing against his chest for a moment.

Golden tendrils spilled from her fingers, curling up in the air. Sebastián raised his left arm and another golden tendril rose from his hand. He glanced at Daniela and she pointed at them, a gold ribbon extending and touching the two ribbons hovering near the ceiling. They knotted themselves together.

The room glowed golden for a second, as though a small sun had installed itself over their heads. Then little flecks of gold began to fall like snow. Their little sun was chipping away into nothingness.

The needle lifted itself and Sebastián brushed his hair from his face.

"We are going to tear the town up," he muttered.

"What?" Meche said.

"We're going to tear the town up, baby!" he yelled, grabbing Meche by the waist and lifting her up.

"Yeah, baby!"

Daniela giggled, jumping up and down. "How much money will we get? How will we get it?"

"Treasure. Hidden in some distant location and we'll

need a shovel to dig it out," he told them, still holding Meche up. "Aye, aye, Jim Hawkins."

"Jim, who?"

"Really, Meche?" he said, putting her down. "You don't even open my birthday presents, do you?"

"Not if I have to read them."

"You suck."

"Sticks and stones, Sebastián Soto," she said, standing on her tiptoes and jamming her finger against the hollow of his throat. "Let's find that cash and spend it."

They rushed down the stairs together, trying to see who made it out of the factory first.

MECHE FOUND THE old boxes where her mom said they would be and pulled them open. There were ancient textbooks there, old toys. A video game she had not played in years and years. Meche scooped them all out and set them on the floor.

She found Sebastián's books at the bottom. *Treasure Island*. Shakespeare's complete works. *El Lazarillo de Tormes*. Sebastián had definitely been an optimist, thinking one day she might develop a taste for reading.

The smallest of all the books was the last one he had ever given her: Auden.

She opened it to the first page and looked at the inscription, the letters crisp and very straight. Sebastián's handwriting.

Suppose the lions all get up and go,
And all the brooks and soldiers run away?
Will Time say nothing but I told you so?
—Always and always your best friend. Sebos.

"Always and always," she muttered.

Meche lifted the book and a picture fell out. She thought

it might be another snapshot of her with Daniela and Sebastián. But the Polaroid was of her father, holding her as a toddler. He was helping her take an uncertain step.

Her mother had gotten rid of many of the photos of her dad. Meche disposed of the ones she had with indifference. This Polaroid had escaped the culling.

There had been no photos of Vicente in his apartment. Meche had only been able to picture him tenuously, like a jumble of half-remembered features. This picture brought his features into the light, sharpened him, made him real.

And damn it, she looked a lot like her father. She'd forgotten that.

Meche wandered into the kitchen and put the kettle on the stove. She would have to go to her dad's apartment again. There were so many things to sort out and another night of food and prayer to look forward to.

"Are you hungry?" her mother asked, wandering into the kitchen and opening the refrigerator.

"I'm fine."

"You haven't had breakfast."

"I never have breakfast."

"That's not good for you. I'll make you some eggs."

"Ma…"

"Just two eggs."

Meche knew it was futile to fight back. She sat down at the kitchen table. The kettle whistled and her mother poured the boiling water into a cup, then handed it to her along with a little box full of tea bags.

"Did you ever feel sorry for dad?"

"Sorry about what?"

"In general."

"Your father made his choices. No, I didn't feel sorry for him."

Her mother turned her back on her, her attention on the eggs she was frying. She grabbed a spatula and flipped them over.

"I have no idea what he was up to these last few years," Meche said.

"The same thing as always. Pretending to write. The bar. Smoking like a train. The last few times he came over…"

"He'd come over?" Meche asked, quite shocked at that.

Her mother turned off the stove and plated the eggs. She set them down before Meche and handed her a fork.

"In the last couple of years. Not a lot. He wanted to know how you were doing. I showed him some of the pictures you sent me, of the Northern Lights. 'Too cold,' he told me."

Natalia sat down across from Meche, holding a glass of orange juice between her hands. Meche really did not want to eat, but she took a tiny bite.

"He wanted to write to you. I gave him your e-mail…"

"Why would you do that?" Meche asked.

She had told Natalia not to give her personal information to her father. He'd had it before and they had few, sparse conversations over the years, generally on Christmas and her birthday. When she lived in London he phoned one night, teary and drunk, talking about music. An incoherent babble of self-pity, of "Let me explain a few things to you about myself," and all of it mixed with lyrics from songs. A mess. She told her mother not to give her phone number to him again and changed the number.

"He was dying, Meche," Natalia said, palms up. "What

else was I supposed to do? He said he was going to write to you from an internet café. I guess he didn't."

"Nope."

Meche added a couple of spoons of sugar to her tea, stirring it slowly.

"Do you miss him?" her mother asked.

"My father?" Meche asked. "How could I miss someone I hadn't seen for half my life before he died?"

"Because you look like you miss him."

MECHE CONTINUED CATALOGUING her father's albums. Around noon, she realized she should have eaten the eggs instead of just taking a bite. Her father's cupboards were barren, the kitchen minimally stocked. Above the sink she found a big box of animal crackers. There was also powdered milk.

She thought of eating the crackers, but the memories of her father and a younger Meche enjoying them with a glass of milk made her pause. She grabbed her jacket and walked two blocks away, to a narrow Chinese café. She asked for tea, but this being a Mexican-Chinese café, there was none. She settled for café-au-lait and fresh bread rolls, watching the woman half-asleep behind the cash register; thinking that this café could be right from the 1980s, so old and worn it looked.

Meche grabbed her earbuds and pressed play, but despite the cheery assurances of Elvis Presley the world seemed dim and grey. She paid, went back to her father's apartment, and found it dimmer and greyer than the café.

She did not feel like sorting his records. She was tired

of looking at album covers and decided to put his other things in boxes. The typewriter, to begin with.

It was impossible to believe a man would continue to use a typewriter well into this decade, but he had. It was a heavy beast, many keys worn with the passage of time. Meche set it in the box, then began to gather his manuscript pages. There was, literally, a pile of them and many more scattered all over the house.

While looking for more pages, she found a dozen shoeboxes under the bed. Each box was packed with tiny little notebooks, inscribed with her father's spidery handwriting. Most of the notebooks contained songs. Songs he'd written. A few things for the book, but it was mostly his songs and his random thoughts.

Meche had never seen any of her father's songs. She knew he'd written them and she knew he'd stopped. But he hadn't stopped. There were notebooks from the 70s, but others were labelled from the 80s and 90s, and as recently as a few months before. She pulled out a bunch of yellowed letters and discovered these were the love letters he had written to her mother years before, when he was courting her. He had written lyrics in the margins.

Secretly, under his bed, Vicente Vega had collected decades worth of lyrics and of his life.

Meche grabbed one notebook from 1973 and opened it, turning the pages curiously, looking at the careful, small letters, the tiny script with almost no spaces in between words.

Natalia and I agreed that if we have a boy, she'll pick the name, and if it's a girl, I get to pick. I know we are going to have a girl. I know she will have my eyes. I have been thinking of a proper name for her. There are many pretty names from songs which she could have. At first I thought maybe Emily because of the song For Emily, Whenever I May Find Her, but then I changed my mind. I thought about Julia because of The Beatles' song from The White Album. *Then I figured maybe I should name her after a singer instead of a song, and oh boy, anyone who knows me knows my first choice was Janice. But yesterday I was listening to Mercedes Sosa singing Gracias a la Vida by Violeta Parra and I think I will call her Mercedes Violeta, in honour of two great Latin American writers. Life has not given me many things, but it will give me the most important thing I can ever have: my very own Mercedes.*

Meche looked around the house and found the record she was looking for easily. It had been in the stack next to her father's bed: Mercedes Sosa singing Gracias a la Vida. She put the record on and sat on the floor in her father's bedroom, looking at the painted palm trees.

Meche took out the picture of her in her father's arms and she wondered about this man she did not know, this stranger who had passed away and left nothing but papers, records and songs.

Mexico City, 1988

SEBASTIÁN AND MECHE were both sitting on the floor and leaning over the book, carefully absorbing every word. Daniela, meanwhile, sulked in a corner. She had videotaped episodes of *El Extraño Retorno de Diana Salazar* and had intended to watch them that afternoon. Meche had invented a mathematics study session, pulled her out of her home and dragged her to the factory. What they were studying was magic and Daniela was not willing to help with their research, preferring to sit on the couch and immerse herself in a bodice ripper with a sexy pirate on the cover.

"But here, what about this part?" Sebastián asked. "An amulet. An object of power."

"What does it mean?"

"Like witches with wands. Only not that stupid, I guess."

"Art-ha-me," Meche said, turning the page of the book. "Dani, aren't you even going to look at it?"

"Not if it has demons in it."

Sebastián had found a used book about witchcraft with plenty of extracts from *The Key of Solomon*. It mentioned a bevy of demons and the garish cover with a bug-eyed woman had scared Daniela away. She insisted she was not going to read it, study it or anything of the sort.

"It's not Hollywood demons," Meche said.

Daniela shook her head and Meche rolled her eyes.

"Okay, so objects of power. We can't be carrying staffs around Mexico City. What can we keep to be our object?"

"I don't know," Sebastián said with a shrug. "Couldn't we keep whatever we want? Whatever matters to us?"

"That's fine with me. We should keep it a secret. Never tell anyone. Not even each other."

"Why would we keep secrets from each other?" Sebastián asked, frowning.

"Ugh. Don't you listen when you speak out loud? Didn't you just tell us about Merlin and that chick Vivi?"

"Vivien."

"That one. She figured Merlin's weakness, tricked him and made him sleep forever."

"But we wouldn't trick each other."

"Yeah, but it feels kind of personal."

"Fine."

"I'll write this thing about objects of power in the grimoire," Meche said taking her pen and opening the notebook. "Did you hear about objects of power?"

"I heard," Daniela said.

Meche began writing, neatly labelling the entry with the date and a heading. Sebastián stretched his feet and reached for the large bag of chips Meche had brought. There were also a couple of sodas and some chocolate. He munched the chips loudly and wondered what object he might pick. A book. Would that be too obvious? Where would he put it? He shared his room with Romualdo and that didn't leave many chances for privacy. There was a loose tile in the kitchen which could be loosened a bit more. Or perhaps he should just tuck it at the back of his closet. Under the bed.

"We still don't have the money," Sebastián reminded Meche.

She held the pen between her teeth and nodded.

"Maybe it takes longer to take effect when it's cash," Daniela suggested.

"Well, we're going to need it if we want to buy new clothes and stuff," Sebastián said. "Are your parents even going to let you go, Dani?"

"Yeah. My mom thinks it'll be good if I go. As long as I'm back early, by ten. She can pick us up and drop us off."

"Wanna hitch a ride with Dani?" Sebastián asked.

"I want to stay late," Meche said. "Can't we take a cab?"

Sebastián considered his reduced finances. Bagging groceries was not a lucrative operation and a cerillo had no regular wage or contract, just the tips he could gather. On top of that, it was near the end of the month and that meant money was short. He didn't have cash to splurge on a cab and since their spell hadn't actually worked yet, he was reluctant to promise a taxi, even if they split it.

"We can take my motorcycle or the bus," he proposed.

"I don't want to mess my hair and clothes on the bus," Meche said.

"We could walk..."

"All the way to Isadora's house?"

Sebastián did not want to sound like he was cheap. He

hated putting his situation into words, so he simply sat on the couch, picking up a couple of records and examining them, hoping Meche might drop the point for now.

Meche went back to her grimoire. After a while she sighed and sat between Daniela and Sebastián.

"Rodríguez is so going to fail me," she said.

"Why?" Daniela asked.

"Because he's a freak. Didn't you see him in class today, 'Miss Vega, can you tell us one of the important symbols in *Anna Karenina* and then he kept drilling me and drilling me, like it was the Spanish Inquisition. I did the reading and he still told me he's giving me a bad mark."

"I'm not doing too great either," Daniela said.

"What are you talking about? You always get an 8."

"Yeah, but my dad doesn't like me getting anything but 10s," Daniela said. "And I'm seriously studying hard."

"Isadora is passing with flying colours," Meche said. "Maybe I need to flash my panties at the creep more often."

Sebastián gave Meche an irritated, sideways glance, his jaw growing tense at the mention of the girl he liked.

"She does not flash her panties at anyone."

"Oh, hoho. With that short skirt?" Meche said, snorting. "She flashes plenty. And her squeaky little voice. 'Mr. Rodríguez, I don't understand why Anna Karenina throws herself in front of the train.' Newsflash: because it's fucking foreshadowed like pages before. Even *I* got that."

"If you're going to be a bitch why don't you do it alone?" Sebastián said, grabbing his backpack.

"Where are you going?" Meche asked.

"I've got a shift at the supermarket."

"At *six*?"

"Yeah, I think I'll leave early."

"Ugh, Sebos, don't be a dick."

"Bye," he muttered.

NINE O'CLOCK and two more hours until he could take off his vest and roll into bed. Sebastián bagged groceries robotically, tossing onions and avocados and potatoes together, stretching out his hand and waiting for the clock to advance another minute.

He felt the headphones pressing against his ears as Meche stood behind him, standing on her tiptoes. He turned around and raised an eyebrow at her.

"What?"

"You said you wanted to borrow my Walkman so you could listen to music at work tonight," she said.

"You didn't have to…"

"It's got The Who on there. Which is probably like giving pearls to a pig, but knock yourself out with it."

Sebastián shook his head. Even when Meche was trying to apologize in her own Meche-way, she had a way of insulting you once again. And yet, looking down at the girl with her oversized green jacket, the sleeves covering her fingers, the collar of her shirt sticking out at an odd angle, he thought she was the only person who ever got him.

"You shouldn't talk shit about other people," he said.

"That's what they do. What do you think they say about us?"

"Yeah, well. We've got to be the better persons and all. I suppose."

"Says who?"

"I dunno. But I don't like gossipy people."

Meche snorted, shuffling her feet.

"Fine. I won't talk crap about Isadora if you don't want me to."

"Thanks."

Meche saluted, a mock-serious expression on her face. She stepped back and started walking away.

"Thanks. I'll get it back to you later," he called after her.

Sebastián pressed Play and the drums began to roll as The Who proclaimed this was their generation. Sebastián bagged his groceries to the rhythm, bobbing his head up and down.

WALKING HOME THAT night Sebastián decided to cut his way through the neglected, concrete wasteland of the park. It was arranged in the shape of a large rectangle with four paths leading to the centre, where the hobos and the hoodlums tended to gather. Sad trees and ugly bushes looked at the large cement benches. The northeast corner was an impromptu waste disposal facility: people who missed or did not care to wait for the morning garbage truck dumped their supermarket plastic bags filled with garbage there, attracting stray dogs looking for a meal.

As he walked by a cement bench he noticed a wallet on the ground and picked it up. It had no identifications inside, only bills. Lots of bills. Sebastián looked around, checked nobody was watching him, and tucked it in his trousers.

THREE TIMES A week Vicente Vega stopped by a little travel agency and met with Azucena Bernal for an hour of sex. He could not say it had started innocently but he had never intended for it to become what it had become. Unlike many other Mexican men—fixated with the idea of being macho, with a desire for a casa chica, for a mistress and its ensuing complications—Vicente had never seriously considered establishing ties with another woman.

Yet there he was, with Azucena. Three times a week and just as many phone calls when they did not meet. They were into the fourth week of their relationship and it showed no signs of stopping or ceasing in intensity. Meanwhile, Natalia stared at him across the table at nights, ate him alive with her words, piled indifference and scorn upon his shoulders. Azucena, as plain as his wife was beautiful, was sweeter, more understanding, did not yell at him demanding he turn off the reading light or ask him to explain why he was still working on that worthless book. Vicente was seriously considering moving out. If he had a little money he would definitely do it. They could move to Puerto Vallarta and he would play his records until late at night with no one to tell him to turn the music down.

Vicente looked at the brochures he'd picked from Azucena's office: beaches, happy couples holding hands.

And he, still young, not yet old, trapped in the middle of his life with a woman who resented him, growing greyer and uglier by the day. To escape... to start anew...

If only he could finish his book. Vicente had thought that by now he'd have it all edited and proofed. Then he could sell it. He might not make a fortune, but enough to ditch Natalia.

Natalia who had never allowed him to go to Puerto Vallarta because the sun was bad for her skin even when, back then, her father had agreed to pay for the trip. Instead, they went to Cuernavaca on their honeymoon and Natalia spent the money her dad had reserved for the trip on a new wardrobe. When her father passed away, leaving Natalia a bit of money, she refused to take a vacation in Cancún. She had bought herself a new car— not *their* car, because he was not allowed to drive it—and some jewellery.

There was still enough money left from that time to go on vacation—at least a little one, at least Puerto Vallarta— but it was all in the family savings fund. Money which one day would go to Meche for university. Not a penny could be touched. Vicente didn't have a say in the matter. Vicente didn't have a say in anything.

Smoking his cigarettes in a corner of the apartment and nursing real and imaginary wounds with a few drinks, Vicente felt himself growing old.

"I DON'T KNOW," he told his wife that night.

"You're never going to finish that book."

Vicente smiled and lit his cigarette.

"At the very least you should see about a promotion. Announcers don't make shit. You should be a show producer."

"I like being on air."

"Announcers are becoming obsolete."

"How are the acting classes going?" he asked, throwing the ball at her.

For the past year his wife had been taking acting classes at a little school downtown. He had seen the coach and could almost vouch she was also having an affair, but he wasn't about to hurl stones. If it kept her off his case, he was frankly okay with it.

"Fine," Natalia said, looking sour.

Vicente smiled. She had never been able to act her way out of a paper bag. At least Vicente could play an instrument, write songs, write a book (though it remained unfinished, remained an eternal work in progress). Perhaps that was where the animosity was first born. A bitter jealousy over his superior artistic talent. Talent which didn't amount to much, but it was better than nothing, and that was what Natalia had: nothing. Not a splinter of artistic ability.

"Mmm," Vicente said. "I'm going to listen to music before going to bed."

"Turn off the lights when you are done. You are always wasting power and then the bill is very high."

"I'll turn them off."

HE SAT IN the dark, listening to The Temptations and smoking.

He thought about what anchored him to this city, to

this apartment, to this chair and found very little, the thread of his existence stretched thin.

Vicente saw himself exiting in the middle of the night, grabbing his leather jacket and his old guitar, and simply getting on a bus and heading to nowhere. He pictured himself as a shadow melting into shadows and disappearing.

He closed his eyes.

Vicente opened them when he heard voices. Male and female. Young.

"I found it in the park, just laying there. It's full of money."

"How much is in there?"

It was Meche talking to the tall boy, the one she was always with: Sebastián. He didn't know what they were discussing. He checked his watch and saw it was late, stood up to remind them Sebastián should be home by now and promptly sat back down. Their voices sounded so content and happy. He remembered sounding like that.

He let them drone on until he heard the door close and Meche shuffle towards her room.

He thought what he might do if he was that young again, of opportunities lost and moments which pass you by.

MECHE LOOKED INTO the mirror, critically analyzing the neon yellow skirt. This was foreign territory. Her regular daywear included jeans, t-shirts and the occasional jacket, sleeves rolled up, with a pair of really heavy, masculine boots. There was no money for the latest fashions so she made do with leftovers from her older cousin or opted for cheap, unfashionable items. Meche looked positively… dainty in this outfit.

"Are you sure girls wear this stuff?" she asked Daniela.

"Look," Daniela said, handing her one of the teen magazines tucked in her backpack.

She matched the girl in the picture. But Meche didn't look like her—she was far less attractive. Meche felt like she was a cheap copy sold in La Lagunilla. This despite that they were shopping at a nice store because the money spell had come through in the shape of the wallet from the park, its contents promptly plundered. Finally, they could shop in Polanco. Sadly, nothing seemed to fit Meche properly.

"I like it. Do you like mine?" Daniela asked.

Meche glanced at her friend's outfit. It was predictably pink and purple. Daniela resembled a large meringue, but Meche supposed it *did* look like the stuff the girls in the magazine were wearing.

"I guess it's alright," Meche said. She leaned towards the mirror, zeroing on the zits around her mouth, and sighed. "I need to fix my skin."

"You should put on a nice avocado mask before going to bed."

"I need a major intervention, not an avocado mask. How can so many pimples appear every damn day? It's like they know I want to go to a party."

"It's no big deal."

"You say that because you don't look like me," Meche muttered.

"Do you want to see what Sebastián is wearing?" Daniela asked.

"Okay."

The girls stepped out of their changing room and knocked at one of the other doors.

"Seboooos," Meche said.

"What?" came the gruff answer.

"Show us."

"No."

"Sebos..."

"No!"

Meche tried jumping to get a look over the door, but could not reach high enough. Over the stores' speakers What I Like About You began to play and Meche began knocking on the door to the rhythm of the music.

"Come oooon."

"Fine!"

He opened the door unexpectedly, making Meche stumble back. He glared at both girls, crossing his arms over his chest. Sebastián—he of the minimalist, all-black attires—looked like he had stepped out of an episode of *Miami Vice* and was going to give Don Johnson a run for his money. He was wearing a bubblegum-pink t-shirt, a white jacket with wide lapels and loafers sans socks.

Meche couldn't help it. She laughed. This caused Sebastián to immediately retreat into the changing room.

"I'm sorry," Meche said, following inside and laughing. "I'm sorry."

"I knew I shouldn't follow Daniela's stupid advice," Sebastián muttered, taking off the jacket and putting it back on the hanger.

"It's not bad."

"Yeah. Your reaction proved it."

"Daniela, come here," Meche said.

"What?" Daniela asked, poking her head in.

"Do you like it?" Meche asked, her thumb pointing at Sebastián.

"I think he looks nice."

"See? You look nice."

"I'll change into something else. The trousers are too damn tight," he muttered.

"I can ask for a bigger size," Daniela said, happily scampering off in her pink and purple tutu-like dress.

Meche looked at the shirts and jackets Sebastián had piled on a chair, raising a skeptical eyebrow at a pastel-coloured tie.

"That skirt is short," Sebastián said.

"It seems to be the purpose of mini-skirts," Meche replied.

"Yeah, but you hate skirts."

"I know."

"I can see your ass."

Meche resisted the impulse to pull the hem down, but she did give Sebastián a pronounced, irritated look.

"The point of this whole thing is to look cool," she said. "You know, unlike we regularly do."

"I think you shouldn't confuse 'cool' with 'mildly obscene.'"

"Thanks, Grandpa Smurf."

"No… I mean, it's… disturbing," he concluded.

Meche didn't even know what to say to that. She opted for nothing and went back to her own changing room. She picked a pair of neon green leggings and sighed.

* * *

THE GIRLS WANTED to get haircuts. That's when Sebastián pulled the brakes. He was willing to go shopping for new clothes, he was even willing to show them the clothes he picked, but he was not going to the hairdresser with them.

Daniela looked crestfallen. She had brought numerous cut-outs from magazines showing various hairstyles she thought would look good on him. Sebastián's longish hair, however, was going to remain exactly as it was.

As the girls wandered towards the hair stylist, Sebastián quietly made his way to a jewelry shop. He stopped before the displays, peering down at the sparkling diamonds and the flash of gold until he spotted a gold heart on a chain. He took out the wallet and counted the remaining bills.

"UGH... I DON'T feel very well," Daniela said.

"That's because you drank the milkshake too fast," Meche said. "Brain freeze. When are you going to learn?"

"I suppose..."

Meche saw Sebastián's spidery hand reach towards her plate, plucking a fry, dipping it in ketchup and throwing it in his mouth. She retaliated by reaching for his burger and giving it a big bite, then opening her mouth and showing him the food.

"Gross," he said.

"Gwa," Meche said, turning to Daniela and also showing her the food.

Daniela did not react. She blinked in confusion. Meche shrugged, closed her mouth and chewed.

"I want to go see a movie," Meche said. "We should buy a big bucket of popcorn."

"No more food," Daniela muttered.

"Bah, I thought you had more stamina," Meche said, pointing a fry at Daniela. "Do you want to watch a movie?"

"I want to go home," Daniela said.

"Don't be a spoilsport. Sebos, what do you want to do?"

"Finish my food."

"After you finish your food?"

"Why don't we go to the arcade?"

"How much money do we have left?"

Sebastián pulled out a bill and placed it on the table. Meche nodded thoughtfully. They'd get more bang out of their buck if they went to play with the machines in the pharmacy near home because it was cheaper, but that meant Meche might bump into her mom. Plus, there were only two machines and the little kids around the block tended to get on them pretty early in the afternoon. The arcade wouldn't have these issues but it was more expensive.

"I think the arcade's a good idea. Dani, you want to come?" Meche asked.

"No. I think I want to have a nap."

"Alright," Meche said. "Suit yourself."

AFTER THEY FINISHED their hamburgers, Sebastián and Meche saw Daniela home. They dumped their purchases at Meche's house before rushing off to Arcadeland, the arcade closest to their home. It had over twenty machines and two bored, young attendants who sold tokens and exchanged tickets for tiny plastic bracelets and other assorted crap. In a corner of the joint, there was a stand selling stale pizza and candy.

Sebastián and Meche ignored the bad food and bought a bunch of tokens, dumping them into the machines of their choice. For Sebastián, that was Pac-Man. For Meche, it was something which involved shooting.

Eventually they both got behind the steering wheel and competed in several driving games. The pixelated car did the Monaco circuit, animated girls in bikinis holding up signs saying 'Number 1' and 'Race On!' while some muffled music—Meche thought it might well be Eurythmics—pumped through the arcade.

"Win, win, win!" Meche yelled.

"Let's try the air hockey table."

Meche knew Sebastián wanted to play air hockey because he could easily beat her and rub it in her face, paying her back for her previous wins at the racing machine, but she felt like being a good sport and followed him.

They both stopped in their tracks once they were near the table: Constantino and some of the other boys were gathered around it.

Sometimes, when Meche looked at Constantino, she could almost feel her brain flying through her skull and exiting her body. Coherent thought escaped her and she was left with a terrible longing.

This was one such moment. The lights and sounds of the arcade seemed to dim, leaving only Constantino, standing by the table, looking down, a lazy smile on his lips. She had the urge to extend her hand, touch his shoulder or brush her fingers through his hair. To hold a minuscule part of him, just for a few seconds. To cup the sound of his laughter against her ear.

The boys, taking note of them, looked at Meche and Sebastián and grinned. One of the boys chuckled and someone—she did not know who—must have said something funny because they all started laughing.

Meche and Sebastián moved away, back to a corner of the arcade and she threw a coin into a slot, her fingers trembling as she gripped the joystick.

The sugar-high she had been on had emptied out and she felt herself crashing down, her stomach heaving and turning with the unpleasant taste of sadness.

Would they also laugh at them at Isadora's party, when they wore their new clothes? If they did, they could curse them, make their teeth fall out; the benefit of becoming teenage witches.

From now on, Sebastián, Daniela and Meche were the ones with the upper hand. Which is why she had a hard time understanding why obstinate tears were prickling her eyes.

No crying. Ever. That was her motto.

Sebastián leaned down, rested his chin against her shoulder and whispered into her ear.

"It's fine," he said.

She turned her head by a small fraction and tried to smile.

Meche looked back at the arcade machine. Sebastián also threw a coin into the slot and pressed the start button.

Now that she paid attention, Meche was pretty sure Eurythmics was what they were listening to. It sounded like Here Comes the Rain Again.

*   *   *

PEOPLE WHO HAVE never spent time inside a radio cabin cannot understand the appeal of that small enclosed space, its turntable and its microphone. Behind insulated walls and tape reels hides a spark, a magic, you can't find anywhere else.

Music.

Vicente sat in the cabin, closed his eyes and the world spun away.

Television, movies—they can't compare to radio. To the music over airwaves. It's like a portal to another world.

He was needing other worlds more and more these days. Things at home were nastier than ever and the book was going nowhere.

Vicente smoked his cigarette and opened his notebook, re-reading his notes from yesterday. He had his great ideas, all scribbled tight, but when it came time to type them out he seemed to lose his rhythm. The brilliant sentence turned limp and stale. The turn of phrase was dull.

Maybe his wife was right. Maybe he was never going to finish the book. It would be just like his musical career: down the drain and away.

He quietly pulled out the hip flask he had taken to carrying inside his coat's pocket and saw his face, distorted against the metal, before taking a sip.

ANIMAL FETUSES OF different kinds sat in jars filled with formaldehyde. They floated in the yellow substance and seemed to stare at the students. There was a big vat with whale ambergris in a corner, which you could supposedly use to make perfumes. A large poster of the periodic table was pinned to the back wall. The blackboard was filled with symbols of a vague, alchemical cast.

Everyone was supposed to have a chemistry partner during lab work, but Meche, Daniela and Sebastián worked as a trio. Miss Costa already had enough trouble trying to enforce the necessity of lab coats and safety procedures, so she let them have their way.

But Daniela was missing today.

"Remember to put on your goggles," the teacher said in a monotonous drone.

Sebastián placed the stirring bar in the large beaker and began pouring the potassium iodate.

"You think she's had another episode?" Meche asked.

Daniela was often sick and they knew the drill. They'd bring her candy, sit by her bed, maybe even take turns reading one of those horrid romance or Gothic novels to her—Sebastián often read parts of *Flowers in the Attic* or *Corazón Salvaje*, which took much aplomb on his part—then pat her hand and she'd be back in class in a day or two.

"Maybe she just caught a cold or has an upset stomach," Sebastián said. "It could be nothing."

"We should go see her, after school."

Isadora laughed. Sebastián raised his head and looked in her direction. Their pretty classmate was playfully sitting next to Constantino, in a position which was strategically hiking her skirt up. Meche thought Sebastián was going to turn into jelly and collapse upon the floor, foaming from the mouth. She wondered if she shouldn't finish the chemistry demonstration for fear he would blow them up.

"Turn on the stirring plate," Sebastián said, checking his notes.

"Stirring plate," Meche muttered.

"I need the hydrogen peroxide."

Meche passed him the diluted solution. They watched as the solution in the beaker turned amber and then a deep shade of blue.

Isadora was laughing again, chirping about some inanity or other. She spoke too loudly and she did it to get the attention of the class. Judging by Sebastián's reaction, it had the intended effect.

"Well then, that's a chemical oscillator reaction," Meche said, carefully writing in her notebook. "You know, chemistry is a lot like magic."

"Huh?" Sebastián asked.

She would have blamed his blank stare on the fumes, but Meche knew better.

"Well, chemistry was started by alchemists. All of them with their formulas and books and secrecy. I think they were a lot like us."

"I suppose so."

"Except we are not looking for the philosopher's stone."

"The what?"

"You know, the substance that turns lead into gold."

"Maybe we are. In a way," Sebastián said.

Meche glanced at Isadora and she thought she wouldn't have Sebastián, not even if he was plated in gold. Sebastián was stupid.

Then Meche remembered Constantino and realized she was as dumb as her friend.

THEY WOULD HAVE taken the motorcycle, but Sebastián was out of gas and didn't have money to fill the tank. So they walked instead. He did not mind. It meant they would spend more time together.

"Are you going to need help with your literature homework again?" he asked.

"Why? You need help with math again?"

"Even trade," he said. "My lit for your math, as usual."

"Throw in a bar of chocolate and it's a deal."

"I'm not throwing in a bar of nothing."

"Blah."

"Stay and watch TV with me. That's your extra payment."

Meche made a face, like it would be such a chore to sit with him and watch two hours of whatever stupid programming was on, but he knew that was exactly what she wanted to do. They could make cheese sandwiches and grill them on the stove. As far as Sebastián was concerned, that was his definition of happy.

By the time they reached Daniela's house they had decided Meche would purchase the Cheetos, seeing as Sebastián was in the gutter money-wise. Sebastián would make the sandwiches and they would fix themselves lemonade.

They agreed to stay with Daniela for an hour before setting off together. They regularly brought Daniela her homework when she was not feeling well and they did not expect anything but the usual "hello" and "come in."

But when Daniela's dad opened the door he looked very tired and he had this sad, sad look on his face.

"Can we see Daniela?" Meche asked.

"Daniela is in the hospital," her father said, shaking his head.

Daniela's lupus flared up now and then. Last summer she had spent a whole month in bed. When Daniela was sick, little purple bruises appeared all over her body and her face. She got tired and had to stay inside because sunlight made her sicker. Her mom was always afraid she'd get a kidney infection and die.

"Is she super sick?" Meche asked. "Can we go see her?"

"She has a fever... she... Her body is attacking itself. She needs to rest."

The words floated in the air, stinging their ears. Meche did not say a word, twisting the cuffs of her sweater. Sebastián took the reins and spoke.

"We're very sorry. Can you tell her we came by?"

"I will."

Meche and Sebastián looked at each other. They walked quietly back home, kicking an empty juice bottle. After a few blocks, Meche looked up at Sebastián.

"But she can't be sick. We are going to the party together next week. Her dad even gave her permission to go, which is a major win," Meche said.

"Yeah, but she's really ill," Sebastián muttered. "She might have to stay in bed for several days."

"We need to help her. We have to cast a spell."

"Just the two of us?" Sebastián asked.

"We don't have much of a choice. Come on, hurry."

She ran towards the factory and he ran behind her.

* * *

GETTING MONEY THANKS to a spell was one thing, but Sebastián was not sure they could actually cure Daniela. He did not dare to air his doubts to Meche. She seemed very determined to find a solution and he let her keep her hopes up.

"I feel something here," Meche said, showing him a record.

"Elvis Presley," Sebastián said. "What song?"

"Jailhouse Rock."

"Okay."

Meche put the record in place. Presley's voice boomed across the factory. *Dun dum. Dun dum.*

Meche tiptoed around in an imitation of Elvis Presley, hips swinging to the beat of the music. Though Sebastián knew nothing about the dance moves of this time period, and though he had rarely laid eyes on Elvis on the TV, his feet seemed to know the necessary moves. It all felt really fine, all the pieces coming together, and there was that flare of energy that rose from some deep place inside him, rose and became a golden thread, a vapour which reached the ceiling and dissipated. But this time, unlike the previous ones, he felt a stabbing pain in his stomach, as though someone had kicked him.

Sebastián groaned and hugged himself. He saw Meche bending down, also touching her midsection.

"Ouch," he muttered. "What is that?"

Suddenly the room seemed to grow too cold, even for autumn and even for an abandoned factory. It was as though someone had opened a refrigerator door.

Sebastián felt tired. He licked his lips and sat down.

"Man, it's like I just ran a marathon."

"It's so... odd."

"What's happening?"

"I don't know," Meche said. "When I did that first spell by myself I slept for a long time and it was also very cold. But it hasn't happened again."

"Maybe it's easier when we are all together," Sebastián said. "Maybe we shouldn't ever cast spells by ourselves."

"Maybe that's the whole point of the Witches' Sabbath," Meche said. "We are stronger together. Like a bunch of batteries in a remote control."

She crossed her arms over her chest, teeth chattering.

"Come," Sebastián said. "You can have my jacket."

"I don't want your jacket. I have my jacket."

"I don't want it," he said, taking it off.

Meche hesitated. Then she sat down next to him, the jacket around her shoulders. She still shivered.

Sebastián's eyelids felt like they were made of lead. His muscles ached.

"I need to rest," Sebastián whispered.

He lay flat against the hard floor and though it was uncomfortable, he was too exhausted to care.

"You're going to fall asleep here?" Meche asked.

"I can't reach the door."

"Okay."

She lay next to him. The floor felt as cold as a block of ice. The only source of warmth was Meche's body, curled up against him, as she hummed a tune he didn't know. Sebastián rested his chin upon her head and closed his eyes.

He had this dream about a woman who was looking at him. She was standing on the other side of the street, and the sight of her made him very nervous, half-afraid. Her hair was short, her eyes dark and cold. Slowly he recognized her as Meche. An older version of Meche. He tried to open his mouth and say hello, but she walked away and he said nothing.

When Sebastián woke up it was dark. The factory looked spooky when it was shrouded by shadows like this. Light trickled through some of the window panes, creating puddles here and there. He looked down at Meche and for a moment he was afraid she had changed, that she changed into that strange woman with the short hair. But it was still his Meche, still a teenager, still the girl with the very long dark hair and the resolute mouth.

He stared at her, wondering if one day she might become that other Meche who did not seem to know him.

Meche opened her eyes slowly and stretched her arms.

"What time is it?" she asked.

Sebastián checked his cheap plastic wristwatch. "Past seven."

"Ugh, we better head home."

"So why are witches always in groups?"

"Is it time to talk about spells again?" her grandmother asked.

Meche had Miguel Bosé's Aire Soy on the record player and a glass of milk with her. She sat next to her grandmother, watching her as she knit.

"Yeah," Meche said.

"A circle is the most perfect shape, isn't it? A witches' circle uses this perfect arrangement. It is wholeness, persons joining and connecting."

Meche thought about records being essentially circles. Power harnessed into the right shape.

"But you can have lone witches?"

"You can. If they are powerful enough."

"Did you know any lone witches?"

"Well, one hears a lot of things in a small town."

"What did you hear?"

"I heard there was a girl in town who could talk to the stones."

"That's useful," Meche snorted.

"It was. Every stone has a story. Imagine speaking to the stones in a house and learning the secrets of the people who live there."

Meche decided that was actually a useful skill. She wondered if what they were doing with the records was something similar. Like listening to what the records were really saying while regular people could only hear the songs.

"Did you ever try to cast a spell?"

Her grandmother did not reply.

DANIELA WOKE UP feeling... odd. Not bad, as she had been feeling all day, but odd. The pain was gone but its absence was strange. She touched her lips, pressed a hand against her forehead. The skin felt cool. No trace of a fever.

This had never happened before. Curious, she tiptoed into the bathroom, careful to not wake up the girl sharing the hospital room with her. She looked at herself in the mirror. Her skin was normal. No telltale marks, no 'butterfly' rash across her cheeks. Daniela looked whole and healthy, as though she had not had a bad flare up.

Impossible. And yet theirs was now a world full of impossibilities.

Daniela smiled.

"IT'S AWESOME!" DANIELA said. "It looks great!"

"Duh. Did you doubt it would?" Meche said.

Meche and Sebastián had strung streamers around the room. Balloons dotted the floor and were taped to the walls. There was a big sign that said 'Welcome back Dani.' They had even baked a cake and frosted it pink.

"That's not all. Sebos, are you ready?"

"Yep."

"Okay, sit down," Meche said.

Daniela sat on the couch and smiled, her hands in her lap.

Sebastián started the music. It was an old song. Volare. Meche and Sebastián hummed together and when the singer said, "Volare, wohoo hohohho," they moved their arms and two of the balloons bounced in their direction.

Daniela gasped. Meche pointed at a balloon and it flew through the air, towards her. Sebastián made a wide sweeping motion and a whole cluster of balloons ripped themselves from the walls and bounced around him, like a wave of colours.

Meche and Sebastián lowered their hands and the balloons gently settled to the floor.

Daniela stood up and clapped, feeling giddy.

"How did you ever learn to do that?" she asked.

"Oh, we figured it out by accident when we were putting up the decorations," Meche said.

"Can you teach me?"

"Sure. It'll be better with you," Meche said. "Sebastián and I get a bit tired if it's just the two of us."

"It's like running for several blocks and getting a charley horse," Sebastián explained.

"I so want to do it!" Daniela said, rushing to their side.

"Okay," Meche said. "First you focus on what you're going to move."

MECHE WAITED WITH Daniela at the coffee shop for her sister to pick her up. They had foamy coffees and shared a large cookie. Daniela seemed very perky and she chatted noisily, her hands fluttering up and down.

Meche smiled and checked the notes in her grimoire.

"Hey, that's Constantino across the street," Daniela said.

Meche turned her head. It was. He was walking with Isadora. Meche sighed, leaning back and brushing the hair off her face.

"She's got every boy in school running after her. Man, can't I get just a little bit of that?" Meche muttered.

"Not every boy," Daniela said, probably trying to perk her up.

"Sebastián thinks she's hot."

"Yeah?"

"He practically drools over her."

"She's pretty."

"I want someone to drool over me."

"Well... maybe someone will. At the party."

Meche nodded, but with little enthusiasm. Wasn't there magic that could make you irresistible? Something to spellbind another person? There had to be. The trick was in finding it.

THEY WALKED INTO the party around nine, glancing around the house with curiosity. The floors had been waxed and Meche walked slowly because she was wearing heels and was afraid of falling down. She glanced at a large mirror by the entrance, making sure her lipstick looked fine. She'd borrowed the makeup from her cousin and painted her nails with a bright pink nail polish Jimena insisted was all the rage. Meche looked different, odd—but wasn't that the point of it? To transform into someone else entirely.

Meche followed the sound of the music, her heels carefully clicking against the floor.

"Man, Isadora's dad must be loaded," Daniela said.

That was something coming from Daniela. Meche had to agree. The house was not only huge, but there were uniformed waiters walking around with trays in their hands. One of them offered them tiny little sausages and Meche took one, nodding. Sebastián grabbed three, tossing them in his mouth in quick succession.

Meche looked at the heavy furniture, the large windows, the air of opulence drifting from every corner of the room. Ugliness had no place there. Real taste, however, seemed to have escaped Isadora. The sweet, candy pop sound of Timbiriche—the mark of a limited, mundane imagination—threatened to give Meche a headache, but she decided to stand firm, smile, and try to have a good time.

"Let's get a drink," she said to her friends.

They drifted around. Meche had the distinct feeling that everyone was staring at them. She had not, in the end, picked the mini-skirt, instead donning tight stirrup pants in a light yellow and a long-sleeve shirt with a very wide black belt.

Sebastián had opted for the *Miami Vice* look, but with a more subdued baby blue t-shirt under his jacket. Daniela, having no qualms about her wardrobe, went for a metallic pink dress and a black, studded bolero jacket.

When Meche finally found something to drink it turned out to be beer. She handed one to Sebastián and another to Daniela. Daniela took a sip and made a face.

"Can't we have a soda?" Daniela asked.

"Do you see anyone else drinking soda?" Meche asked.

Daniela looked around and shook her head.

"Drink your beer," Meche ordered.

"Shouldn't we find Isadora?" Sebastián asked.

"What for?" Meche said.

"It's her birthday party."

"We're not here because of her."

"It's rude not to say hi."

Meche shrugged. Constantino was across the room, next to a window, hanging out with a circle of classmates. Damn it. Meche had copious makeup and hair gel, and was hoping she'd be able to get a chance to talk to him in all her finery. She positioned herself strategically, next to the hallway which led to the washrooms.

"I'm going to find her," Sebastián said.

"Good luck," Meche said, dismissively because—as far as she was concerned—Isadora mattered squat.

Daniela bobbed her head up and down and smiled. "What do we do now?" she asked.

"Hang out."

"Do you want to dance?"

Meche considered her high heels, the possibility of slipping and falling on her ass. She shook her head. Nope.

Daniela looked a little crestfallen. Meche did not have time to baby her, so she simply sipped her beer and tried to strike a pose, ready to chat with Constantino when he happened to walk by.

SEBASTIÁN FOUND ISADORA in the kitchen. She was trying to drag a large box towards the table.

"Hey, let me help you," he said, cheerfully grabbing the box and hauling it onto the table.

"Thanks," she said.

"No problem."

Sebastián opened the box and found more beer bottles inside. He smiled.

"You must be making Tecate rich."

"Well, it's Saturday."

"That it is," he said.

Sebastián wiped his hands against his jacket and nodded. He had nothing else to say and felt his mouth clamming shut.

The heart necklace, he thought. *I should give it to her.*

"Well, you came," she said, plucking a bottle. "Bye."

Sebastián was going to say something witty, but he couldn't string the right words together. Isadora turned around and walked away, leaving him by himself.

He looked down at the floor, furious with himself. He felt the little necklace tucked in his jacket and knew he was a coward and a fool.

Sebastián grabbed a bottle and drank it quick.

CONSTANTINO WAS STILL chatting with his friends, apparently glued to his spot. Meche had been standing very straight but after a while she began to tire and sat on a chair next to Daniela.

He had to walk by eventually. Unless he was planning on peeing in the bushes.

Meche leaned forward, resting her chin against her knuckles.

She had pictured it all before coming to the party: he'd walk by, notice her beautiful outfit, her improved appearance, and immediately start talking with her. She did not expect to be sitting in the same spot after one hour with no Constantino, exactly like the loser she'd always been.

DANIELA TRIED TO be a good sport. She tried to chat with Meche. But she was so stiff, so unpleasant. She gave up and decided enough was enough. Daniela placed her little pink purse on the chair she had been sitting on and headed towards the centre of the room.

"Where are you going?" Meche asked.

"I'm going to dance."

"By yourself?"

"If I have to."

Meche opened her mouth, probably to protest, but Daniela did not want to hear it. She had come for the party and she was not going to go unless she had one good dance. At first she danced by herself, but eventually a couple of classmates joined her and the three of them began joining in with the song's chorus.

MECHE LOOKED AT the clock. Nine thirty. An hour and a half and Constantino had not even moved close to her. It was impossible for her to approach him, not when he was shielded by all his friends. When he finally did move, he was intercepted by Isadora.

Meche watched them as they spoke. Isadora seemed upset. She was shaking her head and making little motions with her hands.

Sebastián plopped himself next to her, in the chair Daniela had been occupying, long limbs spreading carelessly.

"What's up?" he asked.

"Nothing," she muttered.

He nodded, lifted his beer and before it touched his lips, he frowned.

"Is that Daniela over there?"

"Yeah."

"Dancing."

"Yeah."

"Ha! Good for her."

The swirl of bodies—more people kept arriving—made it difficult to see if Constantino was still at his place by the window. Had he moved? Had he gone somewhere else? Was he still talking to Isadora? Meche began to panic.

"Do you want to dance?"

"My shoes hurt."

"You could take them off."

"I'm not taking them off."

Sebastián took a swig. He offered her his bottle. Meche had not touched her own beer. It was still sitting beneath her chair. She shoved his hand back and the beer spilled all over her new pants.

Meche shot up, horrified.

"You ruined them!"

Sebastián stood up too.

"I'll get a napkin," he said.

Meche did not reply. She rushed towards the bathroom, locking the door behind her. She grabbed a towel and tried to clean the pants; the stain was bad. It looked like she had peed herself. Her lips, under the glare of the light bulbs, looked a horrid crimson. Meche hurled the towel into the sink.

She leaned against the door, feeling the beat of the happy music outside, and winced.

Meche slid out, crossing her arms and walking across the room, evading Sebastián and sneaking outside, into Isadora's walled garden. She stepped away until the ridiculous pop music was nothing but a faint whisper behind her.

Meche closed her eyes and took off her shoes, just like

Sebastián had suggested, holding them in her left hand and staring up at the moon.

"You're not having fun?"

Meche glanced to her left and saw Constantino leaning against the ivy-encrusted wall. His cigarette glowed faintly in the dark.

"Not a lot," she admitted.

"You don't like the food."

"The music," she said. "And you?"

"I'm having a smoke."

Meche nodded, licking her lips. Surprise had overridden her nervousness but now as the seconds dragged by she tried to recall the dialogue she had rehearsed. But she had not rehearsed any dialogue. She had thought he'd be struck by her looks, would ask her to dance, and they'd place their arms around each other, swaying gently to the music. A good song. Not something stupid and corny.

Alas, there was no decent soundtrack playing and Meche clasped her hands together behind her back.

"What don't you like about the music?"

"It's trite."

"What would you play if you could?"

"It would be Jimmy Fontana singing Il Mondo."

"Wanna see if they have it?" he asked, tossing his cigarette butt on the ground.

"Okay."

Meche followed Constantino back into the house and he guided her towards the sound system and the big shelving unit with lots of records.

"Do you see it?"

It's not going to be here, Meche thought.

But she forced herself to think the opposite. To think it *would* be there. That all she had to do was reach forward and her hands would alight upon the right record. Meche closed her eyes and pulled a record sleeve...

... and it was Jimmy Fontana.

"Il Mondo," she whispered.

Meche lifted the lid from the record player, lifted the needle.

She felt all the heads in the room turning, surprised by the sudden interruption. Meche placed the record in its place, lowered the needle.

And Jimmy began to sing in Italian.

There was a collective groan from the crowd, but slowly they began to shuffle their feet. Slowly the teenage boys slid their hands around their partner's waists, slowly the girls began to follow the boys' lead. Slowly they stepped left and right. Sway. Rise. Fall.

Ask me to dance, she thought and she willed it just like she'd willed the record, feeling that it could, *would* happen.

"You want to dance?" Constantino asked.

Meche nodded. She put one hand on his shoulder and clasped the other. Forward, step to the side, and then a step to close the feet together. She realized, as she glanced down, that she had not put her high heels on again, had misplaced them at some point, and was dancing barefoot.

Constantino glanced down, chuckling at the sight of her bare toes. A good-natured chuckle matched with a good-natured smile.

She looked up at Constantino and smiled back at him.

As she turned, Meche saw Sebastián, standing by himself, holding a napkin in his hand. He stared at her. No smile adorned his face.

THERE WAS NO reason for Sebastián to be upset. But he was upset. On Monday, when they walked together to school, he did not speak a word to her. He failed to appear during recess and after school he walked back alone.

Meche did not understand what was going on in his head. She did not care to find out either but Daniela— quiet Daniela, who seemed to know very little of what happened around her, but who in this case seemed to know much—said he was hurting.

"He tried talking to Isadora at the party and she rebuffed him," Daniela said. "And then you danced with Constantino."

Ah, so that was that. He was jealous of her. Jealous because Meche had achieved what Sebastián could not: the attention of the object of her desire, followed on Monday by the briefest of nods, the briefest of affirmations proving that she now existed, that he knew her, remembered their stunted chat.

If Sebastián had been too tongue-tied, too stupid, to achieve similar results with Isadora, then Meche was not to blame for his lack of success. Meche decided to have a chat with him. Around six p.m. she went to his apartment building and sneaked inside when she saw a lady come out.

Sebastián's elevator was perpetually broken, ever since she had been eleven and first walked into his building. Meche walked up the six flights of stairs, humming to herself, and knocked loudly—three times, as was their practice.

"I know you're there!" she yelled.

The door opened and he looked down at her, all in black and all gloomy depression.

"What do you want?"

"I'm seeing what you are up to."

"I'm doing my homework. You should be doing the same."

"Uy, so serious."

He moved towards the kitchen. Meche closed the door and followed him. Sebastián filled a bowl with Choco Krispis and poured himself some milk, then turned around to look at her.

"What crawled up your butt?" Meche asked, tilting her head a little and smiling at him.

"You know, Meche? You think you're cute when you behave like this, but you are annoying and bratty."

"Good, because I wasn't trying to be cute. Why are you angry at me?"

"A pastar fang!" he cried, setting the bowl down on the counter, then stomping towards his room.

"Did you just insult me in Catalán?" Meche asked, scoffing, because Sebastián had picked a few choice words from his grandfather, the yellow, weathered gentleman from Barcelona.

"Ah!"

Meche was more energized than angry at his welcome, so she simply followed him, right into his room, chuckling and shaking her head.

"You *are* jealous," she said. "You just can't take the

fact that I got what I wanted and you didn't. It's not my fault Isadora dissed you."

"Rub it in, won't you?"

"Loser."

Sebastián was picking his sneakers from his bedroom floor. He promptly dropped them and hurried towards Meche. She was leaning against the door frame, her arms crossed, smug and confident. Sebastián stretched up his whole, tall, bony length and glared down at her and for the first time in her life Meche felt much smaller than her friend. Meche tilted her head up, staring back into Sebastián's eyes, her teeth bared in a harsh smile.

"What?" she asked.

Sebastián leaned down and she thought he was going to bark another insult at her. Maybe in Catalán, maybe in Spanish.

He opened his mouth and said... nothing. Sebastián stomped away as quickly as he had come, falling onto his bed and pulling the cover around his shoulders.

"Just go," he said.

Normally, that wouldn't be enough to shoo Meche out. But there was a new intonation in his voice that afternoon. It prickled Meche's skin and made her step back, confused, and she left without another word, not bothering to close the front door behind her.

ROMUALDO ARRIVED AROUND eight. Sebastián was still in bed. He had not moved an inch, curled up under the covers, staring at the wall and feeling like there was a piece of lead in his stomach.

"Are you sick, asshole?" Romualdo asked, his usual, cheery hello.

"No," Sebastián asked.

"The front door was open."

"Nobody would come in to steal."

"It doesn't matter. Get up and go to the living room. I need to phone Margarita."

"Why don't you use the pay phone down at the corner, asshole?"

Romualdo punched him in the ribs, hard. Sebastián sat up, rubbing his side and glared at his brother.

"What?" Romualdo asked. "Wanna fight?"

Romualdo was a lot stronger and beefier than Sebastián. Any fight would end with Sebastián bleeding. For a moment, though, he considered it. Then it all seemed like such a bother. Sebastián shook his head, too worn to bother with his brother.

"No. Excuse me, my cereal must be getting all soggy."

Sebastián walked past his brother and headed into the kitchen. It was beyond soggy. He threw the cereal down the drain and poured himself a fresh bowl.

"So what did you fight with Meche about?"

"How'd you know that?" Sebastián asked, his spoon frozen in mid-air.

Romualdo laughed. "Oh, come on. You're having chick trouble. And the only chick who ever hangs around with your sorry self is Meche. Or maybe Daniela. And I know Daniela wouldn't rile you up like this. So what's going on with you two?"

"Like I'd tell you."

"Fine," Romualdo said, lifting his hands in the air.

Sebastián rolled his eyes, he thrust the spoon into his mouth and spoke while chewing at the same time. "I dunno. She irritated me. Sometimes Meche thinks she's so much better than me. It's like she rubs it in my face. She can be such a major bitch."

"Then stop being friends with her."

"Well... it doesn't mean I hate her," Sebastián said carefully. "It's just we've been talking about this magic... um... music and magic thing and it all kind of started with this spell—"

"You are so funny."

"What?"

"Look, you are fucked up in the head. Meche is too. You're just both really weird."

"Thanks," Sebastián said dryly.

"It's true. I was never like you and you're definitely not like other kids. But it's okay because Meche gets you. I don't know why or how, but she totally does get you. And that's a good thing. Most people, they'll never understand you. So, after you deal with this hormonal attack or whatever it is you're having, make up."

"Yeah," Sebastián said, running a hand through his hair.

He stirred his cereal and smiled a bit, then glanced at his brother, feeling contrite.

"I'm sorry. You should phone Margarita."

"Ah, it's okay," Romualdo said. "I already know what she's going to say."

"Is she... is she really pregnant?"

"Yeah."

"What are you going to do?"

"I have no idea."

They stood in silence, nodding. Sebastián felt, for a brief moment, like he was actually close to his brother.

"Did you really fix my old motorcycle?" Romualdo asked. "Mom told me you were out riding it the other day."

"I did."

"How?"

"Magic," Sebastián said taking another spoonful of cereal.

DANIELA WAS DREAMING of an adventure in the South Seas. A ship. Pirates. Marooned on an island. She imagined herself in a flowing 19th century dress, a parasol between her hands, the blinding sun scorching the sky. White sand dunes and a man approaching from afar, his shirt open to his waist. Mr. Rodríguez in the role of the hero.

"Maybe I should just ignore it. I don't have to apologize. Do I?" Meche asked.

Daniela sighed. Meche had been going on about Sebastián all morning. She did not like it when they fought because Daniela often ended up in the middle, a courier between two upset parties. But she was not willing to play mediator this time. Besides, Meche was cutting into her daydreaming.

"I don't know," she said.

The bell rang. Meche grabbed her books. Mr. Rodríguez raised his voice, trying to be heard over the drone of teenage voices and the shuffling of feet.

"Remember. I have two tutoring spots left in the afternoons," he said.

Daniela and Meche hurried to the bathroom. They had chemistry lab next and that meant they had to change into their lab coats before climbing the narrow steps to the classroom. If the coat was not spotless Miss Costa would deduct points from their lab work. Meche, as usual, had neither washed nor ironed her coat, and was trying to quickly clean a ketchup stain which had landed smack on the front of the coat.

"I was thinking of taking some tutoring sessions with Rodríguez," Daniela said, checking her hair in the mirror to make sure her bangs were still stiff with hair spray.

"Man, I hate Rodríguez. He smiles too much."

"There's nothing wrong with being friendly."

"It's annoying. Okay, what's good for cleaning ketchup stains?"

"I don't know. Bleach?"

"Ugh!"

"You asked."

Meche tossed the coat in the sink and pressed both hands on each side of it, staring into the mirror.

"I hate Sebastián."

"Meche…"

"He's being unfair!"

"He's hurt. The girl he likes doesn't give a crap about him and then you are all mean to him."

"I didn't think he *really* wanted to dance," Meche protested.

"Oh, I don't think it's the dance that's bothering him… he told me you went to see him and called him a loser."

"What a tattletale! That's why he can't get a girlfriend."

Meche opened the faucet, pumped some soap onto the

coat, and began scrubbing it vigorously.

"I'm not apologizing," Meche said firmly.

That was the thing about Meche and Sebastián. Both were too proud and too damn stubborn to simply make up.

Meche put on the coat, which was soaking wet. Instead of a red stain she now had a pink stain. It still looked terrible.

"I wonder if I can turn it inside out?" she muttered.

"I think Costa's going to deduct points no matter what you do. We've got to go or we'll be late."

"Fine. Worst day ever," Meche muttered. "Constantino didn't even look at me today. It's like he noticed me once and now I'm back to being invisible."

"You're not invisible," Daniela said.

Meche said something about boys, but Daniela was already flying away into her daydream. Pirates and South Seas and a dashing admiral saving her life.

THREE KNOCKS. MECHE, of course. Sebastián could ignore her. But he knew how persistent she could be. If she was back after what happened two days before, that meant she was back with a vengeance. He opened the door a crack.

"We need to talk," Meche said. "And spare me the dirty look."

"We do?" Sebastián said, raising an arm and resting it against the door frame.

"Don't…"

"No, *you* don't," he replied.

"You are such a baby," Meche whispered and held out a piece of paper. "Here. Take it."

Sebastián looked at the paper warily. She kept waving it in front of his face so he grabbed and unfolded it. It was a rail map of Europe. He looked carefully at the jumble of colours, the red and yellow and blue lines, and back at Meche.

"It's for the wall. For your collection," she said.

Sebastián was quiet. Meche sighed.

"I'm trying to apologize to you," she whispered.

He did not budge. It had come to this. She had to use her trump card. Meche didn't want to. He could tell.

She gave in.

"My object of power is the Duncan Dhu record," she told him. "The one we played that time in the factory. I selected it after we were done. I keep it my room in a box with some toys."

"You're not lying?"

"What do you think?"

Sebastián opened the door wider, letting her in. Meche walked in and they looked at each other.

"Um... I'm sorry too," he admitted. "I made a big deal out of nothing. Do you want... I can put the map up right now and we can go for a ride afterwards."

"Sure."

Sebastián made his way around a mound of dirty clothes Romualdo had piled up near the entrance to their room. He found the box with the thumbtacks and put the map right above the one of France, where he could look at them before going to sleep at night.

"It's really awesome. Thanks," he told her.

"Sure."

"I'm going to spend a whole year in Europe after high school. I'll travel all the countries and see all the major cities. All the way up north, so I can see the midnight sun."

He knew he'd talked about this a million times before, but he liked to hear himself say it. It sounded more real when there was somebody listening to him. Like it could really happen; that these were not the ramblings of a kid. He had the guidebooks; he had the maps; all he needed was a bit of money.

"Cool."

"You should come with me," he said.

Meche sat on the floor of his bedroom, stretching her legs and smiling.

"All the way to Europe?"

"All the way. We can run away together."

"I think we tried that three years ago."

"We went to Coyoacán without permission. Daniela forced us to turn back and kept bawling her eyes out because she was afraid her dad would find out she had skipped class."

"It was pretty silly."

"No, but we should do it. This time for real."

"What the hell would I do in Europe?"

"What wouldn't you do?" he said, sliding down next to her. "It's not like we've got it super amazing here in Mexico City."

Really, what was there for them? For him? This miserable apartment. The school where nobody liked him. Isadora, who didn't even know he existed. The accumulated tedium of hundreds of days piling on top of each other.

"Yeah, but going looking for the midnight sun sounds…"

"… crazier than casting spells with records?" he asked. "I don't think so."

"It sounds cold."

"We'll buy parkas. Blankets. What do people wear in Norway?"

"Bear furs, probably. What do people eat in Norway?"

"Bears."

Sebastián laid down on the floor, his hands behind his head. Meche also lay back, her hands folded over her chest.

"People don't eat bears," Meche said.

"They do. But you shouldn't eat polar bear liver."

"Why not?"

"It'll make you sick. Too much vitamin A."

"You're making it up."

"I am not. I read it somewhere."

"There's a song by Ella Fitzgerald called Midnight Sun," Meche said.

"Everything is a song with you."

"At least it's not bear meat."

Sebastián felt himself getting sleepy. This was their usual banter. This was their usual selves. He could relax now. He could be happy. The pain gnawing him all day long would subside.

"How does the song go?"

"Mmm… let me see," Meche said. "There's a meadow in December, ice and oh darling… something about lips close by. People kissing basically…"

Meche coughed.

"Of course, she sings it much better than I do," she concluded.

"You'll have to play it for me sometime."

"But jazz is boooring," she said, imitating him.

Sebastián let out a loud *hmpf* and turned his head to look at her. They were side by side, but Meche's legs were pointed in the opposite direction and she was tapping her foot to the beat of an imaginary tune. Probably Fitzgerald's song. She was staring at the ceiling.

He pictured Meche walking down a long hallway, towards an airplane. She was ahead of him by a long stretch. With every step he took the distance between them seemed to grow until Meche was just a tiny little smudge against a bright opening. Then she was gone.

"Can I ask you something?" he said.

"What?"

"Something serious."

"Then definitely not."

Meche glanced at him. When he didn't laugh, she turned her body completely towards him, leaning against her elbow and looking down at him.

"What?"

"Promise you'll never leave."

"Leave where?"

"Anywhere," he said. "Without me, that is."

"Gee. Should we stitch our sides together like artificial Siamese twins? Hey, isn't there an episode of the *Twilight Zone* where that happens? Or is that the one of the guy with two heads?"

"I'm not kidding."

Sebastián sat and looked down at her sternly. Meche looked like she was about to laugh. But then she nodded instead of chuckling.

"Alright."

"Never go."

"I won't."

Sebastián hugged her and did not understand why he suddenly felt so sad. He closed his eyes.

"You're lying."

"I'm not."

He thought he could hear the chords of a song. Fitzgerald's song as he imagined it without his ever having heard it. Slow and lovely and somewhat painful.

"There is a *Twilight Zone* episode called Midnight Sun," he said as he stood up, offering Meche his hand.

"What's it about?"

"Earth has moved from its orbit and is heading into the Sun. Everyone will be cooked alive."

"Creepy."

He pulled her up and Meche smiled.

"Let's go for a ride," he said.

They trotted downstairs and grabbed the motorcycle. Meche jumped behind him and placed her hands on his shoulders, then rested them on his waist.

"Ready?" he asked.

"Yep."

They roared away together, through the darkened streets of the city.

Mexico City, 2009

JIMENA HAD A placid smile on her face. A smile Meche knew well. The smile said *I know something you don't.* Meche drank a cup of atole and ate a piece of tamal, trying to ignore the smile. It had never boded well in her youth and she did not think it could bode well now. There were sweet tamales and salty ones, some filled with chicken and others with pineapple. There were even tamales chiapanecos, wrapped in a banana leaf and stuffed with pork.

All this business of eating and praying was having a narcotic effect on Meche. When her mother came to her side and spoke she did not hear her. On a shelf, a photograph of her father looking younger than he had ever been presided over the dinner. He stared at Meche with a sad, startled expression.

"Huh?" she asked.

"Are you going to put on another record?" her mother said again.

Meche realized the turntable had gone quiet. Meche nodded. That was her job: keep the music going. Jimena was in charge of the food, her mother, the greeting of people, her stepfather seemed to be managing the distribution of the atole and the soft drinks. All Meche had to do was keep some soft, pleasant music playing. She had decided she could not stomach CDs. Her father would have hated that. So she had hooked up the old turntable.

Meche picked a collection of jazz songs. She started with Stormy Weather.

She mouthed the lyrics to the song and felt comforted by the familiar tune, the trumpet and the piano and Billie's voice.

"Hey, Meche, come here."

Meche raised her head and saw Jimena motioning to her, by the kitchen door.

"What?" she asked, wondering if she was going to have to distribute tamales. She didn't want to. Meche was happy standing in her corner, blending in with the curtains and avoiding chatting with her relatives and former neighbours.

Jimena gestured more emphatically and Meche hurried to her side.

"What?" she muttered.

"Here she is," Jimena said brightly. "Meche, your buddy is here."

Jimena was grinning from ear to ear. Sebastián stood next to her, looking very sober, a cup of atole in his hands; well-dressed and well-groomed.

"Hi," he said, stretching out his hand.

Meche shook it stiffly.

"Hello."

"I've come to pay my respects to your mother," he said, like a perfect gentleman.

"I can find her for you," Meche offered.

"Oh, I'll find her," Jimena said. "I need to get this tray out, anyway. I'll be back. Don't you move."

Jimena flashed a wide smile to Sebastián and shoved Meche, carrying her large tray with the tamales. Some things never changed. Jimena was still able to flirt with anything that had a pulse.

Sebastián looked at his cup.

"I thought I saw you the other night but I wasn't sure it was you."

"Then it probably was me," Meche said.

"I would have said hi—"

"No worries," Meche said brusquely. "Didn't Daniela talk to you?"

"She phoned me promptly yesterday."

"Then you still like being a dick."

Sebastián looked up at her, lifting the corners of his mouth into a wry, small smile.

"Daniela's coming tomorrow. We're long past being teenagers and we're not afraid of you. We have a right to say hi to your mom and pay our respects."

"And I have every right to ignore you. Eat up, it's all free."

Meche pivoted on her heels, slowly walking out of the kitchen.

"Cry Me a River."

"Excuse me?" she said, turning around and placing her hands on her hips.

"That's what's playing. Ella Fitzgerald is singing Cry Me A River."

Meche realized he was right. The previous song had finished and Cry Me had started to play.

"Did you become a jazz fan at some point?" she asked, with that easy, snide tone she liked to employ with him from years and years back.

"No. But I do know my Ella."

"Congratulations. Should I give you a medal?"

Sebastián chuckled. "Daniela was right. You're exactly the same."

Meche walked away.

"Did you know he was coming?" Meche asked her cousin.

They were tidying up the apartment. Moving empty glasses to the kitchen, tossing any garbage which had found its way onto the floor into a bin, and trying to implement a degree of order. Meche had positioned herself behind the sink, dutifully scrubbing dishes, while Jimena brought her more dirty cups.

"No," Jimena said.

"Are you sure?"

"I said no. What's wrong? He's cute, isn't he? Why, if I could get my hands..."

"Aren't you married?" Meche asked sharply.

"That doesn't stop me from looking at the menu," Jimena said with a shrug. "What about you? You're single, no?"

Meche's last serious relationship had taken place two years before and lasted eight months. She knew it caused her mother much anxiety to know she remained unmarried and childless. In Natalia's eyes, Meche was a spinster, doomed to a life of unhappiness. She viewed her as dangerously contaminated by foreign traits. Marriage and motherhood were a woman's ways. Anything else was an aberration stemming from too many imported shows. If Meche chanced to remind her mother that she herself had divorced her husband and was therefore not exactly a paragon of Catholic virtues, Natalia would deny any wrongdoing.

"I am single," Meche said to her cousin. "I am also uninterested in Sebastián Soto."

"And I thought you'd be glad to see him."

"I haven't talked to him since I was a teenager. Why would I be glad to see him now?"

"Well, seeing as you did like him back then..."

"I also painted my nails neon green one time. It doesn't mean I'm rushing to buy puke-coloured nail polish this instant," Meche muttered.

"Uh, you know who was hot?" Jimena asked. "That C kid... um, Constantino Domínguez."

"Yeah."

"He's married now. He's fat and married and balding," Jimena said. "He's got three kids and they're all damn ugly. Who would have thought?"

"Does he still live around here?"

"No. I saw him at the mall a couple of times when I was working in a pet shop. He chatted with me for a little bit. At first I didn't recognize him, but then when he began talking I remembered. Constantino Domínguez."

"Do you remember a girl named Isadora?" Meche asked. "She was in my grade, so maybe you didn't know her."

"In the Queen? Before you went away?"

"Yeah. She was pretty. Skinny, tallish."

Jimena snapped her fingers. "I remember her! She was Sebastián's girlfriend, wasn't she?"

"I wouldn't know," Meche said.

But Meche did know. Even though Meche did not speak a word to Sebastián after the spring of 1989, even though she moved to a different city that same summer, she was aware of it. It was hard not to be aware of it when she lived three blocks from him. Three blocks and three knocks. But those blocks stretched miles long, separated them as though they were oceans, and she did not take the path which led to his apartment building after that time at the factory.

That time...

"Well, she married him."

"Isadora is married to Sebastián?"

"He's not married," Jimena said. "Weren't you paying attention? I said he's single."

"Yeah, but..."

"They got married right out of high school. We all thought she was pregnant. It's the same thing as with his brother, we thought, but no. It lasted maybe a year. Was it two? It wasn't long. They divorced, she moved back in with her parents and he ended up moving away. You know, he was living in Monterrey in 1998. I thought for sure you guys had met up then."

"I wasn't living in Monterrey in 1998," Meche said. "I had already moved to Europe."

"Oh, well. Then you missed each other."

"Probably."

Meche squeezed more liquid soap onto her sponge.

"He's in marketing now," Jimena said.

"I didn't ask," Meche replied.

"You were wondering about it," Jimena said with all the aplomb of the neighbourhood gossip. "Same as you're wondering if he's seeing someone: I don't think so."

"Man, your mental powers suck, Kalimán," Meche said.

"Well, then what are you thinking?" Jimena asked, giving Meche a little bump with her hip.

Meche frowned, looking at the murky, soapy water and the cup she was washing.

"I'm thinking about music," she said.

Mexico City, 1988

DECEMBER BROUGHT THE Nativity play. Sebastián, Meche and Daniela had non-speaking roles, playing shepherds. Isadora, Constantino and their friends were the angels and the demons in the pastorela, as befitted their station.

Meche sat with her friends at the back of the room and watched her classmates rehearse their lines, her eyes fixed on Constantino. The handsome boy had not talked to her again. The party, the dance, remained a freak occurrence. Had the magic driven him to her? Had it been something else? She did not know.

Meche could not spin fantasies in her head like Daniela; she could not feed on phantom lovers. She wanted Constantino and she wanted him now. What to do? A love spell? Would the others agree to perform it with her? Meche felt too ashamed to tell them about it. She could imagine the face Sebastián would make. He would laugh. But there seemed no other way.

Meche rested her elbows against her knees and leaned forward.

"Is your grandma going to bake a rosca de reyes?" Sebastián asked.

Food. A primary topic for Sebastián.

"Yeah."

"Nice. When is she making it? I'll come over."

"I don't know."

"You can also buy a slice at the posada in two weeks," Daniela reminded him, lowering her romance novel for a moment.

The posada was part of the play. Or, rather, the play came before the posada. After the performance was finished, the students and their families were ushered out into the school courtyard, where food stands offered typical Mexican Christmas foods and treats: mandarins, tejocotes, sugar canes, tamales, tostadas. Punch made with guava. Chocolate and atole to stay warm. There was a Nativity complete with life-sized figures of Joseph, Mary, the baby Jesus and the three kings. A piñata dangled from a rope, ready for the kids to smash it to pieces and collect the candy. People bought tickets for a raffle and purchased holiday knick knacks made by the mothers of the students. The more intrepid students found this a perfect time to make out in the washrooms, marking a yearly tradition.

"Why would I buy it when I can eat it for free?" Sebastián asked.

"She's not even a good actress," Meche said, raising a hand and pointing at Isadora.

Despite the simple dialogue required, the pretty girl was wooden. She did not even seem able to stand still and look credible, though Meche had to admit the white robes she was wearing fitted her well.

"Like you'd do better," Sebastián said.

"I might," Meche muttered. "Only we'll never know, will we?"

Isadora placed a hand on Constantino—he was a devil, though he had not cared to don his costume for this rehearsal, only the horns—and whispered something in his ear. Meche felt her gut churn.

"You always have to complain, don't you?" Sebastián said.

"Yeah, and you always have to defend her," Meche replied.

"Don't fight," Daniela said.

"Look, the school posada is going to blow. Let's go to my cousin Jimena's place after the play. She'll have a real posada. What do you say?"

"Are we invited?" Daniela asked.

"You are if you bring your own booze."

"Will she have rosca de reyes or ate de tejocote?" Sebastián asked.

"How should I know?" Meche said feeling irritated. "There will be *something* to eat."

"I don't know," Sebastián said.

"Fine. Go to the school posada and make googly eyes at Isadora. Like that's more fun. I'm going home. It's not like we're even needed at this stupid rehearsal."

Meche grabbed her things and hurried outside.

She put on her headphones; Edith Piaf was singing about a life in pink. She wasn't even sure why she was angry. Lately Sebastián's interest in Isadora just rubbed her the wrong way. Like it was a bit, well… it was frankly insulting that he liked such a simpleton. Because, let's face it, Isadora was a bit of a simpleton and for all of Sebastián's intellectual talk about "Oh my God, how come you've never read that book," it didn't seem to trouble him that the only thing Isadora read was the daily horoscope and the graffiti in the lavatories.

When Meche arrived in her apartment she waved a weak "hello" to her grandmother, who was knitting in the living room, and headed for the kitchen, pulling out the milk from the fridge. She dunked animal crackers in the glass, listening to more music in French because it was the day for that kind of thing.

Her father walked in and patted her head.

"What's up, Meche?"

"Hey," she muttered.

He sat down across from her, pouring himself a glass of milk and grabbing a few crackers.

"What are you listening to?"

"Eh," Meche said sliding the headphones off and shrugging.

She ran her hands over the plastic table mats with ugly yellow flowers on them.

"What's the most powerful love song of all time?" she asked him, scratching one of the flowers.

Meche thought the most romantic album cover of all time was *The Freewheelin'*, which showed a very young Dylan walking arm-in-arm with his then-girlfriend. There was something about the composition, the street, the sky, the smiles, which made her think falling in love should be like that snapshot.

"Mmm. Good question," her father said, rubbing his chin. "Well, it would have to be A Whiter Shade of Pale."

"Procol Harum?" Meche said with a frown. "It doesn't talk about love."

"It doesn't have to. Are you alright, Meche?"

"Yeah. Just tired," she said, smiling.

"Okay. I have to write for a bit. Do you want to listen to some Rolling Stones later?"

"Sure."

"Okay."

Her father gave her another pat on the head and grabbed his glass, taking it with him. Meche wandered back into the living room and sat next to Grandmother Dolores, resting her head against her shoulder.

"Grandma, why won't you teach me to cast spells?"

"You haven't asked, but also I can't."

"Why not?"

"I've forgotten."

"You're lying."

"No. Things drift away when you age. One moment the memories are clear as typed words on paper, the next you can't make sense of the past. It's all crushed together. All witches forget."

Meche frowned. She thought she wouldn't forget this sort of stuff. It was way too important.

"Can you at least tell me another story about witches?" she asked, grabbing the ball of yarn and putting it on her lap.

Grandmother Dolores nodded, her needles clicking.

"There was a girl in my village who once fell in love with a nahual. He came to her house one night, in the shape of a fox to steal some chickens and she..."

Meche closed her eyes and listened to her grandmother, her voice transporting her from the little apartment to other lands.

*   *   *

IN ADDITION TO his job bagging groceries, Sebastián had picked up a seasonal gig at the mall wrapping gifts. It paid more than his supermarket gig but he had to wear a ridiculous plastic crown which was meant to identify him as one of the Three Kings.

But he needed the money, even if he looked like a dork.

He planned to use the money to buy small gifts for his family, Daniela and Meche. Sebastián had considered returning the necklace he had bought Isadora for her birthday and using the cash for something else, but he decided to keep it. Maybe one day he could give it to her. Maybe he could give it to another girl. He wished he had a girlfriend like all the other boys.

It didn't even have to be an amazingly beautiful girlfriend like Isadora. It could just be a regular girl. Someone to talk to, hold hands with, kiss, make out with. He envied the easy confidence of his peers. They could go up to girls and ask for their numbers. Sebastián had tried asking a girl—a fellow grocery bagger—out but she just stared at him like he had said an insult. Afterwards Sebastián stopped even thinking of asking anyone out. It seemed like a futile enterprise.

Sebastián cut wrapping paper and folded it, his long fingers carefully taping the sides.

He decided to think about something else. Meche's Christmas present. He usually bought her books, which she invariably hated, but he tended to complement those with mix tapes, which she liked. He was thinking of buying her a book of Auden's poetry and he could make a mix tape of songs from the 60s because Meche liked that time period.

He pasted bows and cut more wrapping paper. Once in a while he looked down at the list of songs he had written on a little piece of paper and struck one out.

"I didn't know you worked here."

He looked up. Isadora was carrying a couple of boxes in her arms. She set them down on his counter. Sebastián felt terribly embarrassed to be caught looking like such a fool, wrapping gifts for a few pesos an hour.

"Just 'til Epiphany," he said. "Those two?"

"Yes."

Sebastián tried to cut the paper as quickly as he could, his fingers flying over the boxes.

"Are you excited about the play tomorrow?" she asked.

"Not really."

"Me neither. It's always the same deal every year. The posada might be fun," she said with a little shrug.

"I am not staying for the posada after it."

"No?"

"There's a party at Jimena Estrada's house later. Do you know her?"

"I don't think so."

"My friend Meche thinks the school posada is kind of lame so we're going to Jimena's posada. You're... ah... welcome to join us."

Isadora did not say anything. Sebastián regretted his attempt at small talk. He should have just kept his stupid mouth shut. Like Isadora would care what he did in his free time.

"Well, here you go," he said, putting two red bows on the packages and handing them back to her.

"Thanks."

"Bye," he said cutting more little pieces of tape and readying himself for the next client.

"I'm sorry if I was rude to you at my birthday party."

Sebastián looked up at her, shocked to hear her say that.

"You weren't really rude," he said.

"No, I was. You were just trying to be friendly. It's just, Constantino was being annoying... ugh, anyway, you're always nice to everyone."

"I don't try to be nice."

"That's why you are."

She grabbed her presents and paused for a moment.

"Where is that posada? I might go."

"Do you have a piece of paper? I can write it down for you."

"I don't have paper."

"Give me your arm."

Isadora put down her packages and he grabbed her arm, carefully writing the address with blue ink.

"Thanks," she said.

"Cool."

He watched her walk away and smiled.

SEBASTIÁN DID NOT listen to a single line during the performance. He stood in his place at the back of the stage with Meche and Daniela, simply staring at Isadora and willing the performance to end so they could all escape to Jimena's apartment.

After the show, they decided to go home and change. Sebastián said he would pick Meche up. He was late because he'd taken special care in choosing his clothes. He wore a nice black shirt and jeans and had combed his hair back with a lot of gel.

He jumped on his motorcycle to pick up Meche. She climbed behind him and they sang Los Peces en el Rio at the top of their lungs. Sebastián had never understood the significance of a song which talked about fishes drinking river water while the baby Jesus was being born, but it was one of the few Christmas songs he knew from beginning to end, so he was happy to sing it.

When they reached her apartment, Jimena greeted them with a loud, festive hug, planting a kiss on each of their cheeks. She was dressed in nearly nothing, belly bared, and tottered on high heels. Pretty much what you'd expect from Jimena.

"I brought beer," Meche said.

"Put in the kitchen, girl," Jimena said. "Your little friend is here."

"Who?" Sebastián asked, perking up.

"Dani."

"Oh."

They dropped the beer in the kitchen and Sebastián served himself fortified punch with a big piece of cinnamon. Meche carried two little plastic cups in her hands, giving one to Daniela, who had found a place near the sound system.

"Hey," she said. "Where were you? I've been waiting for ages."

"I dunno. He took forever," Meche said, giving Daniela a little cup.

"Thanks. My mom said I could only stay 'til nine, so I can't be here for long."

"Aw. That's like nothing at all."

"You know how she is. She's afraid I'm going to have a relapse."

"You just want to go home and watch your soaps."

They pulled up a couple of chairs and sat with Daniela, drinking their punch until it was time for her to leave; then they walked her downstairs and waited for her dad to arrive. They waved goodbye when Daniela got in the car.

"Man, Jimena sure poured a lot of booze in that punch this year."

"Yup," Sebastián said.

"We should have more," Meche snapped her fingers. "Oh, Jimena gave me money to buy more ice. Wanna go with me?"

"Okay."

"Race you to the store."

Sebastián was ready to chase after Meche but then he saw Isadora and Constantino approaching. She was wearing a very nice red coat with large brass buttons. Her hair was pulled back in a ponytail and she was smiling at him.

"Hi," she said. "I brought Constantino with me. I hope that's okay."

"That's fine," Sebastián said.

"Third floor?"

"Yeah."

"We're going to buy ice," Meche said sharply.

"See you inside," Sebastián added.

Meche and Sebastián walked briskly, hands in their pockets.

"You invited her to my cousin's posada?" she asked.

"The whole neighbourhood is invited to your cousin's posada."

"Yeah, but you didn't even ask."

"Sorry."

Meche shook her head, walking to the corner store and back in a regal silence which spoke volumes. Sebastián felt bad briefly, but once they reached the door of the apartment he was actually pissed at Meche for being so selfish. She made it worse by pulling away from him and going to stand next to Jimena, like he did not exist. Sebastián put the ice in the kitchen, mixed a couple of rum and Cokes, and went in search of Isadora.

She was sitting by herself, looking out the window and smoking a cigarette.

"Um... I didn't know what you wanted, so I brought this," he said, handing her the cup.

"Thanks," she said, placing it on the window sill and smiling again. "That's very thoughtful of you."

"No problem. Where's Constantino?"

"Somewhere," Isadora said with a little huff. "I wanted to come alone but when he heard I was heading here he insisted on coming. Sorry about that. I didn't want him here."

"I thought you were friends," Sebastián said.

"We are," Isadora said, looking at her nails.

Isadora and Constantino had gone out for six months but broke up before the school year started. From what Sebastián understood, Constantino had dumped

Isadora to go out with Miroslava, one of Isadora's friends. Sebastián thought this was pretty stupid because Miroslava wasn't half as pretty as Isadora.

"I think he's jealous that you invited me," she said. "He's silly like that."

"He doesn't have anything to be jealous about," Sebastián paused. "Are you guys together again?"

"No," Isadora said.

"Sorry. I shouldn't have asked that. I mean, who am I?"

"No, it's okay," she replied. "Everyone thinks Constantino is so great but he's not that awesome."

"I guess."

"Sorry. I know he's a bit of a dick with you."

"I guess it's a night for 'sorries.'"

Isadora finished her cigarette and flicked the butt out the window, giving him a half-smile.

"You know, I don't think I've ever spoken more than half a dozen words with you," she said. "Why's that?"

"We orbit around different suns, I suppose."

It was the type of corny line that Meche would have rolled her eyes at—no sense in discussing suns, stars, moons and similes with her—but Isadora did not seem to mind.

"I kind of like that," she said and the smile grew.

He decided, right then and there, to mail the golden heart on the chain to her and to hell with the consequences.

MECHE HAD BEEN surveying the room from Jimena's side, studying the crowd and keeping an eye on Isadora and Sebastián. When the girl started giggling she'd had enough. Meche rolled her eyes and rolled herself into the kitchen, pouring herself an obscene amount of punch and drinking it in one long gulp. She poured herself another and walked out, holding her drink, and saw that Isadora and Sebastián were still talking.

"I think your boyfriend is making a pass at Isadora," Constantino said.

He was by himself, eyes fixed on their beautiful classmate.

"He's my buddy," she said. "Not my boyfriend."

"Honest mistake."

"I think your girlfriend wants to make out with my buddy."

"She's not my girlfriend."

"Honest mistake," Meche replied as she finished her drink. "Thirsty?"

"Yep."

"Let's get you a refill."

They went to the kitchen and Meche filled their cups. Constantino leaned against the refrigerator, drumming his fingers against its side. Meche sat on one of the kitchen counters, swinging her legs and thinking thoughts as deep and dark as black holes.

"Why did you dance with me the other night?" she asked him.

"What? Did I need a permit?"

"I'm curious."

"I felt like I should."

Meche chuckled. "You want to go out and see what they're up to?"

"Yes."

"You still have a thing for her?"

He did not admit it, but didn't need to and she got why he'd danced with her at the party—to piss Isadora off.

"Don't let me hold you back," she said, jumping off the counter.

They moved towards the living room. Constantino flew to Isadora like an arrow, installing himself by her side. Meche watched as Sebastián pulled away, slowly drifting from them as Constantino wrapped an arm around the girl, beginning what looked like a very animated conversation.

Sebastián looked in Meche's direction. Their eyes locked together.

Meche felt a bitter knot in her stomach. It was not the product of the cheap alcohol in the punch; Jimena's apartment was too crowded, the noise too much. Beneath the buzz of the conversations played Total Eclipse of the Heart. She could not make out the words, barely could hear the music, just felt the beat. She wanted pain and loneliness and everyone to stop talking and Sebastián and no one, all at the same time. Meche grabbed her jacket and headed downstairs.

She did not expect Sebastián to follow her, but he did.

"Hey, what's up?" he asked.

"I'm getting more ice," she said and hoped he'd leave it at that.

"I'll help you."

"No!"

"I'll get my jacket."

"I said no!"

She rushed down the steps and hurried out into the

street. When she heard him behind her she ran. She rushed towards her home, turned a corner and bumped into a mound of garbage, tripped over something and fell.

She felt the glass cutting her hand and looked down to see she had sliced her palm with a dirty beer bottle. Meche groaned.

"Are you alright?" Sebastián asked.

He looked concerned. His anxiety irritated her. Meche stood up, wiping her hand against her jeans and nodding.

"I'm drunk," she announced. "That's all."

"You shouldn't be walking by yourself like this."

"Shouldn't you be back at the posada? You've left your guest all alone."

"Fuck that, I'm taking you home."

"I have two legs and can walk it."

"I'm not letting you go without me."

Meche was going to tell him to fuck himself but then a wave of nausea hit her and she turned around, vomiting all over the sidewalk. The bitter taste in her mouth seemed like a fine coda for the night and she promised herself she would wish for a different life come morning.

"Here, it's alright," he said.

Sebastián brushed the hair out from her face and offered her a tissue. Meche dabbed it against her mouth and smiled.

"You're so thoughtful," she said. "I fucking hate that."

"I hate you too, Meche."

Meche laughed. Sebastián joined in. He curled his fingers around her shoulder.

"Come on," he said. "Let's get you home."

"What about your motorcycle?"

"I'll pick it up tomorrow. Right now we are going to walk back to your place, where I'll give you a big glass of water and tuck you in."

"And will you sing Ne me quitte pas to me?" she asked, the words slurred together.

She liked that song. She liked how Jacques sang it and the line about beads of rain from faraway countries.

"What?"

"Jacques Brel. You don't know *anything*."

"Not about music."

She looked down, at his sneakers with all the inked drawings and words.

RELEASED FROM THE chains of school, winter break holding its arms wide open, Daniela and Meche dedicated their days to watching TV together and—in a smaller measure—Christmas shopping. This was the third record store they had hit that morning. Daniela was starting to get tired and she still did not know what Meche was trying to accomplish.

"I found it," Daniela said. "Procol Harum, right?"

"Right," Meche said.

Meche grabbed the record, touched it carefully and dismissed it.

"No. It's not right," Meche said, shaking her head.

"What's wrong with it? It's the record you wanted."

"Yes. But it needs to be very powerful."

"It feels warm."

"Warm. Not hot. I know there's a copy of that record somewhere and it's searing hot."

"What do you plan to do with it when you find it?"

"A love spell."

"Really?" Daniela asked, eyes wide. "Who do you want to fall in love with you?"

"Same guy I've always wanted. Constantino."

"I heard he was getting cozy with Isadora at Jimena's posada."

"Funny, I thought Sebastián was getting cozy with Isadora. It must have been after we left."

"Sebastián and Isadora? Really?"

"Tell me about it. It's disgusting."

"Why?"

"*Obviously* she's just teasing him."

"You don't think she likes him?"

Meche looked at Daniela with a *really?* expression. Daniela put the record back.

They drifted around the store and Daniela pulled out one of Luis Miguel's records, smiling at the blond, attractive young man. She ran her fingers over his photograph.

"Maybe I could wish to be swept off my feet by Luis Miguel."

"That's not very realistic," Meche replied.

"Magic doesn't have to be realistic. Does it?"

"I wouldn't push it too far."

"Then maybe a kiss from Mr. Rodríguez."

"Eww. He's our teacher and like a billion years older than us."

"Mr. Rochester was older than Jayne Eyre."

Daniela wished life were more like books. Well, not all books, but at least the books she read. Caridad Bravo Adams was her favourite author, though she also appreciated the work of Danielle Steel and Barbara Cartland. Her fantasies were embroidered with details from a multitude of novels, but they all concluded with a handsome man, a wedding, a kiss and a picture-perfect happy ending. All she wanted was a little tiny taste of that.

"Wouldn't it be wonderful if life were like the novels?" she said. "Then Constantino could be the handsome general who saves you from a band of robbers. Mr. Rodríguez could be a dashing pirate who kidnaps me for a ransom but ends up falling in love with me. Sebastián could even be the daring young man who wins over a princess."

"No way."

"I'm going to buy this," Daniela decided, grabbing the Luis Miguel record.

"Just promise you won't play it when I'm around."

"Awww. Hey, do you want me to make cupcakes?"

"Real cupcakes or Easy-Bake cupcakes?"

"Real. If my mother doesn't catch us in the kitchen and panics, afraid I might cut myself."

"We could always cook at my place," Meche suggested.

"And play the Luis Miguel record?"

Meche threw up her arms in the air and shook her head theatrically.

"You're a monster! Only one song, for God's sake. Next thing you'll want to make me listen to Magneto."

SEBASTIÁN AND MECHE sat together atop a table in the courtyard of the mall, right by the Nutrisa store, and ate frozen yogurt. Sebastián was spending all his spare time wrapping gifts for a mob of crazy shoppers, who thrust packages and bills in his face, asked for red or green bows, all demanding it be done in five minutes. If she wanted to hang out with him she had to do it during his lunch break.

Daniela was off to Mazatlán for a week, to spend Christmas by the sea with all the assorted uncles and cousins who lived there. This left Meche to her own devices, with Sebastián as her only companion. Her strategy was to hunt around the record shops in the morning, visit him for lunch, then head home to listen to whatever she had bought while she played on the computer.

That day she was carrying a Queen album under her arm after another failed attempt to find the perfect copy of A Whiter Shade of Pale. She was beginning to think the record was her own white whale, and although Sebastián might be proud to know she had internalized some of his knowledge about *Moby Dick*, she would much rather find the damn thing.

"Do you really have to head back?" Meche asked.

"Yeah. I have another four hours, maybe six if I pick up some extra time."

"You're working like all day long."

"I'm making money."

"Bo-ring."

"That's because you have money."

"I only have my allowance and that ain't much."

"More than I have. It's just a couple more days."

"No, after Christmas comes Epiphany," Meche

reminded him. "You'll be wrapping presents 'til January and we won't get to do anything."

"Well, that's the way it is."

"We could cast a spell to get more money."

"Just the two of us? I thought that wasn't a good idea."

Well, that was the official rule. Not that Meche wasn't ready to bend the rules a bit, though she wasn't sure she should tell Sebastián that.

"Do you want to come over and play a video game later? Daniela lent me her Nintendo and we can rent a game at Chaplin's," he suggested.

"My mom doesn't like me going to your place."

"Do you want her to phone my brother? He's around today."

"I don't know."

Meche finished her frozen yoghurt and jumped down from the table, tossing the plastic container and the spoon in the garbage can. Sebastián also tossed his away and they headed back towards the gift wrapping station.

Meche eyed an instant photo booth with interest.

"Do you have coins?" she asked him.

"What for?"

Meche did not bother answering, she grabbed Sebastián by the wrist and pulled him into the photo booth, swinging aside a tattered red curtain. The compartment was small and long-limbed Sebastián barely managed to fold himself in, Meche squeezing next to him.

She lifted her palm and he handed her a few coins. Meche threw them into the slot and waited.

The first flash went off with Meche sticking her tongue out. The second was much of the same, her hand lifting behind Sebastián's head to make a pair of horns. Flash a third time and she smiled sweetly.

"Last one," Sebastián said.

Meche turned to look at him and Sebastián picked that moment to also turn his head and look at her.

Time slowed down. The seconds crawled, lazily, and she looked at Sebastián and Sebastián looked at her for what was maybe two, three months. A whole season passed in his gaze and her heart—which she knew should beat at 60-100 per minute, knowledge gleaned from her science textbook—beat maybe once or twice.

The walls of the booth, which had imprisoned them in its narrow space, drifted away further and further and the roof melted, all of which caused Meche to panic.

Then the flash went off, bathing them with its white light, illuminating every corner of the booth and making Meche gasp in surprise.

The light faded, the walls crept back together and Meche's heart regained its usual healthy rate, time suddenly returning to its normal course.

"Let's look at the pictures," she said, hastily exiting the booth.

Sebastián remained inside, behind the tattered red curtain, while Meche leaned down near the little opening which was supposed to spit out the photos. She tapped her foot impatiently, wishing the photos would just develop.

Sebastián stepped out of the booth just at the moment the photos appeared. He opened his mouth and she held the photos for him to see.

"They came out okay," she said.

"Yeah," Sebastián muttered.

"I'll pay you back the money... um, I'm going home now."

"Alright. Are you coming over for the video game?"

Meche just wanted to get home fast, so she nodded and stepped back, stuffing the photos in her back pocket.

"I'll meet you at Chaplin's around six!" he yelled.

CHAPLIN'S HAD A big, ugly sign outside which showed a silhouette of the famous comedian raising his hat. The store's full name was Chaplin's Movie Emporium, but nobody called it that. It rented videos in Betamax and a small selection of video games. Videocentro was bigger, but they charged more for rentals and it was further away. Plus, the clerk at Chaplin's usually threw in a free bag of microwaveable popcorn. The clerk was only a couple of years older than they were and he was dating Jimena, which explained the added bonus.

"So are we going with *Castlevania*?" Sebastián asked.

Meche was looking over the videos, not paying much attention to him. She wore her heavy, green jacket and her matching green sneakers. Every once in a while she bit her lower lip, like when she didn't know an exam question.

She didn't look very happy to be at the video store and Sebastián wondered what was up with that.

"*Castlevania* is fine."

Sebastián paid, feeling a bit glad that he could do this. He grabbed the game and the popcorn and they walked back to his apartment.

The elevator did not work so they trudged up the stairs.

Inside it was as dirty as usual even though Romualdo had promised to clean up when they had spoken during breakfast. Sebastián sighed.

"Romu!" he yelled.

No answer. Sebastián put the keys on a hook by the door.

"He's probably gone to buy something for dinner. Do you want juice?"

"I'm fine."

They sat on the couch in front of the banged-up television set. Sebastián plugged in the Nintendo and pushed in the game, grabbing a controller. Meche sat at the edge of the couch, the heavy jacket firmly buttoned up to her neck.

"Do you have a cold?" he asked.

"No," Meche said.

"You look funny."

"I'm just tired."

"You don't have to play with me if you don't want to."

"I'm here, am I not?"

"Okay."

Meche took off her jacket and tossed it on the back of the sofa. She was wearing one of her oversized t-shirts. It said 'Blondie' with big, pink letters on a black background. Sebastián thought she looked very small in it, like she was about to be swallowed by the shirt.

"What?" Meche asked testily.

"Nothing."

"Just push play."

He did, guessing that Simon Belmont might be the solution for whatever weirdness was happening that day.

Because he did feel weird. In the phone booth there had been this uncomfortable moment when he had looked at Meche and she had looked back at him, and it didn't feel like looking at Meche. Hell, he looked at Meche every day of the week and he knew exactly what she looked like, but when the flash went off he thought, for a second, that he didn't know her. It was… bizarre.

A few levels later Romualdo still had not showed up but at least Meche seemed more relaxed. She pressed the buttons on the controller, trying to manipulate Belmont's whip, then handed it to Sebastián when she got killed.

"Your turn."

"Can I ask you something?" she said, as he grabbed the controller.

"What?"

"Do you really like Isadora?"

"What do you mean?"

"Just that."

Sebastián frowned. "Are you going to tell me she's a ditz?"

"No. I'm just asking."

"She's cute."

"Yeah, so is Cindy Crawford."

"Cindy Crawford doesn't go to the same school I go to."

"So it's convenience?"

"It's… ah… well, you like Constantino, no?"

"Don't you sometimes think we're chasing after mirages?"

"What's so awesome about reality?" he asked, turning and looking at her.

"It's what we have."

"We have magic."

"I'm getting the feeling that doesn't work as often as we expected."

Meche leaned back and rubbed her eyes, shrugging. The music on the video game played loudly, the rhythmic electronic beats repeating themselves. Sebastián pressed the pause button.

"What do you mean?"

"I've been looking for this stupid Procol Harum record for the past few days so I can cast a love spell... have Constantino fall in love with me."

"What? You think if you play a song from that band he'll go nutty and start making out with you in a flash?"

Meche blushed, looking down, as though she were trying to find out if the lettering on her t-shirt was still there.

"Would that be so bad?" she asked. "I was also thinking maybe a glamour spell..."

"A what?"

"Something to make me look pretty."

"Meche, you *are* pretty."

Meche raised her head, her eyes dark and cold. "I'm not and I don't like it when you lie to make me feel better," she said flatly.

"I'm not a liar."

Meche said nothing, though skepticism danced in her eyes. Fine. Maybe he was trying to be nice; was that such a big crime? When had a kindness become a slap in the face? The truth was it would take some spell for Constantino to pick Meche over Isadora, but he didn't want to say it outright.

"I'm polite."

She was getting ready to come back at him with a quick, witty jab and Sebastián found himself holding his breath, waiting. Before Meche could speak and needle him with a cynical line from a song, he leaned down and in a sudden case of insanity—maybe because he felt bad about her, maybe because he felt bad about himself, maybe because Constantino was never going to pick her but Isadora was not going to pick him either—kissed her.

Meche opened her mouth, no doubt to insult him, but all this did was deepen the kiss.

Sebastián knew he probably wasn't doing it right because the only time he had kissed another girl before had been in sixth grade, when he'd been invited to a dreadful game of Spin the Bottle and ended up locking lips with a classmate who seemed utterly grossed out by the fact that it was Sebastián instead of the boy sitting next to him.

Meche's sharp intake of breath made him pause and he drew back, staring at her in utter confusion.

Meche looked like she had been run over by a truck, her eyes all big and wide.

"I'm sorry," he said. "I didn't mean it." He paused and added, "Are we cool?"

"Jesus," Meche said, reaching behind the couch and grabbing her jacket.

"Meche…"

"My backpack. Where is it?"

She looked around the couch, finding the backpack on the floor and quickly zipping it closed.

"Why are you mad?"

"Because you're right. You didn't mean it," she said.

Sebastián raised his hands, unable to articulate a proper response. She slammed the door shut on her way out.

MECHE DID NOT understand. The room was dark, the apartment was quiet. She had her Walkman by the pillow, the cassette tape turning, playing Leonard Cohen. This was a quick recipe for sleep but sleep did not come.

She got up and brushed past her poster of The Police, her hands dancing over her records, the familiar shapes of the action figures sitting on the shelves.

She peeked out the window and tried to find the moon but she did not see it and sat back on her bed, wondering if Sebastián was also awake.

Meche did not understand what happened. Had Sebastián gone mad? Why had he done a thing like that? And then, he had been sorry... obviously.

She pressed a finger against her lips and opened the window.

VICENTE SAT LISTENING to his wife and his daughter. It was like tuning into one of the old radio dramas on XEW. All it lacked was the appropriate, tear-jerker music. He wasn't in the mood for dramas and every word was like a nail into his skull. He wanted to tell them to fight outside.

"What did I say?"

"I don't know," Meche replied, ignoring Natalia and opening the refrigerator door.

"I said I don't want you to spend so much time with

that boy. Catalina Coronado saw you together."

"Oh my God. Is that woman with the Federal Police or something? Can I go work on my computer now?"

"It's not funny. Catalina happens to be a good friend—"

"She's a nosy bitch," Vicente said, folding his newspaper. "Go work."

Meche huffed and stomped towards her room. Natalia gifted him with one of her deadly stares.

"Thank you. Now she'll never get the point."

"The point being, what?" Vicente asked.

He was playing a record by Joaquín Sabina and did not want to get into an argument, but Natalia's tone and the way she was shaking her head at him irked him to the core.

"If she keeps hanging out with teenage boys she'll wind up sleeping with them."

"Don't teenagers generally sleep with each other? Or are we selling her off to a feudal lord?"

"Watch her get pregnant."

"Get her condoms, for God's sake. You work at a pharmacy."

"She'll pick the wrong kid and ruin her life."

Natalia didn't say "just like me," but she did not have to. Vicente burst out laughing. He could not help it.

"You are useless," Natalia muttered.

Vicente just kept laughing. He clutched the record's liner notes and sank into his chair, feeling all the misery of his marriage dripping down his shoulders and pooling at his feet.

* * *

SEBASTIÁN FELT LIKE he was reading a map which had all the street names erased. Lost, confused and surprised, he replayed the events of the night with Meche in his head. He had offended her, he understood that much. He also understood he must fix it.

Sebastián could think of only one way to make amends with Meche. He walked the three blocks from his building to her apartment, listening to the sound of fireworks going off in the streets.

He pressed her buzzer, was given access and climbed the stairs, taking care to light the sparkler before he reached her door.

"Happy New Year!" he said, waving the sparkler before her face.

Meche rested her head against the door frame. "It's not New Year's yet."

"Well, it will be in two hours."

"I'm supposed to be putting away the ham."

"You had ham?" Sebastián asked.

"What do you want?"

"I want to take you for a ride around the block."

"I want to put away the ham."

"Look, I'm sorry if I offended you."

"You didn't... ugh," Meche slid out and closed the door, resting her back against it. "You didn't offend me. But it's not nice... look, I don't like being the leftover turkey sandwich you feel obliged to eat after Christmas."

"You're not a sandwich. Come on."

"Do you *really* think I'm pretty?"

No, he thought. That was his natural reaction. A box he had long ticked off.

But he looked at her and she *was* kind of pretty. Not like Isadora, not like the other girls. When you looked at Meche the first impression was that she was going to punch you in the face; she was made of such strong angles. However, if you looked long enough there was a delicate softness beneath her which manifested in the very long neck, the graceful fingers which were meant to play instruments, the petite frame. She was a knot of contradictions and these, thrown together, created an interesting composition. When she grew up, he thought, people would see it more clearly.

"Yeah," he said faintly and then growing more self-assured, he nodded. "Yeah, you are."

Meche smiled a little. She turned her face and tried to cover it by pretending to cough, but he saw her smile and it made him smile too.

"Can you go with me for a ride?"

"Yes," she said.

They rushed downstairs, the sparkler still in his hands.

HALF AN HOUR later Sebastián parked the bike in front of Meche's building. He searched in his pockets and found the cassette he had neatly labelled that morning.

"I made a mix-tape for you, for Epiphany. I also got you a book, but I can give you that tomorrow."

"Books," Meche muttered, opening the cassette and reading the song list. "Forever Young."

"It's like a soundtrack for us. The soundtrack of our lives."

"And Alphaville will be singing on our soundtrack?"

"Among others."

She reached for her Walkman—always tucked inside her jacket, always there—and put the cassette inside, pressing play. She put on the headphones and nodded, tapping her foot.

Meche reached up and hugged him. For three minutes he danced with her to music he could not hear, a song which rang only in her ears.

Two DAYS LATER Meche pinned the pictures from the photo booth against the factory wall, right beside the cover of Dylan's *The Freewheelin'*.

It was a declaration of some sort, although she did not understand what she was declaring. Just that she needed to tell Sebastián something and since she could not write it down she tried putting it the only way she could: in shorthand.

Mexico City, 2009

MECHE WOKE UP early and stopped at the corner store to buy a small bag of peanuts. The shopkeeper stared at her, just like his grandfather had, as though she were a kid trying to steal merchandise. Of course, she *had* stolen merchandise back in the day but it was not like she was going to run out without paying now that she was a grown woman. Meche placed the money on the counter, the shopkeeper counted every coin and then handed her a receipt, still frowning.

Meche hopped on a bus. It was safer than taking a taxi and she didn't mind being squeezed into a tight corner. But she was lucky: the bus was half empty and she had a chance to sit in the back, listening to her music.

Meche kept an optimistic outlook for the first couple of hours as she classified records and moved around her father's apartment. It looked completely doable. She could tidy everything up in a day. Another hour later and Meche had despaired. Reality kicked in. It was impossible to go through all of her father's stuff in just a few hours. He had too much crap and frankly, she was tired of the whole thing, bled dry and exhausted as she tossed another record onto a pile and tried to remember what was the purpose of this. Meche lay down on the floor, in the middle of the living room, knowing she should make herself a cup of coffee because she needed it. Maybe she also needed an injection of sugar.

Someone knocked three times and for a moment she had a sense of displacement, because that knock should have come at her mother's apartment, like it always did when Daniela or Sebastián visited.

Meche opened the door and he was there, wearing a long, dark coat and looking very proper with a tie and all.

"Can I come in?" Sebastián asked.

"How did you find me?"

"Daniela and I paid a visit to your mom this morning. We gave her our condolences and chatted for a bit. She suggested I come over because you need to lug some heavy boxes."

"Aren't you the thoughtful, kind moving man?"

"I didn't mean to upset you the other night."

"Nah, of course not," she said, smiling with her sharpest smile.

"We just wanted to pay our condolences."

"And help me carry boxes."

"Heavy ones."

Meche opened the door wide, banging the wall in the process. She spread her arms open.

"Hey, walk right in. I mean, what the fuck, you're already here. Might as well be useful."

Meche should have offered to put his coat away. She didn't and hoped it got wrinkled. She headed to the kitchen and filled the kettle with hot water. He didn't follow her into the kitchen and she was grateful for that because as soon as she stood in front of the stove she felt the desire to yell and break into a fit of giggles, all at the same time. Meche stared at the kettle, crossing her arms, wondering if she shouldn't have told him to get out of the building.

Shoulda, woulda.

The kettle screamed and Meche poured two cups of tea.

Tea, after all.

Habits die hard.

She headed into the living room and placed his cup on top of a Bee Gees record, sitting herself on the floor because the couch was buried beneath piles of records. Sebastián grabbed the cup and also sat on the floor, carefully folding his long legs. He'd always been more legs than anything. This thin scarecrow of a boy.

"How many records do you think your dad had?" he asked.

"Thousands," Meche said, tired of the question. "It'll take forever to go through it all but I only have until next week."

"Are you leaving after the novena is over?"

"As soon as I can book the flight."

"To Oslo?"

"That's home," Meche said, sipping her tea. There was no milk and no sugar and she made a face when she tasted the chamomile.

"Your dad was always nice to us. Daniela and me... we just felt we should visit."

"He's dead. Saying a couple of prayers is not going to get him out of hell and it's not earning you brownie points."

"All the same, Daniela and I would like to pray with your family tonight or tomorrow."

"With my mother and my cousin," Meche said. "I don't pray. My father was an atheist. He would be offended if I started with the Hail Marys. Hey, maybe I should pray after all."

Meche smiled and took a big gulp of tea, downing the hot drink. She would get something else later. Maybe some food.

"What did you have for breakfast?" Sebastián asked, as if reading her mind.

"I don't have breakfast."

"That's not good for you."

"Says who?"

"Let's go have lunch. I can put those boxes in my car later."

"Don't you have stuff to do?"

"Yes—I have lunch with you."

He sounded like when they were teenagers and he wanted to skip school. And she knew he'd won this round already, probably from the moment she opened the door.

Meche thought of tossing the remains of her tea in his face, watch it stain his nice, crisp shirt and equally nice tie. But she was tired and she was hungry, and the desire for a fight was already dying back to a simmer.

"You're buying," she said.

EVEN THOUGH JIMENA had gushed about Sebastián's new wheels, Meche didn't really like the car. Frankly, she missed the motorcycle. It had been a piece of crap, ugly, worn and unreliable, but she liked sitting behind Sebastián, twining her arms around his waist and riding around the block on it.

Meche flicked on the stereo and Lena Horne started singing Stormy Weather. Meche raised her eyebrows and scoffed.

"Are you trying to impress me?" she asked.

"I like jazz."

"What would you know about jazz?"

"Quite a bit, actually. I started with Fitzgerald."

"Like I suggested."

"Yeah."

"Who wrote Stormy Weather?"

"Are you testing me, Meche?"

"Answer the question."

"Harold Arlen and Ted Koehler. Ethel Waters first sang it at The Cotton Club."

He gave her a smug sideways glance and Meche felt like pinching him. Where the hell was the restaurant? She was starting to get impatient and shifted in her seat, wiggling her toes inside her shoes. Traffic in Mexico City. Dear God. It was murder. They should have walked somewhere nearby instead of jumping in his fancy vehicle.

"Well, if you really like jazz you should take some of my dad's records. You play vinyl, right?"

"I don't, no."

"Then you're not a real aficionado," she said, feeling like she had the upper hand again. "You can't compare an MP3 to vinyl."

"I don't like vinyl."

"You shouldn't believe the crap they say about sound

fidelity and CDs. Vinyl is not inferior to your digital files."

He glanced at her, looking very sombre all of a sudden. "I don't play vinyl because it reminds me of you."

Meche frowned and stared at the stereo.

SHE DECIDED TO pay herself back for all those lunches Sebastián had eaten. All those free meals he had stolen, the pieces of sandwich he had pinched away, the times he sipped from her bottle, the popcorn he grabbed from her bag. A big freeloader, that's what he had been, but now he had shiny, fancy shoes and she bet there was a nice, fat wallet to go with them. She ordered the most expensive item on the menu—steak—and added a cocktail for good measure. A double, because she needed it.

The restaurant was stylish, but the tablecloths were too white and the chairs too stiff. She was used to eating her meals by the computer or at a little café around the corner from her apartment.

Meche leaned both elbows against the table and took out her iPod, looking at the playlist. Force of habit. She listened to music when she ate. Well, she listened to music all the time. When she coded and when she went for a jog. Music was there, the constant in her life.

"You always have dark circles under your eyes?" Sebastián asked.

"It depends on the project."

"Were you working on a big project?"

"Yeah. Now I'm here. Unfortunately."

Meche shook her head and attacked her steak, cutting off a piece and chewing on it with gusto.

"I didn't think I'd ever see you again," he said.

"Yeah, me too. It kind of spoils the thing. I was trying very hard to keep that enemy-mine thing going but I don't know if Mothra ever had lunch with Godzilla."

He smiled and it reminded her of the goofy smile of his youth. Goofy but charming because it was so dumb. But there was a dusting of grey in his hair, faint but marking the passage of time and the long stretch between the teenager and the man she was eating with.

"You're still funny."

"I'm a fucking riot," Meche said. "So?"

"I don't know. I thought about contacting you before but I didn't think enough time had passed."

"For me to forget?"

"For you to remember."

Meche lifted her fork and looked at the piece of meat sticking from it.

"Remember, what exactly?"

"How we used to be friends."

"Two decades ago. Before," Meche made a little circular motion with the fork, "the whole stabbing in the back thingy."

"We had fun times."

"We were teenagers. Scoring enough coins to play at the arcade for an hour was the crowning achievement of the year. What do you want me to do? Get all teary-eyed and tell you I've missed you?"

"I'm not sure how you remember it, but I remember that the world used to stop spinning when we were hanging out and it felt like everything was possible."

"Magic," Meche said. "Magic was possible."

"Not magic. Not spells. Before the magic. We got each other."

"And then?"

"And then I don't know," he said. "I wanted to see you again."

Meche put her fork down. The steak looked kind of bloody and not so appetizing anymore. She grabbed the glass of water and took a sip.

"There's nothing to see."

"I know you hold grudges. Hell, you like to hold them."

"Compartmentalizing works. You build systems like that."

Sebastián sat back. He tilted his head just as she remembered he used to, like he was taking a mental pause to process something.

"You're really going to hate me forever?"

"Forever is a very irrational concept. Let's just leave it at a very long time. Can I order dessert? I need more tea and some sort of pastry."

Meche waved to the server, not caring if it was a crude way to get his attention.

"I can believe that," he said.

"Catching on, are you?"

"Well, holding grudges was your forte."

"It does wonders for the complexion." Meche looked at the server. "I'll need a strawberry tart and tea with milk."

"What movie are we watching tomorrow?"

Meche looked at him with an *are-you-fucking-insane* look in her eyes. He looked back at her with an innocent smile.

"A what?"

"I owe you a movie. 1989. I promised we'd go out and we never did."

Ah, yeah. *That* night.

"Um, it's okay? You can do your own thing and I'll do mine," Meche said.

"We can go to the latest show."

"You really think I'll go with you," she said flatly.

"What was my forte?"

"I don't know," Meche said with a shrug.

"I was stubborn. I gave you eight books for presents even though you said you did not want another book."

"I'm still pissed about that."

"How does *The Ambassadors* end?"

"Not a clue," Meche said. "I never read it."

She was lying and he knew she was lying. She had actually spent a whole weekend trying to find that same book the first time she went to Paris, just because she thought she ought to read it in the damn city where it took place. But she was not going to prove his point.

"I like comic books and albums from the 60s," she said.

"And Jacques Brel."

Ah, touché. He remembered that.

The server put the tart and tea before Meche. She poured a bit of milk into the cup and smirked.

"You can just take them and drop them off at my mom's place."

She shoved the box aside with her foot.

"I can drive you back to your mom's place."

"I'm not leaving right now."

"I could wait."

"Aren't you going to get in trouble at your job?" she asked. "You've been with me for two hours."

Not that she cared what his job thought. She just wanted him out of the apartment. When she was with him she had the bizarre sensation that ants were running up and down her arms. It was terribly irritating.

"I'm not a surgeon. People are not going to die if I show up late. It's marketing."

"Oh, yeah. Marketing," Meche said, folding the flaps of another box. "What do you do, like peddle potato chips and shit?"

"I'm a Creative Director. I oversee the copy chief, the art director, and—"

"Wasn't that what I just said? Peddle and shit."

He looked amused as he sat on the floor of her father's living room. Like he was having a really good time though she had said nothing nice to him all morning long.

"What do you do in Oslo?"

"I'm a coding monkey. Didn't I say that?"

If she had not told him, then she was sure her mother had.

"When you're not coding."

"I don't know. I watch TV. I take care of Svend."

"Is that your boyfriend?"

"It's a very big fern. I have several ferns but I only baptized one because if you name more than one inanimate object you're heading into crazy cat lady territory."

"That's the rule?"

"Yeah."

He smiled and she felt herself smiling back, which was not what she had been going for. Unfortunately, Sebastián had a way of disarming her. He'd had it when they were kids and he still had it now. Even though she knew she shouldn't allow herself to be disarmed, that such behaviour led to shameful ruin, she was smiling.

"As much as I'd love to have a long chat about Pteridophyta, I really need time to work and you're distracting me."

"Just how distracting am I?" he asked scooting closer. The question was warm and mischievous and he was like the notes of a familiar song. It made her want to hum and that triggered a blaring alarm inside her brain.

Meche slammed a record against his chest, her eyebrows knitted together.

"Just carry these downstairs and get out, will you?"

He grabbed the boxes looking mightily amused, like that time when he had all the answers to the Spanish Literature quiz and she got none, so she sat at her desk in a panic while Sebastián smirked at her. Later she threw a piece of sandwich at the back of his head, but she didn't have a sandwich at the moment.

"Don't forget I'm taking you to the movies."

"Go back to planet deluded," she muttered.

She closed the door behind him and plucked a record sleeve from a pile.

"What do you think, Steve Perry?" she asked, smirking at the single—it was Oh Sherrie—and then tossing it to the floor because she realised she was talking to an inanimate object.

Mexico City, 1989

THE FIRST DAY back in class was usually a quiet, lazy progression of hours which everyone—teachers included—took easy. They were all recovering from the festivities. It was not a day for great happenings. But this year something very big did happen.

It took place right after English class. Sebastián, Meche and Daniela were sitting in their usual configuration.

Isadora Galván walked over towards them and in plain sight of about half a dozen other students, paused before Sebastián's desk.

"Thank you for the nice Christmas present," she said. "I'm wearing it today."

"You're... ah... welcome," Sebastián said.

"A bunch of us are going to the movies tonight. Do you want to come?"

"Yeah. Sure."

"Good. Let's talk after school."

Just like that Isadora bounced away, short skirt swaying, dazzling smile lighting the classroom. Gone and leaving half a dozen students—as well as Meche and Daniela—completely stunned.

"Did I miss something while I was away?" Daniela asked.

"I'd say we both did."

"I bought her a necklace," Sebastián replied.

Meche's voice was caramel-coated razors. "Gee, purchasing affection."

"What do you know about it?"

"She just invited you to make Constantino jealous," Meche said.

Daniela noticed how Sebastián twitched at that, as though he'd been zapped with a small taser. His eyes fixed on Meche and Meche rolled her eyes in turn.

"We need to change into the lab coats for chemistry. I have to wash mine again. I spilled something on it," Meche said.

Daniela and Meche headed to the bathrooms. Meche grabbed the coat and placed it in the sink, rubbing it quickly.

"Do you think he'll really go out with them tonight?" Daniela asked.

"What am I? A mind-reader?"

"I'm just asking."

"Ugh," Meche said. "Hey, how do you get rid of an avocado stain?"

"Beats me. When were you eating avocado?"

Meche put on the coat and looked in the mirror, brushing the hair away from her face.

"I don't remember. Did you have a nice time in Mazatlán?"

"It was real nice. I wish we could have stayed longer."

"Tell me about it," Meche muttered. "How the hell does Rodríguez go about giving us an assignment during winter break? What am I saying, you don't have anything to worry about. You'll be doing the tutoring thing with him and he'll give you an A just so you keep paying him."

"I don't know," Daniela said. "It might not be so easy. We have our first session Friday and he's already given me reading material."

"I hate his little beady eyes."

"He does not have little beady eyes."

"Does too."

They walked out of the bathroom and went up the stairs, following the flow of students moving at the sound of the bell.

"Did you have fun with Sebastián while I was away?" Daniela asked.

"It was alright," Meche said, giving Daniela a sideways glance. "He..."

Meche trailed off and Daniela waited patiently for her to complete her sentence.

"Yeah?"

"Oh, nothing. Something dumb."

SEBASTIÁN WATCHED THE screen without watching it, his eyes out of focus, and when they stepped into the lobby he could not have said what movie had been screened.

"We're going to the washroom," Isadora told the boys.

She walked away, followed by the other girls. Sebastián stood a bit to the side, not really engaging the boys in the group. Constantino and the other three clones glanced in his direction, smirked and talked amongst themselves.

It was to be expected. But then Constantino motioned to him and Sebastián walked towards them, shuffling forward, his shoulders hunched; a lumbering giant.

"Yeah?" he asked.

"We're glad you could make it tonight," Constantino said.

Sebastián nodded, a bit surprised by that.

"I'm glad too."

"But don't make a habit out of it."

"What do you mean?"

"I mean we don't want you going out with Isadora again."

"We or you?" Sebastián asked, surprising himself with the boldness lurking in his voice.

The boys glanced at each other, then back at him. Constantino's lips curled into a smile.

"What's your friend's name?"

"What friend?" Sebastián asked cautiously.

"The one who likes music. She wears her headphones all the time."

"Meche."

"Yeah. She's a good dancer. She's got good moves."

Sebastián recalled the night at Isadora's party, when he'd seen Meche twirling in Constantino's arms and the sick feeling in his gut. He said nothing.

"If you fuck with my girl, I'll fuck with yours," Constantino said. "I'll give it to her up the ass."

Sebastián stood straight, unfolded to his full length and glared down at Constantino, his fingers pressing against his throat, making the shorter boy gasp with shock because Sebastián had never before put up a fight. The others must have also been in shock because they did not interfere.

"Never, ever try that," he whispered. "Or I'll cut off your dick."

He released Constantino and stepped back. The boys, normally itching to pile insults on him, seemed to have lost their will and looked dully at him. Constantino straightened up, his handsome face ugly with anger.

"I'll teach you a lesson some other time."

"Try it," Sebastián said.

He thought how they might fare if he cast a spell. Maybe Constantino could contract a nasty disease. These dark thoughts must have been reflected in his eyes for the boys looked away and Constantino pressed his lips tightly together and did not speak again.

The girls returned. Isadora smiled at him and Sebastián smiled back. There was talk of going for a bite and Sebastián, tight on finances as usual, looked at his watch and pretended he was expected for supper back at home.

"I should go," Sebastián told her. "But thanks for the invitation."

"Maybe we can go out some other time," she said.

"Yes."

The boys glared at him. Sebastián walked out of the movie theatre.

GRANDMOTHER'S NEEDLES CLICKED together as she knitted, fingers steady, always knowing what movement would follow. Practice, she'd told Meche. All it takes is a little practice.

Maybe it was the same with magic. Meche thought

they were getting better but there was still the need for practice.

They should have been in the factory that evening. But Sebastián was out with Isadora and her friends.

Meche glanced at the clock. The little hand had scarcely moved.

She sighed and looked at her homework. She had finished the math problems ages ago and was now stuck on short story readings. The words seemed to jump and dance before her eyes. She could not concentrate.

"Can you tell me the story of the girl in the well, grandmother?" she asked.

"Aren't you working?"

"I'm tired."

"There once was a little girl who lived deep in a well. The chaneques had taken her when she was little, stolen her from her mother and placed her deep in the middle of the forest, inside a well—"

The phone rang and Meche rushed to pick it up, breathlessly holding the receiver.

"Yes?"

"Hey, Meche," her father said.

Oh. She thought it might have been Sebastián. He would tell her the evening had been crap and they would laugh together about it.

"I'm going to be home late tonight. I've got some business over here."

"Do I leave your plate out?"

"Just put it in the refrigerator. Thanks, sweetheart."

"Okay. Night."

Meche went to the kitchen and put some picadillo on

a dish, then began covering it with plastic. Her mother walked in and glanced at her.

"Dad's coming late."

Her mother did not say anything. She dropped her glass in the sink and walked out, but Meche could see it in her eyes: she was angry. Dad was probably at the bar, getting drunk. She hoped she was not going to be sent out to find him. But, as was regularly the case, an hour later she was putting on her green jacket and gnashing her teeth.

She poked her head into the bar and looked around. Her father was not playing dominoes and he was not chatting with the regulars. He was not there.

Meche walked back home and poured herself a glass of milk before going to bed. Her mother, nestling a cup of coffee between her hands, was reading a magazine.

"He wouldn't come," Meche lied, though she did not know why she did.

Her mother turned a page and nodded.

VICENTE LAY IN the arms of his mistress and thought of his wife. It was the worst time possible to be doing this, but he could not get Natalia out of his mind.

He needed to leave her. He was tired of sneaking around. He was just plain tired. When he woke up in the morning he saw a middle-aged man with grey hair and a forlorn expression in the mirror. He hated that man. He hated himself.

But there were practical things to consider. Their daughter, for one. And, though it might sound crass, there was the issue of the money.

Vicente had none. His desire to move to Puerto Vallarta, to live by the beach and spend his days watching sunsets, drowned in the reality of his scant possibilities.

He wished he was fifteen, even ten years younger than he currently was. He wished he had never met nor married his wife. Then he didn't wish that because that would mean Meche would not exist.

Azucena had told him about a business venture of a cousin of hers, something guaranteed to bring in dough. Vicente imagined himself rich, with a house in el Pedregal and a brand new sports car. Meche could live with them. She'd like it there. He'd buy her nice clothes and take her to eat out every night of the week.

"What is it that your cousin does, again?" he asked Azucena.

Mexico City, 2009

MECHE BOUGHT PISTACHIOS and a Coke at the corner store. Catalina Coronado was there too, buying eggs. The old woman stood gossiping and Meche had to wait ten minutes as the gnarled witch informed the shopkeeper of the movements of everyone in the colonia. Finally, Meche was able to pay, dumping her coins on the counter. Then it was onto the bus, headphones on, until she reached her father's apartment.

The apartment seemed to be getting more depressing every day and Meche was sure the flamingoes were growing anemic. Their ugly, faded, pink bodies blurred into one large pink blob when she stared at the curtains for too long. If she stared at the records the faces on the covers also blurred and changed, becoming faces of people she had known. Becoming her father.

KEEP MOVING. KEEP going. Keep running. Go through another pile of records, toss another box in a corner. Repeat.

Three more nights of prayer and then it was over.

She switched to her father's papers, cramming pages

from his book into a box, slamming the typewriter on the top. She emptied the bedside table and found his diary for the current year.

March's entry. Written with his tight handwriting, filling every centimetre on the page.

I am planning on visiting Meche next year in Norway. She doesn't know it yet. I have decided to save enough money for the plane ticket and go in the summer. I want to see Meche before I die.

Meche went into the kitchen and searched the cabinets for her father's booze. But there was none. The old drunkard was disappointing her: he wouldn't even share his liquor.

Meche laughed. She opened the front door, determined to leave for Oslo right that instant. Determined to escape the dark, dingy apartment, the singers plastered on the covers of an army of records, the notebooks crammed with his life. She was going to die if she didn't get some air.

But back home there would be the food, the prayers, the people, the conversations and her father's picture in a silver frame set high upon a shelf for everyone to see.

She hurried back to the bedroom, lay on the bed and turned up the volume on the iPod, searching for a recent song. Something fresh. Meche closed her eyes.

When she woke up there was a tall, dark shadow in the doorway, blocking the light which filtered from the living room.

"Sebos?" she asked, her mouth dry.

She must be dreaming of him, like she did in Europe, during the long winter nights when he used to come into her room and sit quietly at the foot of her bed. The ghost of a boy who had not died.

"Nobody calls me Sebos anymore," he said and when he stepped forward she saw it was not the young Sebastián who had haunted her. It was the older one. The real one.

"What are you doing here?"

"I went to your home for the novena and nobody knew where you were. I thought you might still be here. We had a movie to watch."

"How did you get in?" she asked, wondering if he still had magic tricks under his sleeve. Turning into mist and slipping under the door maybe.

"You left the door open."

How prosaic. Meche shook her head, still groggy. She pulled out the earbuds, stuffing them in her pocket.

"Is the praying over?"

"Yes."

"Good."

"What are you doing?"

"I was taking a nap until you interrupted me."

"No, I mean what are you *doing*," he asked, the inflexion falling on the last word.

He sat on the bed and she sat up so that she was level with him.

"Thinking," she said.

"I had a hard time when my dad died."

"When did he die?"

"A couple of years ago."

"You hated him," Meche said. "He used to beat you up."

"He did. But he also did nice things. He made toys for me. Little things of wire and tin. I try to remember the good things."

"Then you're a better person than I," she muttered, folding her legs into a lotus position.

"When did you get so sad?"

"Oh, please," Meche said. "Am I crying?"

"No. Then?"

"When I was seven years old I fell down and I said, 'I'm not going to cry about this.' And I didn't. I've stayed true to that. Waterworks don't work for me, all that stupid melodrama..."

"You didn't cry because you wanted to show your dad you were brave," Sebastián said turning his head and looking at her. "You told me that story. I remember."

"Great. So what? Should I start weeping all over your shirt and you can wipe my tears with that God-damn nasty tie you're wearing?" she asked, jamming a finger against one of the buttons on his shirt. Poking his chest. "You get your kicks like that these days?"

"I can go if you want."

"You do that," she said and grabbed the notebook she had been reading before. She tossed it at him, hitting him on the face.

It made her incredibly happy. If only she could pelt him with about two dozen other notebooks. Seized by a desire for destruction, Meche grabbed a bunch of records and flipped them at him. Sebastián evaded them this time, ducking. She kept throwing them, like Frisbees.

"Look! Take On Me. Now that's a classic. And here, La Puerta de Alcalá. It was a big hit back in 1985. Oh, look at this one?" Meche showed him the sleeve. "Mi Unicornio Azul by Silvio Rodríguez. My dad liked that song a lot."

Meche buried her face in the pillow.

She felt Sebastián's fingers on her shoulder; tried to shove him away and failed, then lay still and blinked.

"I hate this city," she told the pillow, because she wouldn't tell him.

Sebastián's hand just rested there as it had many times before: comforting her after the news of a bad grade; the nasty words a classmate spoke at school; even the time when she got so many zits she promised she'd never leave the apartment again and Sebastián had arrived, luring her out with the promise of the arcade.

A phone rang. His cell. The hand left her.

"Yes. Mom? Yeah."

He walked towards the doorway and Meche rolled over, grabbing the blanket and wrapping herself into it. She was not cold in Oslo but this apartment packed the cold of too many winters in its heart.

Sebastián returned and sat next to her.

"Jimena said your mom is sick."

"Cancer. Romualdo and I take turns looking after her. That's why I'm back in the city. The chemo has worked. I'm betting she lives to a hundred."

She thought of her own father, shuffling alone through his apartment in his slippers with no one to watch over him. Nothing but the songs for company.

"You're going to go visit her now?"

"No. I can stay."

"I'm not asking you to stay," Meche said looking over her shoulder.

"You think I'd leave just like that?"

Well, you did once before, she thought. Well, technically she'd left. But only after he completely abandoned her by the curbside.

"I don't know you," she muttered. To the pillow, again. "You're a stranger."

He turned her around and Meche frowned as she looked into eyes which were exactly the same as she remembered them. But the rest wasn't. And this man... she had never ridden down the boulevard on this man's motorcycle, never scrawled idly in his books, never listened to vinyl records in an old pantyhose factory with him.

And that was that. You don't get to rewind your life like a tape and splice it back together, pretending it never knotted and tore, when it did and you know it did.

Didn't he get that?

They'd never be friends again. Never care like they cared, never dance like they danced. Time had sucked the marrow out of her and they were both too old.

He stretched his arms and pulled Meche forward, resting his chin upon her head.

"I know," he said.

Meche squeezed her eyes shut and let him hold her for a good, long time. They'd lain like that on the factory floor, Sebastián wrapping his arms around her as they fell asleep.

"I can't see you again," she said. Her voice sounded dinted and strained.

"Why not?"

"Compartments. Plus, it's not as if I like you."

Sebastián laughed lightly.

"Then pretend to like me for a couple more days."

"Why?"

"Because you'll be gone after that."

Oslo, with the little apartment. The shelves and the books—yes, she had bought them. She even had *The Ambassadors*, damn it—and the vinyl records proudly displayed on the walls instead of photographs of her family. Yellow walls and little white dishes as she sipped her tea and looked out the window, facing north. For half a second she wished he could see the place right now.

Meche shifted and slipped from his embrace. She looked down at him as she stood beside the bed and she shook her head, just the slightest movement.

She headed to the living room, pushed her hands deep in her pockets, brushing a pile of records on her way and making it tumble onto the floor. The front door was two paces away.

The keys.

Meche sighed, heading back towards the living room and bumping into Sebastián, who was standing there, leaning on the doorframe, looking down at her.

Sebastián stretched out a hand, pulling her closer and pressing his forehead against hers.

She felt completely lost and tried to shove him back, gently. He didn't budge, instead pressing a kiss against her cheek.

"Second movement," he said.

He kissed her mouth. Meche shook her head and looked away, staring at the shadows. She stood like that for a long time.

Coda, she thought. *You mean a coda.* She slid her hands up, touched the stubble of his jaw. It was odd, the texture of his skin beneath her fingers. Meche closed her eyes and kissed him harder than he had kissed her, wrapping her arms loosely around his neck.

He smiled against her mouth and she wished he was not so damn *pleased* with himself. Then she smiled too, only a little.

Mexico City, 1989

MID-JANUARY VICENTE Vega withdrew all the savings from their bank account. He was investing them in the business venture of Azucena's cousin. By the end of January, Azucena and the venture had vanished. Natalia found out at the end of February.

Vicente grabbed two suitcases and left on the last day of the month.

FEBRUARY WAS AN explosion of pink and red at Daniela's house. Valentine's Day approached with its excuse for her to indulge in craft-making on a grand scale. She went downtown and bought all kinds of supplies: silicone for the hot glue gun, fabric, shiny paper, bits of lace. She made Valentines for all her family—including the extended cousins in Mazatlán— and for all her classmates, even though they did not give her any Valentines. Then she began working on Sebastián's birthday gift: he was turning sixteen.

Sebastián had been born the morning before Valentine's Day and this gave Daniela the perfect excuse to put her talents to use for a gift which was part birthday present and part homage to this holiday. Her creations were all pink and sparkly, hideous and kitsch, best viewed from afar or not viewed at all. Sebastián, not wanting to hurt his friend's feelings, accepted each with a smile, posed for a picture with Daniela holding the gift and stuck it somewhere on a shelf.

This year she was working on something which seemed to be a cross between an elephant and a zebra, a creature capable of giving Dali nightmares.

Sebastián observed her from the couch, wrapped in a warm blanket while Meche fumed.

"I thought we were going to practise some spells."

"I'm here, ain't I?" Sebastián said.

"I thought we were taking a break," Daniela said, pressing sequins against the head of the deformed elephant.

"That was half an hour ago," Meche said.

Daniela shrugged and Meche turned to Sebastián. It was cold in the factory with the broken window panes. He felt quite comfortable snuggled underneath the blanket, but he relented and walked towards Meche. Daniela, noticing it was now two against one, gave in.

They did not need to dance or hold hands anymore, though they sometimes did. For the past two weeks they had been working on something called a glamour, or as Meche pronounced it—gla-mur. She'd found out about it from a book of fairy tales she pilfered from the school library and was determined to make it work, although the results, so far, were far from perfect. There had been a creepy moment last week when they made Daniela's eyes apparently vanish and she walked around as though she was a mole-person.

"Why don't we try to imitate a whole person?" Meche asked.

"We can't get eye colour right, let alone the eyes. Why bother with a whole person?" Sebastián asked.

"I have a feeling it might be easier."

Magic happened like that for them: in feelings and hunches and surprise insights which came in the middle of the night.

"Okay," Daniela said. "Who will we imitate? A movie star?"

"Can I see one of your magazines?" Meche asked.

Daniela grabbed her purse and pulled out one of her teen magazines. Meche thumbed through it, finally ripping out a page and holding it up.

"This one," she said.

Her choice was a pretty girl wearing a black leotard. Her hair was in a ponytail. Sebastián looked carefully at the photo, trying to memorize her face, her expression.

"Who are we focusing on?" Sebastián asked.

"How about Daniela?"

"Fine."

Meche fiddled with a record. A song began to play. Take On Me. Sebastián tapped his foot, picturing Daniela as the girl. Erasing Daniela and sketching a whole new face on her, a whole new body. Clothes stitched themselves together, hair changed colour and grew, Daniela gained height and the contours of her body were reshaped. The final result was a good approximation but though it looked like an accurate copy of the picture, it also looked a bit glossy, perfect and two-dimensional; too much like the picture in a way, their imaginations producing a young woman whose skin had the rubbery quality of a mannequin.

Daniela walked around the room. It was like she had become a large Barbie doll, taking extremely long steps with her new slender legs. Then the outlines of Daniela's body seemed to fizzle—like one image had been superimposed upon another. Streams of colour cascaded down Daniela's shoulders, tumbling down; the threads of the illusion came apart, golden dust drifting towards the floor and disappearing as soon as it touched the ground.

The three of them sat down in unison. That had been interesting but not exactly what Sebastián had imagined.

"We need to keep working on it," Meche said.

"It's almost four," Daniela said, putting the crafts she had been working on back in her big market bag. "I need to go to my tutoring session."

"Really?" Meche said. "It's Saturday."

"Yeah, it doesn't matter," Daniela said. "I'm paying for it. We can meet tomorrow."

"Can we come by your house around noon?"

"Sure." Daniela rubbed her eyes and yawned. "My mom will make us lunch. Anyway, my sister's picking me up. I better go."

"Bye."

Daniela waved a happy, cheerful goodbye and clomped down the stairs. Meche locked the door behind her and looked at the picture from the magazine, biting her lower lip.

"Maybe we need to look at a moving picture instead of a still image," Meche ventured.

"What are you getting me for my birthday?" Sebastián

asked, flopping onto the couch and grabbing hold of the blanket again.

"You'll have more than enough with Daniela's awesome birthday present. Did you see all that glitter?"

"I did."

"I think she mistakes you for a five-year-old girl," Meche said.

"She means well."

"Of course she does."

"Come here," he said. "I want to show you something."

Meche sat down next to him, propping her legs over the arm of the couch and resting her back against his arm.

"What?"

He cracked open his copy of *The Ambassadors* and pulled out a cut-out from a magazine.

"I got it the other day. It's from a *National Geographic*. The Northern Lights."

"Cool."

"We have to go to the North Cape to see them."

Meche handed back the clipping. She grabbed the blanket and pulled it over herself so that they were both covered. Things were back to normal between them—the December incident vanished—except when they weren't; moments like this when Sebastián felt there was a little splinter in both of their brains.

He opened his mouth to ask Meche something. The trouble was he wasn't sure what question he wanted to ask.

Sebastián sighed.

*   *   *

DANIELA'S SISTER DROPPED her off in front of Mr. Rodríguez's place and told her she'd be back in a couple of hours. Daniela rang the bell and hummed as she waited for him to come down the stairs and let her in.

Her teacher had told her she was progressing well with her essays and Daniela felt proud of herself. She was not a brilliant student, rather average in her achievements, and it felt good to know she could shine at something.

Mr. Rodríguez let her into his apartment and smiled.

"Hi," he said. "How are you doing today, Daniela?"

"I'm good," she said, peeling off her sweater and putting it in the entrance closet, before following Mr. Rodríguez inside.

He had a little apartment with potted plants by the windows. The living room/dining room combo contained numerous shelves crammed with books. Photographs of a girlfriend Daniela had yet to meet adorned one shelf. The furniture was all a bit worn but it all looked rather chic and effortless.

Daniela sat at the dining room table and took out her notebook and her books, piling them all neatly.

"Do you want a soda? Some water?"

"No, sir. I'm fine."

The living room had a view of the kitchen and she watched as Mr. Rodríguez poured himself a glass of water. Daniela opened her notebook.

"I finished the assignment you gave me."

"What did you think of the book?"

"I thought it was fun."

"*Wuthering Heights* was fun?"

"Well... yeah?" Daniela said cautiously.

She realized she should have said dramatic, moving, romantic—any of those words. Fun was such a stupid choice.

"Here," he said, setting a glass before her. "I figure you might get thirsty."

"Thanks," she said, though she didn't need it at all.

"You were saying it's fun?"

"Yes. I mean, I finished it quickly and it wasn't hard at all. I wrote my impressions on it, like you asked."

Mr. Rodríguez stood next to her, leaning down to look at her notes. Sometimes, when Daniela stood in line at the supermarket, boys brushed by her, touching the side of her breasts. Meche would not allow anyone to cop a feel, but Daniela just tried to ignore it. It didn't happen too frequently, anyway, and she tried to tell herself the boys did not mean it, that it was an accident.

When she felt Mr. Rodríguez's hand brush against the side of her breast Daniela stiffened and stared at her notebook, figuring he hadn't meant it.

"What did you think about Heathcliff?"

Daniela's tongue clicked. Yes. Just an accident. "He's a complex character. You'd think he'd be the hero, but he acts like the bad guy sometimes…"

There. She felt it again. Large fingers brushing against her breast.

Daniela looked down. She scooted a bit to the right, reaching towards a book, moving away a little from him.

"… there is a part where…"

The fingers again, though this time they rested on her thigh.

Daniela's eyes went round. She swallowed.

"Mr. Rodríguez, you're making me uncomfortable," she muttered.

"I'm sorry."

The hand tugged at the hem of her purple peasant skirt.

"I'm going home," she said and stood up.

Mr. Rodríguez smiled at her and it was such an innocent smile that for a split second Daniela thought maybe she had imagined it, that her overactive imagination was mixing a plot from one of her books with real life.

"Look here, I know how you look at me," Mr. Rodríguez said. "Let's not be a baby about it."

The shock of his words numbed Daniela and she sat in her chair, motionless, an overstuffed doll. Mr. Rodríguez's hand returned to her thigh.

"I'm doing you a favour."

The books she read did not contain scenes like this; they offered no solutions and no maps through this forest. Daniela tried to think, tried to move from the chair and was only able to utter a weak, "Please stop, sir."

He reached for her shirt, about to take it off, and Daniela raised a leg and kneed him in the balls. He howled in pain, bending down. Daniela pushed him away and rushed towards the door.

For a few panicky seconds she thought the doorknob would not turn, but the door swung open easily and she rushed out like a scared rabbit, running faster than she thought possible. Two blocks from his place she tripped and skinned her knees, but she got up again and ran and ran until she was out of breath.

*　　*　　*

"SHE'S STILL IN bed," Daniela's sister said.

"But it's noon," Meche said. "She told us to come at noon. Is she sick again? Can we see her?"

"Well... you can try. I took her breakfast up today and she wouldn't even open the door. She says she has a cold."

"We were supposed to have lunch together," Sebastián explained.

"Yeah, I know. Maybe she'll come down if you talk to her. She's been acting weird since yesterday."

"Alright," Meche said.

They went up the stairs to Daniela's room. Her door had a colorful sign bordered with flowers which read 'Daniela.' Meche knocked three times and waited.

"What?"

"Hey, it's us," Meche said. "We're here for lunch."

"Go away."

Meche frowned and glanced at Sebastián. When Daniela was sick, she liked having them around. They read to her or played board games. She enjoyed the company and, in fact, felt sad when they didn't show up.

"Stop kidding and let us in."

"I'm not kidding. I don't want to talk to you."

"Come on. We're not going to go. What's up with you?"

"If I tell you... you can't tell anyone else."

"Who are we going to tell?" Meche said. "Open up."

Daniela unlocked the door. Meche and Sebastián walked in. The curtains were drawn. Daniela, in her pyjamas, looked tired and her eyes were red from crying. She shuffled back into bed, pulling the covers up to her chin.

"Hey, what's up with you?" Meche asked. "Did you catch a bug?"

"No," Daniela muttered.

Meche frowned. She sat at the edge of Daniela's bed.

"What's wrong?" she asked very seriously.

Daniela covered her face with her hands and shook her head. "It's embarrassing…"

"We won't laugh. Right, Sebos?"

"No, promise," Sebastián said.

"He grabbed my boob."

Sebastián looked at Meche, eyes wide. She turned towards Daniela.

"Who did?" Meche asked.

Daniela kept her hands over her eyes. She pursed her lips.

"Who?" Meche demanded. "Tell us or we'll find out."

"Rodríguez," Daniela whispered.

Meche knew it! She just knew he was an asshole. There was something unpleasant and oily about him. She wanted to wring his neck like a chicken.

"What?" Sebastián asked.

"He also touched my leg. He said he was doing me a favour."

Meche grabbed her by the shoulders, pulling her up. "Did he rape you?"

"No! But he would have… I ran out and… and tomorrow I'm going to have to see him in school. I can't. I just can't."

"No, you're never going to have to see him again because he's going to get his ass fired," Meche said. "Frankenstrada is going to kick him out on the spot."

"Yeah… yeah," Sebastián agreed. "He won't teach again."

"I don't want to tell the principal."

"We'll go with you," Meche said. "We'll tell her together."

"What if she doesn't believe me?"

"She's got to."

Daniela uncovered her face. She nodded weakly. Meche sat with her and held her hand.

"It'll be fine."

THEY SHOWED UP promptly at Principal Estrada's office on Monday morning, asking for a brief meeting and were admitted into her office. Estrada sat behind her massive desk, photographs of former students decorating the walls, the history and pride of the institution reflected through the decades. She listened to them, hands clasped in front of her, and sat very still as Daniela spoke.

Once Daniela had finished she placed her hands upon the desk.

"That's quite a story," she said.

"It's true," Meche said. "Mr. Rodríguez is a creep."

"Mr. Rodríguez has been with us for five years. He performs very well on his evaluations and has never given us a cause for concern."

"Well, there's a cause here," Meche replied.

"Look, I understand," the principal said.

Meche sighed with relief.

"It's hard being a kid these days. All that sex in music videos on the television. There is very little sense of decency left. It's terribly confusing."

"What does that have to do with Daniela?" Sebastián asked.

Principal Estrada gave Daniela a kind, motherly look.

"Look, I talked to Professor Rodríguez already—"

"You did?" Daniela mumbled.

"Yes. Yesterday. He told me you tried to kiss him. He was terribly ashamed about the whole thing."

"It's the other way around," Meche said. "He was trying to touch her boob."

Principal Estrada rose, circling the desk and standing next to Daniela. She stared down at the girl. Daniela lowered her head, as if she were trying to look at something stuck to the floor.

"Did he really try to touch you?"

Daniela did not answer. Meche saw how she gripped the arms of the chair she was sitting in.

"Can I leave?" Daniela asked.

"I asked you a question."

"No. Can I go now?"

"Yes. That goes for the three of you."

Daniela rushed out of the office. Sebastián hurried after her. Meche stopped at the door, looking back at Principal Estrada.

Estrada sat back behind her desk, tidying her papers and utterly ignoring her.

"WAIT," MECHE SAID, running after them and catching up as they exited into the courtyard. "We can't leave it at that."

"We are going to leave it at that," Daniela whispered. "She doesn't care."

"She doesn't care, but we do," Meche said. "We have to do something."

"Like what?!" Daniela turned around, clutching her books against her chest. "What can we do?"

"Everything," Meche said. "That's what magic is for."

"What kind of spell are you talking about?" Sebastián asked.

"Something to teach him a lesson, so he'll never bug Daniela or any other girl again."

Daniela and Sebastián looked at each other nervously. Daniela stared down at her shoes, biting her lower lip.

"Black magic?"

"Oh, black magic is the shit they say in movies," Meche said with a chuckle. "Magic is magic."

"It's not the same to ask for money as it is to hurt a man," Sebastián said, feeling terribly uncomfortable with the whole conversation.

"Like I don't know it?"

"No, I don't think you do."

Meche's eyes narrowed. She grabbed Sebastián's arm, digging her nails into his skin. Like when they played together and mock fighting got out of hand. Only not really, because there was this glimmer in her eye which he did not like. Sebastián brushed her hand off.

"Rodríguez must pay," Meche said.

"Maybe," Sebastián said. "But magic it's not the way to do it."

"Can we even do it?" Daniela asked.

"Oh, yeah," Meche said. "I'm sure we can."

DANIELA SAT IN the front seat, nervously touching the steering wheel and staring at Meche through the rearview mirror.

"I don't know if I can do this," Daniela said. "I don't have a permit yet. This is not even my car. If my sister finds out…"

"Shhh. I'll be quick."

"Yeah, I don't know about this either," Sebastián said. "You're making an awful lot of assumptions here."

"We practised."

"Um, barely."

Meche handed him the portable record player, placing the record on top of it.

"It'll be fine."

"Why don't you let me go?" Sebastián asked. "I can do it."

"Nope. I can do this and I can do it better than either of you can."

"How do you know that?"

"Because I know," Meche said.

Meche jumped out of the car before he could say anything else. Sebastián stretched his head out the window. She went around the corner and rang the interphone.

"Yeah?" Mr. Rodríguez's voice came through the speaker.

"Hi, Mr. Rodríguez? It's Meche. I'm here for the tutoring session."

"Oh, alright. Come on in."

The door opened and Meche slipped into the building. She reached the end of a hallway and had hardly knocked when Rodríguez swung the door open, letting her in.

"You're early," he said.

"I caught a ride."

"Good. Come in."

Meche followed him, hands in the pockets of her heavy jacket. She eyed the living room carefully, looking at all the books and the photographs sitting on a shelf. She glanced out a window and saw Daniela's car below. Meche checked her watch. Three more minutes.

"Do you want something to drink? Soda? A glass of water?"

"Water is fine."

Rodríguez went to the kitchen, filling a glass for her. He handed it to Meche and she took a tiny sip, nodding.

"Mr. Rodríguez, you know I'm friends with Daniela, don't you?"

"I'm aware of that."

"Friends tell each other things, Mr. Rodríguez."

He raised a hand, scratching the back of his head and smiling. "I'm not sure what you're talking about."

"I think you are."

The man's eyes narrowed and the smile grew a little crooked. "Are you going to start making accusations against me?"

"Oh, they're not accusations. It's the truth. Ten."

"What?"

Meche turned her wrist, looking at the watch. Tick tick tick it went, marking each passing second.

"Eight."

"What are you going on about?"

"Just counting down. Four."

Meche paused.

"To what?"

"Candyman. Siouxsie and the Banshees," she said.

The little minute hand reached the mark and Meche dropped the glass. It shattered on the nice, oiled floor of Mr. Rodríguez's apartment. He stared at the puddle and Meche shrugged, making an exaggerated pout.

"Oops. Clumsy me."

"What are you... maybe you better leave."

"So fast? You don't want to make a pass at me? Try to rub your dirty crotch against my side?"

"Hey," Rodríguez said, stepping towards her and wagging an angry finger at her.

Meche raised a hand and a book flew through the air, hitting him on the head. Rodríguez stumbled, touching his head and looking up in surprise.

"Now how did that happen?" Meche wondered out loud. "Oh, yeah, it went a bit like this!"

She extended her other hand and a thick dictionary whacked him on the back. Rodríguez turned around, surprised.

"What is happening?"

Meche looked at her nails, flicking a finger, and a third book bounced against his leg.

"Magic," she said.

She couldn't hear the music but she could feel it outside, swimming up and stretching up her arms.

Rodríguez rushed towards her, perhaps thinking he could overpower her. Meche raised the glass shards from the floor, sending them flying into his face like darts. He fell on his knees and began to roll on the floor, crying like a little baby. Meche pressed a foot against his ribcage and looked down at him, feeling rather numb at the sight of his pained face and the blood.

"If we ever see you again, we'll make it *really* hurt," she said. "And if you ever touch another girl we'll make you cut off your balls and eat them. Believe me, we can."

She gave him a kick, for good measure, and slammed the door when she left. The whole building crackled with the power. When she leaned down next to the car, her hand rested against the hood and a little spark of electricity shot through her fingers.

Meche felt like she had just drunk a whole bottle of tequila. She opened the back door and collapsed next to Sebastián.

MECHE SQUINTED. SEBASTIÁN was smoothing her hair. She could feel his long fingers and the familiar smell of him that was... him.

"Mmm," she muttered, smacking her lips.

"How's it going?" he asked. "You've been out for ten minutes."

"Great," she said, feeling groggy. "I guess telekinesis takes its toll, huh?"

"Maybe it's 'cause we weren't in the room with you."

"You were very near, though."

"I don't know the rules of this," Sebastián said with a chuckle.

"Meche, you sure you're okay?" Daniela asked.

"Yup."

Meche sat up. Saw they were in motion already. Good. She rested her head against Sebastián's shoulder, frowning.

"Are you guys hungry? I need to eat something."

"Famished," Sebastián agreed.

"How about tacos?" Daniela asked.

"Where?"

"By the subway station," Sebastián said. "Take a left."

THEY DRANK JARRITOS, lifted tacos with expert fingers while holding little plastic blue plates and elbowed their space around the crowded stand. Meche spoke.

"What are we going to do to Frankenstrada?"

Sebastián wasn't sure he had heard her right with all the people around her, so he shook his head. "What?"

"What are we going to do about Frankenstrada?" she repeated.

"Meaning?"

"We have to punish her too. We can't let her go on her merry way, can we?"

Neither Sebastián nor Daniela spoke. He grabbed a napkin, carefully cleaning his greasy fingers and wiping his lips. Daniela sucked on a lemon and looked down.

"Really? You pussies!" Meche said dismissively.

"Hey, I didn't *enjoy* doing what we did to Rodríguez and I don't want to do it again," Sebastián said.

"Liar," Meche said. "You liked the power as much as I did."

He recalled the rush of power as the music played, the intensity of it coursing through his veins. The taste of raw anger in his mouth, pleasant and sickly sweet. But despite this, he had not enjoyed it. It was not something he would choose again.

"I did not."

"Then maybe you are not a real warlock. Just a second-rate impostor."

It stung to be called an impostor and her tone of voice made it even more painful. Sebastián snatched his Jarrito and sipped it, biting down on the straw.

"I didn't like it either," Daniela ventured weakly. "It was scary."

"It was fucking awesome," Meche said, chuckling.

"No, it was not," Sebastián muttered.

"Okay. Then it wasn't. For you. Whatever. She didn't lift a finger against that pervert. Do you want to let her get away with it? Doesn't that deserve some sort of punishment? I say it does."

"Well, it's three of us," Sebastián replied. "And I vote we let her be."

"Daniela, what do you think? Aren't you still mad at Frankenstrada?"

"I am still mad," Daniela whispered, her thin lips barely opening and letting the words out.

"Then should we punish her?"

"You don't have to do what she says," Sebastián said, reaching towards Daniela.

Meche pressed a hand against his chest, pushing him back. Not shoving. Her fingers just gently pressed against his shirt, the slightest of contacts and yet it had a very clear, sharp meaning. A defiance. It made him pause in his trajectory.

Meche, strong-willed, most often than not led the pack. He didn't like the way she looked at him right now, eyebrow quirked, blocking his path.

"So?" Meche asked, turning her head, addressing

Daniela with dark, piercing eyes.

"I do want to punish her a little," Daniela said.

"Good," Meche said, picking up her soft drink and taking a long sip.

"I'm full," Sebastián said, putting down his plastic plate.

"WHY ARE YOU being a hard-ass?" Meche asked him.

They were standing at the bottom of the stairs to her apartment. She had her arms crossed and looked rather smug, lips slightly curved into a smile. He hated it, hated her, when she got like this.

"You think you're better than us," he said.

"Oh?"

"At magic."

"Maybe a tad," she said with a shrug. "I figured out the whole spell thing, didn't I?"

"At life."

"What are you—"

"I just want you to know, I don't agree with what you are making us do."

"I'm not making you do anything. We took a vote. You lost."

"You can't push Daniela around all the time."

"Loser."

"You think I'm joking?"

"Blah, I'm bored," Meche said, climbing up a couple of steps.

He grabbed her by the wrist, giving her a strong yank. Meche stumbled down, bending against him.

She still stood two steps above him but she had almost lost her balance and was holding on to the collar of his jacket for support. He raised an arm, resting it against her back, holding her in place.

"One day, if you're not careful, all your bullshit is going to bite you in the ass," he whispered.

"Really, mister?" Meche asked, tipping her head at him. "You don't scare me. I can hex the life out of you if I want to."

"Yeah? Let me step back so you can hit your face against the ground," he said.

"Try it," she said, her hand inching up and resting against the back of his neck for leverage.

Though they had played and teased each other in a myriad of ways, this didn't seem like their regular games. He felt an ache—dull and uncomfortable—which made him wince.

Sebastián grabbed her by the waist and deposited her on the ground.

"Coward," she said.

She scared him, the way her eyes gleamed. There was something ugly and much too cold in her, and it made him want to run off. But, as usual, when he took two steps back with Meche he wanted to take three forward. That was her most distressing form of sorcery, the hold she had on them.

On him.

"I'll see you tomorrow at school," he said.

ON MONDAYS THE students assembled in the courtyard for the salute to the flag. The national anthem played, five students marched with the flag and everyone raised their left hand, resting it against their chest. Sometimes the principal said a few words, before everyone shuffled off to class.

That Monday the students marched, the flag went by, the national anthem finished playing.

Sebastián, Meche and Daniela stood at the back of their group and watched as a teacher went to the microphone and briefly talked about an upcoming event.

Principal Estrada took her place, ready to dismiss them, grabbing the microphone.

She opened her mouth and croaked loudly.

The students giggled.

The principal, looking rather surprised, opened her mouth again.

The croak was louder. The giggles multiplied.

A third time and everyone broke down in laughter.

The principle doubled over and began vomiting, a sticky, dark substance. *Ewws* mingled with the laughter as principal Estrada bent down on her knees and continued to vomit. Finally she finished and rose on wobbly legs, stumbling into the school offices.

"Children, children," said the physical education teacher. "Head to your classes. Now…"

Meche, leaning against the wall, grinned in satisfaction and began whistling a merry tune.

"ARE YOU GOING to give me grief just like Sebastián?" Meche asked her.

"No. I just said it was a bit extreme," Daniela replied.

"Why shouldn't we be extreme?"

"You really have no fear, do you?"

"Fear of what?"

"Of what we are doing."

"Why should I?"

"Because it's dangerous."

God, how was it dangerous? It wasn't like there was a magic police force waiting to give them a ticket. Nobody could suspect them. Nothing bad would happen to them. Plus, she didn't feel any guilt over the whole thing.

Power was meant to be wielded.

Meche snorted. "Dangerous for anyone who stands in our way."

Daniela looked at her, shaking her head while Meche shrugged.

"Look, Estrada deserved it," Meche said. "She crossed us one too many times and she got what was coming for her. She's lucky we didn't break her damn back."

"Gee, I hope you never get mad at me."

Meche draped her arm over the shoulders of a cardboard cut-out of David Bowie and eyed the records at the back of the store. It was a wash out. There was no Whiter Shade of Pale in the store and no records with any significant power. This seemed to be the case with most stores which offered new merchandise. Meche had found records with power at used shops, making her guess the power might be related to the previous owner or persons they had come into contact with; a patina that somehow impregnated the vinyl, like thumb prints upon the surface. This was a conjecture she had scribbled in her grimoire, but it made sense. And wasn't most of everything pertaining to the world of magic a conjecture, anyway?

"What are you getting Sebastián?" Daniela asked, giving up the fight.

"I was thinking a Tom Waits album, but then I decided on a movie," Meche said, her hands drifting over the records, flicking through album covers.

"Like a date?"

"Not like a date," Meche frowned. "Why would you think I'd go out with him on a date?"

"Oh… No-nothing. It just crossed my mind. It's all."

"I'm done here," Meche said, tossing the record back in its bin.

"He's going out with Isadora again."

Meche raised an eyebrow at that. "How do you know?"

"He told me. They're going out on Sunday."

"Sunday we're supposed to practice! And why didn't he tell me? This is the kind of thing we need to vote on. He can't just run off…"

"Maybe because you would have asked to vote on it?"

"Ugh," Meche said and bit her lower lip.

It wasn't that she wanted Sebastián to practise every day, but this magic thing required discipline. They were improving at the glamour and although they had triumphed over Rodríguez and Estrada, both spells had worn them down. The one they had cast on Estrada, especially. Meche's body had ached so afterwards she ate a whole roasted chicken on the way home from the factory, famished and exhausted by the experience. But she could feel they were getting better. They needed to practise their powers, to explore the limits of their sorcery. To attempt bigger things. What else might they accomplish, the three of them?

But they would get squat if Sebastián went out on Sundays with Isadora. Of all the girls! Sure, Isadora was hot but that was about it. Meche felt slightly insulted that her best friend would go for the rich ditz. There was a vague, distant possibility, that Sebastián might actually get it on with the girl and ditch Meche and Daniela for full-time pursuit of his wet dream. With the circle broken, Meche was not sure she could make magic. Not to its full potential.

Maybe she needed to study alone, to see if she could cast hexes and spells without the others. She'd cast a hex by herself the first time, after all.

"Let's head out," Meche said.

DOLORES FOUND THE thimble in the back of her clothes drawer, packed along with old postcards, a pressed flower and pictures of her sisters. She smiled at the picture of the girls in their white summer dresses with the hair tied in pigtails. Finally, she took out the thimble and pressed it against her ear. She couldn't hear anything but the faintest of whispers. Magic is for children, for the young. She had forgotten how to cast spells, only bits and pieces remained, like the fog of dreams.

"Grandma, do you want me to make the rice today?"

Dolores blinked and raised her head. Meche was standing at the doorway. Meche had already changed out of her uniform and into her day clothes. Dolores had spent half the afternoon daydreaming and had not even realized her granddaughter was home.

"The rice," Dolores said. "Yes. I've got to boil the rice."

She stood up and the thimble tumbled from her hands, landing on the floor. Meche scooped it up. She frowned.

"Feels warm," she muttered. Meche raised her eyes and stared at her. "Is this—"

"An antique. From days past."

"But—"

"Days past, my girl. Stories I've forgotten."

Meche nodded and handed her the thimble. Dolores placed it in the front pocket of her apron and rubbed her hands together.

"Now, we need to make rice, don't we?"

SEBASTIÁN KNEW HE was a beggar at a banquet, invited only out of pity or as a joke. A new amusement. Perhaps he was an annoyance, simply meant to piss off Constantino, but he still appreciated the chance to go out with Isadora and her friends a second time.

Well, he could do without the friends. The boys hated him and the girls ignored him, but Isadora was what mattered and she listened to him chatter, smiled at a joke and even shared a bag of popcorn with him.

When it was time to part ways, she kissed him on the cheek and he practically sprinted all the way back home. He lay on his bed, lacing his fingers behind his head and wondered if Isadora actually liked him, if maybe, just maybe...

... the phone rang loudly. He tried to ignore it, but it kept ringing and he finally picked it up, pressing the receiver against his ear.

"Yes?"

"What took you so long?"

Meche. Sebastián closed his eyes. "I was sleeping."

"So you didn't go out tonight then?"

"I went out," he said.

"Oh."

Was that disappointment, annoyance or regular variety Meche? He straightened up, tugging at the phone cord.

"What do you want?"

"I wanted to say Happy Birthday. But maybe you're too busy wanking in the bathroom, so good—"

"Yeah, if I was wanking you already ruined it."

"Gross."

"You brought it up."

"You confirmed it."

Sebastián smiled, turning and looking at the wall with his maps and pictures of Europe. He pressed a thumb against Paris, which was a red dot surrounded by smaller black dots.

"Meche, do you ever…"

His finger slid up the wall, following a river and he did not even know what to ask, the words were all smudged inside his head.

"Thanks for phoning."

"I'll see you tomorrow."

MECHE WAS ON the computer when the screaming started. She hated it when they screamed. If only parents could tear each other to pieces in silence, like civilized people. She turned up the volume on her Walkman until Mecano's

Perdido en mi Habitación was as loud as it could be.

It was not loud enough.

Meche decided to make a run for Daniela's house. Daniela would bake her cupcakes which tasted like ass, but it was better than the constant shouts streaming through the walls.

Meche put on her jacket, grabbed the backpack and found her father also preparing to leave. He was pulling two suitcases down the hallway.

"What's up?" she asked, placing her hands in her pockets.

He smiled faintly at her.

"Meche, I've got to move out."

"What?"

Her parents fought. Like, a lot. But Meche could not picture them separated. What, was this temporary? When was he coming back?

"Dad—"

"I'll give you my address, when I have it. You can come and visit. I'm going to be moving to Puerto Vallarta next year and you can come with me for the summer. It'll be awesome."

"Puerto Vallarta?"

"Yeah. It's all part of the plan. The taxi is going to leave if I don't get downstairs."

He grabbed the suitcases and kept on walking. Meche followed him in shock. When they reached the door he turned around and gave her a hug.

"You be good, alright?"

"Dad?" Meche said, watching him head towards the staircase. "Daddy?"

"Get inside!"

Meche turned around. Her mother's eyes were narrowed, her face was as hard as rock; no signs of weakness.

"He's really going?"

"We are getting a divorce."

"Why?"

"You don't need to hear the reasons. Get inside."

SHE MANAGED TO avoid Sebastián for a good number of days, but Friday, when Meche was crossing the street, she felt hands wrap around her waist and Sebastián lifted her, spinning her around.

"Put me down, please?" she demanded.

"Are you going to skip school with me today?" he asked.

"No."

He set her down with a frown.

"Why not?"

Meche looked at her sweater's cuffs, pulling at a little thread and shrugging.

"I don't feel like it."

"I've got a bag of chips and several cans of soda."

"Oh my God, it's my teenage dream," she said, squealing with mock enthusiasm.

"Well, I dunno. You've been mopey all week."

"So an overdose of salt and carbonated beverages will cure me?"

"It's all I've got. Oh, and a record from Hombres G. What do you say?"

She wanted to wallow in private. Plus, if she kept skipping school the principal was going to phone her mom. But then... it might be fun. Meche weighed the negatives against the chance to get a sugar high and ended up sighing.

"Okay."

MECHE AND SEBASTIÁN were hanging out in the factory. They lay on the floor, their feet resting against the wall and little bits of potato chips littering the space around them. The sky was purple like a bruise. They would have to light candles if they wanted to remain into the evening.

"My parents are getting a divorce."

Sebastián put down the book he had been reading and turned his head to look at her.

"I didn't know. When did this happen?"

"Few days ago. Just took his clothes and left."

"Why didn't you tell me sooner?" he asked.

"Because if I told you, you'd tell Daniela and then Daniela would bake cupcakes to make me feel better. And if I told her, she'd tell you and we'd end up having a heartfelt discussion about it. Which is totally not what I want. I mean, I don't even know why they're getting divorced."

"But is it serious? Maybe they're just having a fight."

"My mom changed the lock to our apartment so my dad can't get back in."

He stretched a hand and caught a stray chip which had fallen on his shirt, popping it into his mouth.

"What does your dad say?"

"He called yesterday to give me his temporary address and to say he's seeing about a new job in Puerto Vallarta."

"You think he'll get it?"

"I don't know."

Sebastián found another chip, trapped in the cuff of his shirt and held it up, staring at it. He was glad when his parents divorced. Their separation ended his father's beatings, but Meche's dad did not beat her and he was always nice to Sebastián when he went by the apartment.

"The worst part is my mom is getting totally overbearing. Like we couldn't meet at my place today because then she'd flip out."

"Why?" Sebastián asked, frowning.

"Because she's nuts. She has this fixation; thinks you're my 'secret' boyfriend. Right now, she'd probably imagine we are totally making out. It's gross."

Sebastián frowned. "I'm gross?"

"No, you dummy. My mother's bizarre nightmares about teenagers making out are gross."

Sebastián tucked an arm behind his head, deep in thought.

"So what you're saying is making out with me would *not* be gross?"

Meche turned her head and raised an eyebrow at him, with that *come-again-asshole* look she sometimes sported when a random construction worker yelled an inappropriate comment at her.

"Do I need to answer that one?"

"Yeah. Bad question."

EIGHT O'CLOCK and all hell was about to break loose. Since Vicente had moved out, Meche's mother had apparently decided she would quarrel with Meche in what Meche could only imagine was supposed to be a display of motherly concern. It smelled more like bullshit than love.

"You think I'm stupid."

"Is that a rhetorical question?"

Meche's mother looked like her head was about to start spinning like the girl in *The Exorcist*. In Meche's experience backing down would be an admission of guilt. She was not going to be bullied into the guilty square. It was not the 17th century and she was tired of getting the Inquisition treatment.

"You skipped school again and you standing here, a complete liar, in front of me."

Meche crossed her arms and glanced over her mother's shoulder, at the face of Sting on the wall.

"What were you doing?"

"I wasn't doing anything."

"Out with Sebastián Soto again?"

"Oh my God," Meche muttered under her breath.

"Do you two have to meet every single day? You go to school together. Then you spend every moment outside school together. What is going on?"

"Nothing!" Meche yelled. "God, is your life so boring you have to invent this drama to keep you entertained? No wonder dad dumped you!"

The slap came as a bit of a surprise. This was a new level of theatrics. Meche rubbed her cheek, knitting her eyebrows together angrily.

Her mother gave her a long, cold stare and slammed her bedroom door shut. Meche put on the headphones and gritted her teeth.

*   *   *

SEBASTIÁN DID NOT understand how Principal Estrada knew they had been behind the public humiliation levied upon her during the school assembly, but she knew. That killer instinct which helped her pounce on teenagers trying to smoke in the bathrooms must have also prepared her to recognize the undeniable stench of a hex. Whatever it was, she was onto them and a confrontation was imminent.

Just after recess on Friday, when Sebastián, Daniela and Meche were preparing to drag their feet to Biology class, Estrada appeared, blocking their way, just like the robot in the bad B-movie from the 50s he had been watching on the TV the night before.

"Mr. Soto, I've had enough of that hair of yours. You are getting a haircut."

"Yeah," he said. "Over the weekend. I promise."

"No, Mr. Soto," the principal said. "Right now."

Estrada grabbed him by the arm and pulled him towards the office. Meche raised her voice in protest.

"You can't do that."

"Watch yourself, Miss Vega, unless you want to be in detention for the rest of the school year."

Estrada walked with quick steps, her heels clicking upon the pavement and down the hallway towards her offices. She told him to sit down and Sebastián stared at the woman.

"You'd like to be expelled, Mr. Soto?"

He could imagine his mother's face if that happened. She'd have one son who had impregnated his girlfriend and was dropping out of university, plus another one kicked out of school. It would be too terrible to bear. If his father found out... well, that would be an epic beating. Just because his dad didn't live with them anymore didn't mean he wouldn't make a special guest appearance to kick the crap out of Sebastián.

Between the humiliation of the haircut and the dicey outcome at home, he picked humiliation and sat still as Estrada took out a pair of scissors and unceremoniously chopped off his long hair.

"Now people can see your face," Estrada said. Like she'd done him a favour.

Sebastián saw his faint reflection in a glass display case and quietly disagreed.

He hurried out of the principal's office, only to hear Daniela and Meche calling for him. He ignored them and hurried towards the west wall. There he climbed one of the trees, stood on the wall and lowered himself onto the other side.

Sebastián held on to the straps of his backpack and began walking, head down.

"Hey!"

He did not bother looking back nor did he quicken his pace and soon Meche was at his side, brushing leaves from her uniform and glancing at him.

"What are you doing?" she asked. "We've got Bio."

"I don't. I'm going home."

"It doesn't look so bad," she said, sounding like she was about to laugh.

Sebastián stopped. He looked down at her, wanting to kick her.

"Really?" he said. "Because I have the feeling it looks like a donkey chomped on my head."

Meche sighed and stepped on his toes, then stood on her tiptoes in order to reach him. Her fingers brushed his hair.

"You're still cute."

"I think 'still' and 'cute' are incompatible in that sentence."

"Then you're such an ugly motherfucker that no one will notice the difference, so stop crying like a baby," she said, her hand slipping down and away.

Sebastián caught it and frowned.

"You're serious?"

"The baby part or the motherfucker?"

"The cute."

"Not if you're going to get weird about that. Can you let go?"

"Sure."

He released her hand. Meche stepped down and pulled at her sweater's sleeves, hiking them up. Then she took out her Walkman, tugging at the headphones and he spoke quickly, before she could shield herself with songs.

"Thanks. I never thought you thought... I'm... like, okay looking."

"Gee, should I fax you a notice about it? Forget it," she said, looking uncomfortable.

Sebastián nodded. Later, in the factory, Meche played music and he sat on the floor by the couch, one knee drawn up. He watched her as she grabbed albums, read the liner notes and stood by the record player.

Sebastián pulled himself up and hovered by Meche, feigning an interest in the record she was examining.

"What... which one is this?" he asked.

"Sarah Vaughan. Body and Soul. It's jazz."

"Doesn't ring a bell."

"It never rings a bell for you," she said, chuckling. "Look, you'll know this one. It's Nat King Cole."

Meche knelt down and placed the record on the turntable, dropping the needle. The man's voice was spectacular and it seemed to tickle something in his brain.

"Isn't it from a TV commercial?"

"It's Unforgettable," she said, rolling her eyes. "The day you learn anything about jazz I'll know you've lost it."

"Maybe I will one day. To keep up with you," he said kneeling next to her.

"Start with Fitzgerald."

"Who?"

"Ella Fitzgerald. And then maybe Louis Armstrong. Thelonious Monk. Chet Baker. There are like dozens and dozens of people—"

"It's romantic. This song."

"It was written by Irving Gordon. The arrangement is by Nelson Riddle... you have no idea who I'm talking about."

"No."

"I can put something else on."

"I like it," he whispered.

Nevertheless, she heard him, her head turning slightly towards him. Meche's hands were resting on her lap and he stretched his fingers to clutch one of them. Meche let him hold it for maybe a second before she scooted forward and pulled the needle up.

"I don't think it's a day for Mr. Cole," she said very seriously.

*　　*　　*

VICENTE VEGA HAD fucked up again. With the profits from his investment, Vicente had planned to quit his job at the radio station and dedicate himself full-time to his book, which was bound to become a bestseller once he could find the right publisher.

Now he was back to square one. In truth, he had never even left square one.

He smoked his cigarette and sat in the bar, nursing a double scotch, with his notebook in front of him. He'd been writing song lyrics but they wouldn't come right, so he'd decided to have one drink. That had turned into two and now he was on the sixth.

A couple more and he'd be ready to shuffle back to his apartment. A couple more and he could start smiling at the songs playing inside the joint. A couple more and he could whistle a tune as he walked out.

It was going to be better. One day. Soon.

Mexico City, 2009

MECHE BLINKED AND raised her hand. Sunlight slipped through the curtains, sneaking through her parted fingers as she shielded her face. She turned around and frowned. It was a narrow bed and long-limbed Sebastián was taking up most of the space.

She slipped on her t-shirt, running quickly towards the kitchen. She decided to make tea.

The kettle whistled and Meche poured the hot water into a cup. She sat on the counter and tilted her head, looking at the cheap calendar on the wall, the kind one gets from a grocer every year. It read May 2009 and had a sappy picture of puppies. Her father had forgotten to change the month—or had not been bothered enough to do it.

What would Mr. Vega have said about this development? He would have laughed, no doubt. Her father had a sick sense of humour and he would have found some pleasure in her embarrassment. He might even have pointed out that they shared a genetic code and thus a proclivity to make really bad choices; to fuck people they shouldn't fuck, and fuck themselves into a corner.

She had always considered herself a bit more level-headed, at least since she'd grown up.

Turns out she was wrong.

"Awesome," Meche muttered.

She wish she had music. Her iPod was in the bedroom but she was reluctant to fetch it. She decided to think about songs, go over lyrics in her head. Love Will Tear Us Apart was the first thing she could conjure. No, not *that*. Jazz, that old friend, would do. Sebastián interrupted her before she had even reached the third line of "How High The Moon."

"You always get up so early?"

Meche did not look at him, finding the puppies a good focal point.

"I usually get up around noon," she said. "I code at nights and wake up late."

"And then you don't have breakfast."

"Breakfast in Norway is pickled beets and sweet pickles and Gammelost. Maybe fårepølse. I've never been able to get into it."

He stood in front of her, shirtless, and Meche blushed even though she was far too old to be blushing.

"I can't believe how short your hair is," he said, raising a hand to touch it.

"I'm sorry, this is too weird," she said, jumping down from the counter and evading his touch.

"What?"

"I've never seen you naked."

"You have now."

"That is not... yeah, that's why it's weird. We never had a *thing*. It wasn't like that."

"Of course not. I was too dumb. I barely even kissed you that one time."

"Sorry. I can't talk without my trousers," Meche said. "It's freaking me out."

She marched back into the bedroom and scooped up her jeans, buttoning them and wondering if she shouldn't have just run out of the apartment when she woke up. It might have avoided this very awkward conversation.

"Shoes," she whispered, looking under the bed. Where the hell had they gone? "Okay, yeah, explain that to me."

Meche knelt next to the bed and set her hands upon the sheets, frowning and looking in Sebastián's direction.

"Why are you suddenly developing this bizarre passion for me?" she asked. "You were not even into me."

Sebastián lay on the bed and placed his hands behind his head, looking at the ceiling.

"You think so?"

"Absolutely. I mean, you had a thing for Isadora Galván."

"I did."

Meche tilted her head and smirked. "So is this like a stamp collection or something? Diddle all your ex-classmates and you get a prize?"

"No. I didn't understand back then, what you meant to me. I assumed I could find the same easy feeling with many other people. But time passed, people passed and it was never quite the same. Then the other day I was walking to my mom's place and I saw you across the street. It all just... hit me. I haven't been able to stop feeling... I've felt things I haven't felt in ages. It's all because of you. I was so alive when I was with you. It was like... like it even hurt."

"Sounds like a book I read," she said. "It was shelved under 'sappy.'"

"You didn't feel like that about me?"

He looked at her with dark, steady eyes. Meche had to avert her gaze, sitting cautiously onto the mattress.

She remembered being a teenager, being near Sebastián, very clearly. It had been thrilling. Every single morning, walking at his side to school, their shoes dipping into puddles, their easy smiles and the easier banter. Oh, she had been so in love with him and not in the 'sappy' way. Not the crush a teenager has for a handsome boy, like Constantino. She loved him absolutely and if she never kissed him then—*really* kissed him, not whatever microsecond of a kiss they had shared—never made him her lover, it was because they had already touched more deeply than any youthful caress.

"Maybe. It was a while ago."

"How long have you waited for someone?"

"Oh come on, you got married," Meche said, flipping on her stomach and pressing her chin against the back of her hand. "You probably had two dozen girlfriends after that. You weren't waiting for nothing."

"I have been waiting for something, always without knowing it."

He peered at her from beneath thick eyebrows and Meche half-smiled because maybe—just maybe, this was no admission—she had walked the streets of Paris once-upon-a-time expecting to stumble onto *somebody*. Maybe she sat by the river and read her map and wondered if *someone* would turn a corner and appear there.

"God, the way you talk," she said, trying to rub the

half-smile off her face. "You didn't spew those lines when we were young."

He'd seen it though, recognized her mirth, and was now giving her a sly look.

"An improvement or a drawback?"

"Did you ever visit Europe?" she asked, changing the topic because she would have liked him even if he couldn't string two words together and she wasn't about to tell him that.

"No," he said. "Something always got in the way."

"Even though you could afford it by now?"

"Maybe I was afraid I wouldn't find you. Or I would and it would be different."

She chuckled and he shifted, looking down at her.

"What's funny?"

"I have no idea," Meche said.

There was a scar on his left hand which had not been there before, a long gash which went up his arm.

"What happened?"

"Car accident," he said. "Three years ago."

Meche stretched out a hand, touching his brow, a tiny little line there.

"And that one?"

"Someone cracked a bottle open on my head."

"Really?"

"It was a wild 1999."

He stretched his hand down her leg and tugged at the denim, exposing her tattoo. It was a sentence, circling the ankle.

"'A kingdom for a stage, princes to act,'" he read. "Someone finally read Shakespeare."

Just so I could come back at you when you called me illiterate, she thought and that sounded too much like admitting he'd had some huge influence on her life. Which was not the case. Not really.

"Drunk in Amsterdam, 2000. It seemed like a good idea at the time. At least it's not a Looney Tunes character or some Chinese character I can't read." She glanced at him. "No tattoos?"

"No tattoos and no piercings."

"What kind of damn punk were you?" she asked moving closer to him and he shifted a bit too, closing the gap between them.

"A very low-key punk."

"Your shirts look expensive."

"Some are. Still with the t-shirts?"

"Can't wean myself off them," she said looking down at the one she was wearing. Abba. "My defense is it's vintage-chic."

"That's not chic. They do fit better than they used to though."

"Yeah, well, bras help."

"Do you keep a bag-lady jacket in your closet?" he asked.

"That was an awesome jacket," she said.

"No. It was god-awful."

"You drew on your shoes."

"I still doodle. Not on my shoes. You should come to my place and look at some of my drawings."

Meche scoffed. "That's such a cheap come-on."

"I can try something better."

Meche touched his clavicle, curious. It just looked so sharp and chiseled. He was still very thin, although now there was some strength. Sebastián caught her hand and held it, kissing her lightly.

"I think you're lovely," he said.

"That's still a cheap come-on."

"It's true."

Meche lapsed into silence, pondering, glancing at the palm trees and the flamingoes on the curtains.

"I have a lot of organizing," she said. "I assume you have that job you need to show up for. Mr. Creative Director."

"Not until nine."

"What time is it?"

"Six. Do you want to have breakfast with me? Even though you don't do breakfast?"

No, she thought. *What's the point of that?*

"I should shower," she said, which was not exactly what she had been intending to say.

"Ah," he said, kissing her shoulder. "Not yet."

MECHE LOOKED AT the grapefruit, sinking her spoon into it, toying with the pulpy interior and wondering at what point she had lost her mind and whether she was going to get it back soon.

Breakfast with Sebastián Soto. Not only that, breakfast with Sebastián Soto after she'd had sex with him. Twice. As if to make a point that mistakes were better performed in pairs.

In for a pound, she thought.

"Time?" she asked, twisting his hand, trying to get a look at his wristwatch.

"We have time enough."

"You said you had work later."

"I'll worry about work."

He caught her fingers, turned her hand up to look at her palm and smiled.

"It's good to have you back," he said.

The smile stabbed her hard. Meche wished she could slink under the table and stay there for about a decade.

"Hey, since we missed the movie we could go to listen to live music. Jazz in Coyoacán. It's a small joint. Well, it's really a house and they can only fit like twenty people, but it's good."

She had a vague idea of what a jazz club with Sebastián would look like, a pleasant, blurry sort of image, as seen through a black and white lens. Like the cover of a really nice record. Now who was being sappy?

Meche shook her head.

"I'm flying to Oslo in a few days," she reminded him. "I'd also like to point out this doesn't negate my previous opinion of you."

"You still hate me," he said, digging into his green chilaquiles with gusto. "You still hold a grudge against me."

"Essentially, yes."

"Even though you had sex with me."

God, who cared? Meche tossed three sugar cubes into her cup of tea and raised her shoulders slowly.

"Please. It's not some secret promise. We don't have to be," she raised her fingers, turning them into imaginary quotes marks, "'really, really in love to go all the way.' Last time I checked we weren't exactly blushing virgins. We're grownups and grownups do stupid things."

She drew pleasure from his expression, as though she'd just doused him with a bucket of cold water. He'd started this. It was his fault. What had he expected, anyway?

"Thank you," he said tersely, "for classifying me as a stupid thing."

"Are you going to get majorly offended?"

"No, I'm not going to get," he raised his hands, now making the imaginary quote marks for himself, "'majorly offended.'"

Meche added another sugar cube for good measure and took a sip, then scooped out more grapefruit.

"This is exactly why I didn't want to talk to you. I knew you'd be all melodramatic."

"Me? Melodramatic?"

"What do you call this? 'How long have you waited for someone?' *Pfff*. I make one mistake fuck and I've got damn Romeo at my doorstep."

"Forget it."

He grabbed his fork, busied himself with the chilaquiles. Suddenly, he put the fork down and took out his wallet, pulling out several bills and placing them neatly under his glass.

"Here. That should cover it," he said.

"What? You're leaving?"

"Yes. Phone my cell if you want to see me again. If you don't, I'll just be majorly offended at my place, alright?"

Meche scoffed and crossed her arms. "I don't have your cellphone number."

"Then you are going to have to work for it," he said.

Sebastián leaned down next to her chair, to speak into her ear.

"I'm in love with you. There. Should have said it twenty years ago. Your move."

She watched him walk away and she had a feeling like when they made a house of cards one time and Meche pulled one card and the whole thing came tumbling down.

Meche plunged the spoon into the heart of the grapefruit and pushed her plate away. This was just... insane.

"I hate breakfast," she told the grapefruit.

"WHAT'S UP WITH you?" her mother asked.

Meche was laying on the couch, listening to Wild is the Wind. She shrugged.

"Nothing," she said, her voice clipped.

"It looks like something."

"I'm overdosing on Nina Simone."

"Your dad used to do that."

Meche rubbed her eyes. She turned her head. Her mother was still standing in the living room, holding a cup, as though she were expecting to continue the conversation.

"Why didn't you like him?"

"Who?"

"Sebastián. When we were kids, you were always all over his case. And don't say you liked him. That's a lie."

Her mother smiled, setting her cup on the coffee table. She nodded.

"You loved him too much."

Meche looked at her in surprise. She didn't say anything, tucking her chin down and frowning.

"You love somebody that much, one day it all unravels and... it's just bad. Here, I made tea."

"Mom, you don't have to keep making stuff for me all day long."

"That's what I'm supposed to do. I'm your mother."

"Yeah, yeah," Meche said, reaching for the cup and taking a little sip. "It has no sugar."

"It won't kill you to have a cup without sugar."

"I like sugar. I should go back to dad's apartment and finish with the boxes. I'm practically done."

"Finish your tea."

Her mother got up and moved towards the kitchen.

Meche stretched her legs and listened to the music. Nina Simone sang Where Can I Go Without You.

Mexico City, 1989

ISADORA CHEWED HER nails. It was a bad habit she could not kick. He thought it was cute. It made her flawed and consequently human.

"I think you chew your nails in class because you smoke. It's a compensation mechanism."

She offered him a drag, but he declined. She smiled a little.

"Have you been reading our biology textbook or something?"

"Something," he said.

"Why is it that you don't smoke but you agree to come here with me?" she asked.

"You asked."

Three times. She had asked him three times that month and he had agreed. Normally he walked after school with Meche but he had made an exception for Isadora and walked her to the Pit instead. He didn't know why she asked and he didn't really want to know because most likely it was pity or sick amusement.

"Would you like to go to the movies with me tonight?" she asked.

"Sure. What time are you guys getting there?"

"I was thinking we might go alone."

They had never been together without her friends. He wondered what could possibly inspire her to go out with him by herself as though... as though it were a date.

"Hey, Isa."

Sebastián turned his head. Constantino, along with some of the other boys, was standing on the sidewalk, giving him a very ugly look.

"You coming with us or not?" Constantino asked.

"Gotta go," Isadora said. "Meet me at seven?"

"That works."

"Alright."

"Isa, what the hell? Get your ass here!"

"Coming," Isadora said, dropping the cigarette and stepping on it with the heel of her shoe.

She hurried off with them and Sebastián stood alone, in the middle of the empty lot, heart hammering in his chest.

ISADORA'S DRIVER DROPPED her off right on time in front of the movie theatre. Sebastián watched as she crossed the street, short purple skirt, matching purse and tall boots, looking so very beautiful. There was no reason why she should be hanging out with him. No reason at all. It was a mistake. Pretty girls never looked at him. Hell, no girls looked at him. He was swarthy, which was enough to put off most of his classmates who hungered for the paler boys. He was too tall and odd. When he spoke the words came out wrong.

He watched the movie and ate his popcorn and tried hard to have a good time, but something was off. When the movie was over and they were standing outside, waiting for Isadora's cab to arrive, he dared to speak up.

"Why are you asking me to hang out with you?"

Isadora clutched her purse with both hands and looked down.

"Well, well. So you did go out after all."

Constantino. Sebastián turned around. The boy was there with his buddies in tow, all five of them dressed exactly the same: sweaters tied around the shoulders, polo shirts, even the same haircut.

"Hi," Isadora said. "I thought you weren't in the mood for the movies."

"I wasn't. I just wanted to see if you'd be with him," Constantino pointed a finger at Sebastián. "Why are you sniffing around my girlfriend? Do you have a death wish?"

"I'm not sniffing around anything," Sebastián said. "Besides, she's not your girlfriend."

"Fuck you."

Sebastián dodged Constantino's punch and managed to land one of his own, right in the middle of the bastard's face. Big mistake. This infuriated Constantino, who began yelling obscenities, telling his friends to get him, kick the crap out of him, teach him a lesson. Sebastián had heard that tune before. He did what any rational person would do in this situation—he ran.

He managed to sprint for several blocks before someone tackled him to the ground, flipped him around and punched him in the stomach, making Sebastián gag. Another punch, this one to the ribs. Then it was all kicks. Sebastián rolled, tried to find purchase on a wall and pull himself up, but he was summarily beaten with something—it might have been an empty beer bottle—and stumbled down again, next to a lamp post. He touched the back of his head. It felt damp and he was dizzy.

"Stop it!" Isadora yelled.

She had followed them. Sebastián felt even worse now, knowing she was witnessing the whole spectacle. There was nothing like a good beating with a side of humiliation.

"Please, stop! No more!"

Nobody listened to her. The boys laughed and continued kicking him. Sebastián raised his hands trying to shield his face. He swallowed blood.

The boys paused and Sebastián was able to stand up. He did not know if they were done with him or if they had just paused for a breather. He was not about to find out. Sebastián limped away.

He heard them when he turned the corner, coming his way. Ready for more fun.

A street musician was playing the guitar nearby. Sebastián concentrated on the melody, his eyes fixed on the hands plucking the strings and he changed his face, his shape. Glamour—just like they'd been practising.

When the boys ran by they saw a stooped, old man resting next to a wall and ignored him. A few seconds later, Sebastián sighed and the tattered illusion he had constructed shattered.

He slid down to the ground, curled up on the sidewalk. People who walked by him took him for a drunk or a street kid.

A couple of hours later, Sebastián opened his eyes, got unsteadily to his feet and began walking home.

*   *   *

MECHE SAT WITH her grandmother, sorting scraps of yarn into balls. Her grandmother did not believe in wasting anything and the collected little bits of yarn would be used for new projects.

The needles clicked and Meche set the balls from largest to smallest, then arranged them by colour. She'd done this since she was a child and it was kind of fun, especially if she could play good music in the background and get her grandmother to tell stories.

"Some witches can cut their chests with sharp blades and will not bleed. Others can summon invisible spirits. And then there are those who can fascinate animals with their gaze."

"I'd prefer to fascinate people with my gaze," Meche replied.

"You might be able to do that too," her grandmother said.

Meche placed the balls of yarn in a big bowl and set it down on the floor.

"Grandma, did you ever cast a spell?"

"You keep asking that."

"I want to know."

"I might have tried, once or twice."

"Did it work?"

"It was such a long time ago. I'm not sure," her grandmother said, frowning. "I think I tried..."

Sometimes grandmother couldn't remember all the details or she repeated herself, but Meche knew how to get her talking. "What did you try?" she asked. "Tell me grandma, what did you try."

"I tried to be invisible."

"How did you do it?"

"That would be telling, wouldn't it?"

"Please."

"I knitted a blanket, dark as night, and wore it around me. It made me... disappear. Of course, I wouldn't be able to do that anymore." She paused to look at the cover she was knitting. "My eyes are not what they used to be. Anyway, magic is for the young."

"Maybe you could try again," Meche said. "I could help you."

"You don't like to knit."

"I *would* knit a magic blanket."

"The only problem is I don't stitch spells anymore."

"Why not?"

"I hurt people, once."

"Did they deserve to be hurt?"

Grandmother touched Meche's chin. "Don't they always, when you're a girl?"

Meche thought some people deserved a taste of their own medicine and she didn't see why anyone would stop using spells when they could be so much fun. Why let go of the power? She sure as hell wouldn't.

"Oh, come on. Show me one spell."

Her grandmother smiled and set her needles down. "I'm tired, Meche, and I've forgotten."

She stood up, stumbling. Meche helped steady her.

"Are you alright, grandma?"

"I'm tired," she said, patting Meche's shoulder. "I'm just tired."

* * *

SEBASTIÁN STUMBLED INTO his apartment. His body ached something awful and the coppery taste of blood lingered in his mouth.

The door to his bedroom was closed. By the noises filtering out, his brother was with a girl. He wanted to get out of the dirty, stained clothes he was wearing. Sebastián knocked, pressing his forehead against the door.

"Go away," came Romualdo's reply.

"I need to come in."

"Go the fuck away."

Something snapped in Sebastián. Furious, he kicked the door and it slammed open. A naked girl he didn't know squealed, pulling the covers over herself. Romualdo glared at him.

"What the hell?! What are you doing, barging in…"

Sebastián pulled a duffel bag from under his bed and dumped clothes in it. When Romualdo stalked towards him, Sebastián stretched up his whole length—which was considerable—and looked his brother in the eye. Romualdo took two steps back and Sebastián returned to the duffel bag, tossing in two books and zipping it closed.

He stopped to look at himself in the bathroom mirror. His left eye was very bruised. It would be purple, swollen, awful in the morning. Caked blood dirtied his collar. He opened the faucet and drank from it, spitting out blood. He washed his face and his hands, took off the soiled clothes and looked at the bruises on his chest.

He changed into dark jeans and a dark shirt, put on a clean jacket and hurried out the door. He strapped the bag to the motorcycle and went to the corner, tossing a couple of coins into the payphone.

Meche answered at the fifth ring.

"Yes?"

"Meche, be downstairs."

"You're coming over? Now? It's nearly midnight."

"Be there."

He hung up and by the time he parked his bike across the street from her building, Meche was standing outside, arms crossed and wearing a large grey sweater. She looked annoyed, but as he walked closer her expression changed.

"What happened to you?" she asked. "Did you have an accident?"

"Constantino and his friends beat me up."

"Why?"

"Because I went out with Isadora tonight."

"What the hell? What are you going to do?"

He knew what he wanted. No trouble coming up with a picture. It was black on white, very simple.

"Get on the bike. We're going."

"My mom's not going to let me go for a ride at this time of the night, I—"

"No, I mean go as in *go*."

"What?"

"Run away with me."

MECHE TRIED TO process the four words properly, but they were too daunting. *Run away with me.*

"Let's go to Europe together," he said. "Let's see the Arctic circle."

"Okay, unless you have a super-duper motorcycle that can float all the way to…"

"That's not what I mean."

"What do you mean? You're freaking me out."

Sebastián leaned down, grabbing her hands between his and pulling her up, so she had to stand on her tiptoes to look at his face.

"I hate this place. I hate this neighbourhood. I hate the kids here. I hate the school. I hate the view from my apartment window. You hate it too. What are we waiting for? Let's run away together."

Meche had never seriously considered running away. That's the kind of stuff people did in the movies, like joining the circus. It didn't happen in real life. Meche didn't want to go. She didn't like high school much but there was her dad, mom, grandma. The records and the computer sitting in the living room. Daniela. Her room with the posters of several bands and the narrow bed. She feared abandoning all that.

"Sebastián, that's silly," she whispered.

"Meche, you said you'd never leave me."

"Come on."

His hands clutched her own together and he pulled her forward, her knuckles brushing his chest.

"Come with me."

Meche wondered what was his plan was. Would they just get off in some other city when they ran out of gas? Then, what? What were two teenagers supposed to do to survive? Beg for a coin, wash car windows at the stoplight, sell bubble gum to the drivers? Meche had seen street kids. She didn't hold any wild dreams that somehow they'd make it to Paris whole, get a garret with a view of the Seine and Sebastián could be a bohemian writer while Meche coded some awesome bit of software which made them millionaires. That was the kind of shit to be found in one of Daniela's novels. Shit which never happens because when teenagers run away they end up living in an abandoned hovel which smells of piss, prostituting themselves to make ends meet.

"We can cast a spell. We can get the money. We can do it."

Meche opened her mouth. His face had the kind of need she had never seen in another human being and there was a hunger there she did not understand.

She was fifteen. The intensity of him, of this moment, caught her unprepared. She felt that if she went with Sebastián he'd steal a deep part of her. She would change and she feared this. She feared him, feared what it might mean.

"I am—"

"No," she said jumping back. "No way."

Sebastián didn't believe her. For a long minute he smiled, confident, believing she was just joking. She would laugh soon and tell him of course she was going. His smile died as she backed away, towards the entrance of the building.

He walked back to his motorcycle and jumped on it before turning to look at her.

The look he gave her turned Meche to stone. His face was splintered with pain. He looked ahead and Meche raised her hands, thinking of stopping him, thinking—

Too late. The motorcycle sped away and she walked back into her building.

*   *   *

SEBASTIÁN STOOD OUTSIDE his apartment building, counting the beats of his heart.

How stupid of him. Idiotic. To think he would do something as silly, and Meche, that she might—

He leaned over the motorcycle, thinking he was about to cry.

"Sebastián?"

He looked up and saw Isadora stepping out of a car, pressing her hands against her mouth. Her driver gave him an indifferent glance, as though he were a stain on the ground.

"I'm so sorry about what happened," she said.

"What are you doing here?" he muttered.

"I was very worried."

"I'm alright."

Isadora walked to his side, squeezing his arm. "He's a brute," she whispered. "Oh, I truly am sorry."

"No broken bones," he said, wincing. "Just bruises."

"I should get you to a doctor."

"I'm fine. Really. I just need to sleep."

They were both quiet.

Her hand rose and settled on his cheek. She kissed him there and Sebastián couldn't help smiling, despite everything.

"You're very brave," she said. "Again, I'm sorry. I'll see you at school, alright?"

"Sure."

She slipped back into the car and waved at him.

The car rolled away and Sebastián stood in the middle of

the street, hands in his pockets. He waited there for about ten minutes thinking perhaps Meche might come around.

She did not.

Sebastián took a deep breath and saw the moon hiding, skittish behind a cloud. He shook his head and decided to call it a night, erasing the faint path she had traced in his mind.

TWO DAYS LATER she offered him revenge with the same casual tone a vendor at the tianguis might offer to discount you a bunch of rotting bananas.

He had not talked to her about the incident. Her refusal stung, the look on her face had torn him apart. There were so many things he wanted to tell her and knew very well he shouldn't. So he kept his mouth shut.

"We should hex the guys who beat you," Meche said, licking a chilli lollipop. "Make them pay for what happened."

It was a cheap trick to buy his sympathy or a blatant misinterpretation of his emotions. Either way, it showed she did not understand him at all.

"Why?"

"They deserve it."

"It wouldn't fix anything."

"Well, we could at least heal your wounds."

"The exterior ones don't matter."

"You are so lame sometimes."

"Most of the times," he corrected her.

"Why, if some boys beat you to a bloody pulp, wouldn't you beat them back? Why—"

"Because they don't matter," he snapped at her.

"You're a pussy."

"Yeah, and I'm gay too, no? 'Sebastián Soto, el Joto', right? Thanks. Many thanks."

Meche gave her lollipop a final lick and tossed it away, raising a petulant eyebrow at him. No doubt she thought herself very smart, very talented, because of the spells. Superior to him in every way because he was a coward who wouldn't respond to fire with fire.

"If life offers you something, you should take it," she said. "Life's offering you a chance to get even."

"Take it, huh?"

"Yeah."

"I'll remember next time."

He'd show her one day... yeah.

They did not say anything else the rest of the way home.

Mexico City, 2009

SOMEWHERE BETWEEN THREE and four a.m. Meche rose from her bed and walked across the room, staring at a wall where there used to be a poster of The Police. It had come down many years before but the wall still bore its outline, the marks of yellowed tape showing where it had been.

This, she thought, *is the real meaning of a haunting.*

She grabbed her father's manuscript and went into the kitchen. She made tea and put her earbuds in, idly turning the pages as she took little sips. She ought to read it. Ought to go through the whole thing and yet—

She kept getting distracted.

Around nine in the morning she phoned Daniela.

"Hey," Meche said. "Today is the last night of the novena. I was wondering if you're coming over."

"You've had a change of heart?"

"I'm leaving soon. I'd like to say goodbye to you."

"Sure. I'll be there."

"Um… Sebastián can come too."

"Do you want to see him?"

Meche ran a finger down the page, frowning. Yes. No. Both.

"Just tell him it'll be okay if he comes over."

"I can give you his phone number. You can phone him yourself."

"No, it's fine. I have stuff to do now. See you."

Meche pressed her forehead against the table, slowly straightening up.

GENTRIFICATION HAD SWEPT through the colonia but it had left the factory intact. There was a sign announcing the upcoming construction of an apartment building in its place, but the factory still stood for now. Still ruinous, the outside now sprayed with all kinds of graffiti.

Meche looked at it, looming over her like a strange stone idol. Their usual entry point had been half-heartedly boarded up, and she pulled the plywood apart easily. She slid in, dragging the portable record player with her.

The interior of the factory—definitely no designer's wet dream in her younger days—had become even more of an eyesore. Rusted pipes, peeling walls, debris, bits of glass, all these were familiar sights, but twenty years had made the decay more prominent.

Meche climbed the stairs, creating echoes as she moved.

The door to their room was open.

Meche paused before it, holding her breath, and walked in.

It was empty. Disappointment hit her like a wave. She did not know what she had expected to find, but it wasn't there.

Someone had stolen the couch and the tables. All the posters—the great musical collage she had created—had been taken away.

She moved towards the circular window and looked outside. The neighborhood had changed, but the light filtering through the window still had the same spectral quality and the view was hazy, as though the city were shrouded in mist.

Meche put the record player down in the centre of the room and walked back towards the door, closing it. She smirked, realizing that one poster had been left in place, taped onto the back of the door: Jim Morrison.

Meche took out the bottle of Coke and the records. She took a sip of the sugary soft drink, smacked her lips and placed Time After Time on the player, hesitating before letting the needle touch the vinyl.

She pulled out her dad's manuscript and began reading the whole thing. Twenty years too late but better late than never.

THE AIR SMELLED of rain and thunder. Meche had no umbrella. She eyed the clouds with a quirked eyebrow, wondering if they were plotting to unleash a storm upon her. Her father's restless spirit might be preparing to teach her a lesson. But if he had not haunted his apartment, he probably wouldn't bother with the cemetery.

Meche looked at the grave marker and the wilting flowers.

"Here you are," she muttered. "You left your apartment and your life a mess, you know that?"

Meche turned her head and looked at the rows of tombstones, feeling a bit uncomfortable. She did not know exactly what she was doing there, with a record and a bunch of flowers under her arm. Maybe she was there because he *hadn't* haunted his old place. Stumbling onto his semi-transparent figure might have connected the dots floating in her head. Her father's book, his letters and records had taught her only one thing: she hadn't known him very well. Hell, she'd had done such a good job of forgetting him, she scarcely remembered him.

"I was looking in the mirror the other day and I realized I look a lot like you. I think I *am* a lot like you. Which is very unsettling, to say the least.

"I've missed you. And... I'm in a bit of a pickle right now. It's not the kind of stuff I can talk about with mom or Jimena, so, I suppose I'll tell you."

Meche smiled, her mouth trembling.

"There's something incredibly stupid I want to do. The problem is... well, it's stupid. I can imagine what you'd say about that, "Hey, just do it!" But it's not that easy. What if..."

Meche trailed off. She cringed and shook her head.

"Anyway, I've... I've brought you something. Here are some flowers," she said, putting the bouquet down. "And this is for you."

She placed the record next to the flowers.

"Gracias a la Vida," she said. "You never told me how you came up with my name. I should have figured it out."

Meche leaned down, touching the gravestone with the tip of her fingers.

"Bye, dad."

Mexico City, 1989

"I'M SO SORRY," Isadora said.

They were back at the Pit. They had not exchanged a word in a couple of weeks, but she'd approached him after school that afternoon and he had followed her there.

Sebastián pushed an empty glass bottle with his foot. Back and forth. Back and forth until he gave it a good kick and it went rattling into the bushes.

"It wasn't your fault."

"But it was. I... I've been asking you to hang out with me to piss Constantino off. It started at my birthday party. We were fighting and then he went to dance with your friend and I thought I'd get back at him by going to that posada, and then I've..."

"Kept it up," Sebastián said helpfully.

"Yeah," Isadora admitted. "He says he wants to get back together with me but he goes after all these other girls... I wanted to make him jealous. Give him a taste of his own medicine."

"So are you?"

"Am I what?" Isadora asked.

"Getting back together with him."

Isadora pulled out a cigarette and her lighter. She shook her head as she lit the cigarette.

"I'm not sure."

"Pardon me if I say he's an asshole."

"I know," Isadora muttered. "I know."

"I suppose this means I won't see much of you anymore."

Isadora did not answer. Sebastián slid his hands into his pockets. Of course. What else could he have expected?

"I shouldn't have asked you to go with me," Isadora said.

"It wasn't your fault. You couldn't know."

"I still feel awful."

"Water under the bridge," he said. "I'd still like to show you the factory sometime."

"The what?"

"It's a place where we hang out. It's no big deal if you don't want to go. Or you, know, speak to me again."

Sebastián bit his lip and stepped forward.

"If... if you still feel like talking to me and if you feel like it, maybe you can take a ride with me some time and we can go there. We've made it nice inside and... um... it's just a good place. A safe place."

"You're very nice."

"But?"

"But what?"

"There has to be a but."

Isadora chuckled. "There is no but."

SEBASTIÁN AND MECHE sat in her dining room, doing their homework. The stereo played Botellita de Jerez as they scratched their answers across the notebook. He tapped his foot to the music. Fast, fast, fast.

"You know what the problem is?" she asked.

Sebastián paused mid-equation and looked at Meche.

"We're trying to copy people we don't know."

"What are you talking about?"

"The glamour."

Sebastián, caught off-guard, simply blinked at her. Meche sighed.

"I'm talking about the spells. I think we are failing because we are picking people out of magazines instead of real people."

"I thought we were doing homework."

"Do you think the Mulata de Córdoba went, 'Oh, it's homework time now, I can't think about spells?'"

"The Mulata lived in a time when there was no homework," Sebastián replied. "Besides, she was caught by the Spanish Inquisition. Have you actually been reading history books?"

"Myths and legends," Meche corrected him. "I'm reading everything I can about magic. Someone needs to be the research and development arm of this corporation. Anyway, what we need is to copy a real person. Once we've mastered that we can probably try sympathetic magic, steal a bit of hair and all."

"Hair? OK, Jesus, can I finish this homework before we start talking about this stuff? It's due tomorrow."

"Okay, look. I've been toying with something," Meche said.

She stood up, found a record and put it on. Sebastián was not familiar with the song. Something smooth and jazzy. The singer crooned, "I'm a fool to want you," and Meche sat down again.

She reached across the table and placed a hand on top of his own, then placed the other against her face, covering her features. She slid her fingers down revealing a pair of eyes, a nose, a mouth—a face that was not her own.

It was a crude copy, to be sure. It looked like a rubber mask and it did not resemble Isadora as much as caricaturize her, but there was clear effort and talent put into it.

"Make it go away," he said.

"Wait," Meche said, her hand upon his own, concentrating.

The mask seemed to grow snugger. It fit better. It lost most of its rubbery quality and the skin now had pores. The eyes were the right colour instead of an unusual, artificial shade. Eyelashes grew where there had been none and the lips moistened.

She was close now. Very close.

Isadora smiled.

Sebastián jumped up in his seat.

"Stop it," he said.

"It's good, isn't it? I think we can do much better."

"Stop."

She shrugged and shook her head. Isadora's face chipped and cracked and fell, revealing Meche's real features.

"Why did you do that?" he asked. "Why did you have to imitate her?"

"Why not?"

"You are cruel," he said.

He gathered his notebook, his pencils and pens. Meche watched as he tossed the stuff in his bag.

"You're going?" she asked.

"Yes, I'm going," he said. "You think I should stay and let you torture me a little longer?"

"I thought you'd appreciate it. Maybe laugh."

"It's not funny."'

"Aw. Come on. You're not in loooove with her are you?" Meche asked in her patented mocking tone.

Sebastián did not bother answering. Any answer he gave would be the subject of much snickering. He did not have the stomach for Meche's japes that afternoon.

"You're not serious about her, are you?" Meche asked dryly.

"What does it matter?" he replied.

"I'm just asking."

"She's nice, alright?"

Sebastián zipped his bag closed.

"You go with her to the movies a lot."

"We've gone a few times. And the last time was a disaster."

"You don't ask me and Daniela to the movies anymore."

"Do you want to go see a movie with me? Damn it, I'll take you next weekend."

"Forget it."

"No, I mean it. You wanted to look at some records, no? We'll watch a movie after that, you and me."

"I'm not your fucking charity case. Piss off."

She headed to her room, abandoning him in the middle of the dining room. Sebastián cursed in Catalán and followed her.

It was always like this with Meche. She was like a cat, sometimes purring and letting herself be petted, the next showing her claws and biting your hand. She could never, ever, make it easy for anyone. Sebastián did not understand why everything had to be a battlefield with her, but it was.

"I didn't say you were. What's your problem?" he asked, holding the door when she tried to slam it shut.

Meche sat on her bed, crossing her arms and staring at a poster of Blondie.

"If you have better things to do, go and do them," she said.

"I have nothing better to do," he replied.

"Yeah, well it seems—"

He sat next to Meche and held her hand. They laced their fingers together and looked at the poster.

"Movie, then?" he asked.

"Records Saturday. Movie Sunday."

"Fine."

"Fine."

"You annoy me."

"Same."

Meche rested her chin against his shoulder with a sigh.

MECHE DID NOT know what to think about Sebastián lately. She watched him as they rode the subway, on the way to the record store where they would meet Daniela, and thought he was turning into a stranger. He was not himself. With Isadora this and Isadora that. He never seemed interested in the magic anymore and he sure as hell did not seem interested in spending time with them as much as he did before. He was drifting away from her.

You did this, said a nagging little voice inside Meche's head. *You hurt him and it's not the same.*

Well, she couldn't possibly have run away with him. That would have been idiotic. Who did that kind of thing?

Clearly he did. And clearly she was too chicken to follow him.

She did not want to think about it and, so, pumped up the Walkman's volume, drowning her thoughts with the voice of Joan Manuel Serrat, singing about a man who falls in love with a store mannequin.

They arrived at quarter to eleven, a little after they had agreed. Daniela was already there and greeted them with a big smile, a Timbiriche album under her arm, constant reminder of her lack of musical taste.

It was a small store. The walls were adorned with albums and the ceiling was plastered with posters advertising a number of music acts. The back wall was dominated by a huge, floor-to-ceiling image of Jimi Hendrix.

While Sebastián and Daniela riffled through the cassettes and records at the front, she felt herself drawn to the back, as though she were following an invisible trail.

"Hey Meche, what do you say..."

She ignored Daniela. Meche walked with sure footsteps. Her hands tingled, growing warmer. When she reached the back of the store they were sweating. She drifted towards the third bin to the left. Her fingers danced over the record sleeves, brushing them aside until she touched one which burned like a coal.

She held it up, her mouth opening a little.

Her hands trembled. It was A Whiter Shade of Pale.

"Hey, you found it!" Daniela chirped behind her, looking over her shoulder.

"Found what?" Sebastián asked.

Meche pressed the record against her chest.

Nothing, she was going to say.

"The record for the spell," Daniela said.

Meche closed her eyes, mouthing a curse. Daniela! She couldn't keep her mouth shut.

"What?"

"Just an experiment I'm running. I mentioned it before."

Meche turned around and faked a bored look at Sebastián, trying to downplay the importance of her discovery.

"Like?" Sebastián asked cautiously.

"I think I can use this record to cast a special spell. Of course, it's far-fetched, but—"

"Let me see."

His finger fell upon the record sleeve. Meche pulled it back, frowning.

"What? I can't look at it?"

"*Look* at it all you want," Meche said, holding it up, "just don't get your dirty fingers on it. I'm going to pay for this."

MECHE WALKED TOWARDS the cash register. Sebastián watched her with narrowed eyes, irritated by her secrecy. What the hell? Now he couldn't even touch the records?

"What does she want it for?" Sebastián asked gruffly.

Daniela shrugged. "Um… just a spell. Like she said."

"Yeah. For what?"

"She... I don't think I'm supposed to say."

"Spit it out. I'll find out eventually."

Daniela started chewing on a strand of hair, a sure sign she was about to buckle.

"I think it's a love spell for Constantino," she blurted.

Constantino. She wanted him to fall in love with her. He remembered Meche mentioning something about love spells back in December but he didn't believe she'd *seriously* pursue this, especially if it meant she was going for Constantino. The same Constantino who had beaten the hell out of Sebastián with the assistance of his clones. That piece of shit. Sebastián felt offended. He felt hurt. He felt fucking angry.

Meche marched back towards them, a plastic bag dangling from her fingers.

"I'm ready to go," she said.

"I NEED TO borrow the record," he said.

"No," Meche replied.

The subway was crowded and there was no place to sit down. Meche and Sebastián occupied a narrow space between a street vendor carrying a huge bag packed with salted nuts and a mother with a small child. They were barely inches apart, sweating and uncomfortable. Three more stations to go and it seemed like it might take forever.

"Why not?" Sebastián asked.

"Because it's mine."

"Are you going to use it to get that asshole to pay attention to you?"

Meche chuckled. She lifted a lofty eyebrow. Her words were pure venom.

"Let me guess: you are going to try to get into that ditzy little thing's pants?"

"She's not a ditz."

"And I'm Madonna."

"I'm asking, as a favour—"

"And I'm saying no."

The look she gave him was the exact same look she might use on a grubby beggar asking for a coin. It made his blood boil, to be viewed with such contempt. As though Meche were the queen and he was a serf, a nothing she could jostle around when it pleased her.

"It's a very shitty thing to say, you realize that?"

"The record is mine."

"Yeah, but—"

"You wouldn't be able to use it. You suck as a warlock."

"Yeah? I'm part of the circle, so whatever—"

"Not for long, I'll bet." She shoved him aside, his back colliding with the back of the street vendor. "Don't stand so close to me. You're sweaty and disgusting."

Gingerly, she pulled out her headphones and put them on, switching on her Walkman. Though the subway car was packed to the brim, he felt absolutely alone.

SEBASTIÁN SLAMMED HIS backpack against the bed. He slammed it again and again until he finally understood the futility of this and tossed it away. He slid onto the bed, seething.

Meche was full of shit. She was a bad friend. Hell, she'd

always been a bad friend but he had not really cared until now. Why couldn't she lend him the record? She thought he wouldn't be able to use it properly. She was the real witch and he was just a two-bit imitation.

And the way she talked to him! And the way she had looked at him, shoved him away.

Well, he would show her.

He wanted her to know she was not everything to him, that he was more than her tributary.

"HEY DAD," SHE said.

"Hey, sweetheart. How are you doing?"

"I'm great. How are things?"

"Pretty good. I've got a place, a little apartment. As soon as I've fixed it up you can come and visit."

Her father's voice had always soothed Meche. It was rich and vibrant and pleasant. As she pressed the receiver against her ear she felt comforted just by the tone of his voice.

"So then... you won't be coming back home soon?"

"I don't think so, no."

"But you still care about mom."

Meche bit her lip and waited. He sighed and did not speak.

"Meche, your mom and I have a lot of problems."

"It could get better," she said.

Now that she had the record it would, for sure.

"I wish it would."

Meche closed her eyes, picturing them as they had been a few years before, when she was a small child. When they loved each other.

"Dad, could you come by tomorrow? Maybe take me out to dinner?"

"Well... alright," he said.

"And can I play music for you?"

"I don't know, Meche..."

"Please?"

"Alright."

They talked for a few more minutes. When Meche hung up she felt giddy with excitement. She went to her room, pulled out the record and stroked her fingers across the sleeve, feeling its warmth. This was her secret weapon. This represented her parents' hearts and they would be back together again, as they should be.

Magic could fix anything.

Meche thought about Sebastián. That thought made her curl her fingers and sigh, all the mirth vanishing. She'd been mean to him. Lately she did not know any other way to deal with him. She wanted to be nice. She really did. But things always went wrong and she was so angry... and he made her want to scream some times. He was difficult.

She shouldn't have said that about the circle, but she really felt it was going to end soon. He was going to call it quits. He wanted to spend his time chasing after Isadora. Daniela and Meche would be left to their own devices.

Meche tried to picture the world without Sebastián. She erased him and pictured a vast, white expanse which seemed to her like snow.

Meche lay back on her bed and pressed the record against her face, closing her eyes.

* * *

SEBASTIÁN DID NOT know how this was supposed to work. He had only cast a spell on his own once, and that had been an unexpected event. He did not know if he could manage it again. But he wanted to try. At the very least, he would give Meche a good scare.

Sebastián knocked and Meche's grandmother opened the door, smiling at him.

"Meche's not in, Sebastián," she said. "She's out doing the grocery shopping with her mom."

Sebastián already knew this. Sunday morning was always grocery day for Meche and her mom. Sebastián feigned surprise.

"She was going to lend me a couple of records."

This was not an unusual occurrence and Meche's grandmother nodded.

"Do you want to look for them?"

"Sure," Sebastián said with a smile.

As soon as he was in Meche's room he began pulling at drawers, rifling through her shelves. He found A Whiter Shade of Pale fast enough, resting in a box filled with old toys. He also found the Duncan Dhu record right next to it.

Sebastián frowned. He had not planned on taking Meche's object of power but now that he had it in his hands he thought it might not be a bad idea. If Meche got mad at him, he could tell her to cool it or he would scratch the damn thing. Well… at least he'd let her think he would scratch it.

Satisfied, Sebastián grabbed the records, thanked her grandmother and hurried downstairs.

Isadora was waiting for him next to the motorcycle. She smiled when he came out.

"I'm ready now," he said. "Let's go."

*　　*　　*

HE PARKED THE motorcycle in the alley behind the factory and sneaked in first before helping Isadora through. She looked at the abandoned building skeptically, her eyes darting across the dusty floors.

"It's over here," he said, grabbing her hand and guiding her up the stairs.

He unlocked the door and ushered her in with a sweeping motion. Isadora walked in slowly and her mouth curved into a smile as she saw the posters, the images of singers from magazines, the little coffee table with the candles on it.

"You did this?"

"My friends did," he said, not wanting to take all the credit. "We come here to listen to music. Do you... would you mind if I play some records?"

"Sure," Isadora said, as she sat on the couch.

MECHE DRAGGED THE bag full of vegetables into the kitchen, humming as she shoved the tomatoes into the refrigerator.

"Meche, your friend came looking for you," her grandmother said.

"Who came?"

"Sebastián."

Sebastián was supposed to take her to the movies that afternoon, but not until three. Meche frowned, her spine tingling with an unpleasant hunch.

"What did he want?"

"He came to borrow a few records. I told him to bring them back when he's done with them."

Meche's hands stilled. She slammed the refrigerator drawer shut and hurried to her room. She pulled the cardboard box from inside her closet and immediately saw which records were missing.

"Asshole!" she yelled, giving the box a good kick.

She curled her right hand into a fist.

She should have been more careful. She should have suspected this. Fortunately, Meche had a good idea of where he might be.

SEBASTIÁN HAD PLAYED a couple of songs by Mecano and one by Simple Minds before his fingers grazed the Procol Harum record. He swallowed, not knowing what to do.

"Maybe you could put on something to dance to?" Isadora suggested.

"What kind of music?" he said, raising his head and looking at her.

"Your pick."

A spectral light filtered through the old window panes, filling the room with an odd glow. He grabbed the record, set it down and lifted the needle. There was a tiny little hiccup as the needle slid across the vinyl surface and then the song began.

"It's slow music," he muttered. "We don't have to dance to it. I can put something el—"

"It sounds nice."

Isadora stood up. Despite his greater height, he felt very small as he took her hand, trying not to shake. Such moments did not happen in reality. They were reserved for movies and books. Any minute now he would wake up; it would turn out he was daydreaming again.

Sebastián placed his hands against Isadora's waist, carefully moving his feet to the rhythm of the music. Twice he looked down to make sure he was taking the right steps, but then he began to relax, and even smiled broadly at Isadora as he pulled her closer to him.

"What?' she asked, smiling back.

"I think I'd like to kiss you," he admitted.

Her hands crept up and wrapped around his neck.

"You think?"

"I'm sure."

"Why don't you?"

"I'm not sure if it's the right moment."

"It's right," she whispered as she pulled him down.

When their lips touched it was as though a circuit had been closed and the power which surged in him when he cast spells now manifested once more, except it was different this time. It did not flow out of him, but seemed to flow through him and he was all of a sudden giddy, intoxicated, brimming and drowning in a sea of pleasure.

It lasted for a small eternity and then he lazily opened his eyes only to see Meche standing at the door.

As SHE HURRIED up the factory's stairs, she heard it. First faintly, then growing stronger as she climbed. The door was not locked and she pushed it a little way open, looking through the crack.

Sebastián was dancing with Isadora. They were very

close together, her arms wrapped around his neck as they swayed to the melody of A Whiter Shade of Pale, the lovely, haunting organ pipes echoing through the room.

Sebastián's hands were resting on the girl's waist and he was moving very slowly.

When the singer sang "and although my eyes were open," Isadora reached up and pulled him down for a kiss.

Sebastián closed his eyes, his fingers fluttering up and molding around the beautiful girl's face.

Meche felt her heart grinding to a slow halt, like a broken clock. She smiled, though it was the grimace of despair.

Sebastián raised his head and opened his eyes just in that instant, locking with her own gaze.

Meche stepped back as he opened his mouth. Perhaps he intended to speak, but whether it was to Isadora or to her, she did not know.

Meche, who had prepared an abundance of insults for this occasion, suddenly found herself without a voice. Every syllable stuck to the roof of her mouth. She could not produce a single sound. Even worse, she felt tears gathering in her eyes.

She would not cry; not in front of him. She'd rather die than let him see her tears.

Meche closed the door, very gently, very quietly and hurried down the steps.

Once she was outside she surveyed the sky, trying to blink the tears away and managing only to sniffle. She wiped her nose with the back of her jacket.

A couple of hours later she returned to the factory. They were gone by then.

A Whiter Shade of Pale had been left on the turntable, like the remnant of a shipwreck upon the sand. Meche touched the record, but it felt cold. There was no warmth in it. She played it and heard only ordinary music. There was no magic in the recording. She looked at the sleeve, looked inside it, shook it, desperate to find a crumb of power but the power was gone. Her father was coming over in an hour and the record was useless.

Desperate, she looked for her object of power, thinking perhaps it might fix the problem. It might furnish the useless record with new magic. But Sebastián had taken the Duncan Dhu record with him.

Meche unpinned the photographs taken inside the photo booth and stomped on them.

SEBASTIÁN WAITED FOR Meche, knowing she'd show up that night. She had to. He read for an hour, then shifted to the couch and watched television, zipping through the channels.

He felt nervous. Like maybe he had overdone it. He'd wanted to best Meche, but as the minute hand dragged itself around the face of the clock, he felt he'd made a mistake.

He remembered dancing with Isadora, the kiss. He smiled. But then he also remembered the look on Meche's face. He'd only seen it for a couple of seconds, but her eyes had seemed so pained.

He should apologize. Make it up to her.

Then he frowned, thinking about all her little cruel comments, her coldness when he'd needed her, the indifference which sometimes punctuated their exchanges.

Let her be angry. At least for a little while.

At nine o'clock the knocks came. Three in a row.

He smiled when he opened the door, feeling smug and content, savouring the acid expression on her face, the ways her eyes lit up with righteous fury.

"Hey," he said. "How you doing?"

He expected Meche to launch into a long, angry tirade. To stomp and yell and use barbed words which would sting, lacerate the soul. He was not prepared for the cold, long stare she gave him and the very hard slap that followed.

Sebastián blinked, aghast, and rubbed his cheek, too stunned by this greeting to even speak. She had punched him in the arm before, in jest, but never this.

Meche shoved him away and marched into his apartment.

"Where's my object of power?" she asked.

She headed into his bedroom and began tearing his maps from the walls, ripping the postcards and tossing the sheets from his bed.

"Hey!" he yelled as she opened the doors of his armoire and pulled out his shirts, throwing them on the floor.

"Where do you have it?"

"It's not here and I am not giving it back to you tonight."

"When are you going to give it back, asshole?"

"When I damn feel like it!"

She turned around, shoulders raised, and walked away.

"Come back here!" he yelled.

"Go to hell," came the reply.

He chased her down the stairs, furiously stomping on every step.

"You're jealous, isn't that right? That's what this is about. You're jealous of me."

"Like I'd be jealous of you!"

"Well, you are."

"You knew I needed that record," she told him, stopping on the second landing and turning around, slamming him against the wall even though he was much bigger than her. "You knew it and you stole it!"

"I borrowed it."

"You are a thief!"

"Didn't you say to take what I wanted? When life offers you something, grab it. I've grabbed it, alright."

"How did you dare, to go into my house, into my room…"

"You wouldn't lend it to me! You were being selfish! Now you're angry because I used it, because I have the girl and you don't have the guy."

"What goddamn guy?" she asked.

"Constantino! Which other guy would it be?"

"You thought I was going to play that record to get together with Constantino?"

He grabbed her by the shoulders, gripping her tight and flipping her around so that she was now against the wall, his fingers digging into her flesh.

"Who else?" he muttered.

Meche let out a low laugh which startled him. Confusion, doubt, flashed across his face.

"I wanted to play that record for my parents. So they'd get back together."

His hands grew slack and she brushed them off her.

"I didn't know."

"Of course not. You're too busy being selfish."

"You can have it back. The record—"

"—I tried it. It has no power left."

"What do you mean?" he asked.

"You drained it! You took it all for yourself and for her! Are you in love now, Sebastián?" she asked, pushing him back so that his back hit the bannister. "Does your heart beat a little faster?"

"I didn't know records could be drained."

"Doesn't matter now, does it? Pat yourself on the back. You have the girl of your dreams and I have nothing."

"Don't exaggerate. Look, Meche—"

"You're going to regret this," she whispered.

He closed his eyes for a second, feeling like they were standing at the edge of a cliff and were about to fall.

"Can we pause and rewind?"

"No."

She shoved him away, her elbow hitting his ribs, and then she was gone.

Twin desires, to seek her forgiveness and to ignore her, warred with each other. His pride was hurt by the angry slap. He did not want to acknowledge he had done any wrong. To do so would be to admit she had been right and, once again, his pride would be stomped over.

He would talk to her later. Give her a day or two to cool down. Seek Daniela's intercession if necessary.

But why the hell did he feel like they'd already hit the ground and shattered?

DANIELA WRUNG HER hands and pushed the cupcake moulds into the Easy-Bake oven, trying to focus on her cooking, trying to do things they'd done before and attempt to fake a sense of normalcy. But Meche would not stop. She had been going on about it for nearly an hour and Daniela knew this was not a storm which would subside. This was a hurricane, gaining speed, preparing to rip the ground apart. Daniela did not know what to do. She did not know how to stop it. She felt that with every passing minute she was being engulfed by Meche's nervous energy, dragged along, small satellite that she was.

"I said, will you help me hex him?"

There. The question. Point-blank. Daniela squeezed her eyes shut.

"I need to finish baking."

"Quit playing silly games," Meche said, crouching down and looking straight at Daniela's face. "Are you going to help me or not?"

"What you want to do... it's mean," Daniela whispered.

"You think what he did to me is right? You think stealing is nice?"

"No."

"And ruining my parents' marriage?"

"No."

"And getting together with her, with Isadora, that is nice? How many times has she made fun of us at recess and suddenly she's all over him? And he likes it?"

"I know, it's just—"

"It'll only be a little tumble from the motorcycle. A few scrapes. Maybe he'll need a band-aid. He can take it."

Daniela shook her head and closed the oven door. She set the timer and rubbed her hands against her skirt.

"He'll ache for a couple of days and then he will be fine."

"You should talk to him," Daniela said. "You should talk it out."

"I'll talk to him after we are even."

"Why not talk to him *now*?"

"There is nothing to talk about."

Meche stood up and walked to the other side of the room, standing before Daniela's shelves and looking at her dolls and toys. She grabbed a stuffed bunny and squeezed it between her hands. It was pointless, once Meche had boiled herself up to this state, to expect her to cool down. Daniela knew it. There had been other fights, other times when she had been called on to act as conspirator and ally of one of her friends—mostly Meche. However, this time it felt different. More dangerous. It was not a childish prank, not about cutting holes into Sebastián's t-shirt. This was about inflicting actual physical pain. Even if it was only one bruise and one band-aid, it seemed like a big deal.

"I thought you cared about Sebastián. Loved him. When you love someone—"

"What?"

Meche's quick turn of the head and the way she spit out the words, as though she had just swallowed sour milk, made Daniela realize she had misspoken. She blinked and scrambled to correct herself.

"I... I meant..."

"What did you say?" Meche asked, frowning.

"Nothing. I... we can cast the hex," Daniela said, wishing only to avert Meche's wrath, to make those dark eyes turn away from her.

Her acceptance had the expected effect. Meche smiled, looking smug, and tossed the bunny away.

"We should head to the factory," she said.

Every crack on the pavement spoke words of warning to Daniela as she rushed behind Meche, towards the old, abandoned building. But there was nothing to do now. She was a coward and would obey, bend the knee. She always did.

"ARE YOU READY?" she asked.

"Meche, you can't," Daniela whispered.

The factory was cold. Shadows gathered at the corners of the window. The distant moon turned its face away from them, hiding behind a cloud.

Meche knew they shouldn't do it. She could feel it in every fibre of her being, feel it from the tips of her toes to the top of her head, but she did not care. She would have her revenge. She would have her hex.

"It's Sebastián."

"I know exactly who he is," Meche said.

She held the needle above the groove. There was only one album for such a spell, only one song for this kind of hex and she had known it from the moment her hand had found the record—guided by an unknown force, just like it had been guided in the record shop to find A Whiter Shade of Pale—waiting on the third bin to the left, near the Jimi Hendrix poster.

It was *In the Court of the Crimson King*. Recorded in 1969, it was the debut album by the British rock group King Crimson. Although it contained five tracks she knew which one she needed. Side two. Fifth song.

It was a track to bring down houses and topple

monarchs and surely it would teach a lesson to a teenage boy. A lesson he would not be likely to forget. And though a part of her wanted to leave things alone, to toss the record away and instead knock three times on a familiar door and embrace a skinny boy... Although a part of her didn't want a single bruise, nor a scratch on him, another, wilder, stronger part needed pain.

The music began to play. Daniela and Meche held hands tight as the building groaned, reverberating to the sound of Greg Lake's voice.

DANIELA WANTED TO pull her hand away, but Meche dug her nails into her palm and Daniela stopped fretting.

She was scared. The windows were tinkling, the glass straining in the frames and Meche's hand felt like it was a hot iron poker. When she looked at Meche's face, her eyes looked darker and older.

Shadows seemed to cloak Meche. She was robed in darkness. And the power in her burned, making Daniela wince.

SEVERAL BLOCKS AWAY Sebastián turned a corner as he had done many times before. But this time something felt wrong. Invisible hands seemed to hover on top of his own hands, invisible fingers making the motorcycle speed up, howl and screech and rush down hill.

He knew the hands.

This was Meche's doing. She was trying to scare him.

"Screw you!" he yelled.

He didn't know if she could hear him, but she hoped his defiance reached her.

The pressure of the hands increased, he swerved and almost lost control of the bike.

A cold bead of sweat dripped down his forehead and he was suddenly afraid. He realized she was not playing. It was not a prank.

"Mercedes!" he yelled.

The car hit him right at that instant and sent him flying through the air, tumbling over the pavement.

DOLORES WAS HALF-asleep on the couch, her hands resting over a ball of yarn, when she felt the tugging. The web of magic drifting through their apartment shivered and moaned. She opened her eyes slowly, specks of darkness dancing before her eyes.

And she knew what was happening all of a sudden. Meche was casting a new spell. A very dark spell.

A spell of death.

Unintended, surely. Uninvited. But when is death invited? Doors do not open to him. He sneaks through fissures, slips under doors. Burrows into your heart and poisons the gut.

Dolores stood up and shuffled towards her bedroom without bothering to put on her slippers. She opened a drawer and pulled out her thimble. She looked at her sisters in the photograph and wished they were still around. Lone witches are never much good. Maybe if the others were still alive they could have taught Meche the way Dolores couldn't. Because Dolores had never been the head witch. Just a minor echo for her eldest sister. Always half-afraid of the spells and now unable to remember them. They'd poured out of her one summer, long, long ago.

But perhaps there was one last spell she might remember.

Dolores put on the thimble. She took needle and thread and began stitching a handkerchief. Sweat beaded her forehead as she worked. The needle rose and fell, dipping until she tied a knot and cut it with her scissors.

There was a hiss, like steam escaping a kettle. Dolores winced as the thimble burned her finger.

She felt Meche's death spell eroding and decaying, bits of it falling to the floor. The thimble also slid from her finger, shattering, bits of white dust scattered all around her.

Dolores closed her eyes and sighed.

DANIELA SAT ON the couch, heart beating fast, and stared at Meche. Meche was on the floor wrapped in a blanket, a cushion behind her head, eyes closed and humming. Daniela could barely breathe but Meche seemed to be making a quick recovery.

Watching her from her position on the couch, Daniela knew her friend was dangerous. She felt the same horror she might feel at discovering a scorpion in her shoe and though she was exhausted, hungry and in desperate need for a nap, she pulled her knapsack over her shoulder.

"I should go," she said.

"Go," Meche said, eyes closed.

Daniela walked out quietly, looking over her shoulder before she closed the door.

*　　*　　*

MECHE WALKED HOME listening to los Fabulosos Cadillacs sing Mi Novia se Cayó en un Pozo Ciego. She felt festive, moving to the rhythm of the trumpets, bobbing her head and smiling. By the time she stepped into the apartment she was dancing.

"Hey, mom," she said, noticing that the kitchen light was on.

She poked her head in the kitchen. Her mother's eyes looked raw and red.

"Where were you?" she asked.

"I was hanging out with Daniela," Meche said. "What's up? Is this about Sebos?"

"Sebastián?" her mother said. "No."

Odd. Because Meche thought maybe Sebastián's mother had already called to give them the bad news: that her son had a little traffic accident, that he'd broken his leg, or bruised his shoulder, or had a black eye, and Meche could feign innocence. Buy flowers. Take them to the hospital. The joy of his pain would be like a candy, melting in her mouth. Perhaps he would think twice about messing with her again. He thought himself a warlock? Fine. She was a witch.

"Then what's with you?"

"Your grandmother had a stroke. I came to pick some clothes for her, some things—"

"She didn't have a stroke," Meche said.

"She did have a stroke. This evening."

"But she couldn't have."

"Meche, I need to go to the hospital," her mother said,

rubbing her eyes and reaching for her purse. "I have to get a cab and get back there."

"Can I go?"

"All you'd be doing is waiting."

"I can wait."

Her mother nodded and they hurried down the stairs.

The telephone began to ring when they shut the door, a lonesome and sad cry.

SEBASTIÁN HELD THE receiver and leaned back, trying to find a comfortable position on the couch. He had bruised his knee, had scrapes here and there, a sprained ankle and a broken wrist.

"You are an idiot," Romualdo said. "How come you were driving so fast? Don't you watch where you are going?"

Sebastián pressed the plastic bag filled with ice and wrapped with an old towel against his leg, watching the bruises with a certain detachment, as though this had happened to someone else. It felt like it had happened to someone else. Like he was a character in a video game, controlled by another player.

Meche.

The phone rang and rang.

Answer, he thought, gritting his teeth. *Answer me. Tell me it was an accident, a game; you didn't mean it. Tell me now.*

"You know what's going to happen, right? Mom is going to take away the bike. Not only that, she's going to blame it on me for giving it to you in the first place. She's going to say I did this. That's bullshit."

The phone seemed to pulsate between his hands, like a heart. Sebastián squeezed it, tried to find purchase on its surface, slick with his sweat.

Meche...

He needed her now. There. If she answered now, this might be forgiven. But she wasn't answering. She was hiding from him.

He could see her in his mind, savouring her victory, her eyes indifferent to his pain. Indifferent to him.

He hung up and hung his head while Romualdo brought him another cushion and yelled and ranted.

MECHE WOKE UP feeling very cold, her eyes fluttering open. She had a vague, unpleasant sensation, like the one you might get when you crush an insect and rub your palm against your trousers, trying to wipe it away.

She thought of the hex she had cast with Daniela and for the first time that night seriously wondered if Sebastián was alright. The hospital's clock read one a.m. and she considered, for a few seconds, daring to phone Sebastián.

Then she feared what he would say if she did phone and woke him up. His anger would still be raw.

Even worse, she feared if he did not answer. What if she had really hurt him? What if he did not lift the phone and speak? What would she do then?

Meche took off her jacket and rolled it into a makeshift pillow, laying down on the plastic hospital chairs, staring at the white walls of the hallway.

She knew herself—wicked and cruel, the way true

witches are, as in the stories grandmother told her. She knew herself and curled up into a tight ball, flipping on the Walkman and listening to Starship sing We Built This City, which was corny and sappy. But she needed corny and sappy.

"I'm going to make it all better," she promised herself. "I can fix this."

DANIELA HEARD IT from Catalina Coronado, who was faster than a telex: Sebastián Soto had an accident, ended up at the hospital and was sent home with a cast. She asked her sister to drive her to his apartment, a box of chocolates on her lap. Romualdo opened the door and let her in. Daniela shuffled her feet and bent her head as she walked inside.

"Hi, Sebastián."

"Hi," he said.

He was sitting in the living room, wrapped in a blanket, watching television. She noticed the cast on his left hand and the bruises on his face, blooming an ugly purple.

Daniela handed him the chocolates.

"Thanks," he said, placing them at his side.

"How are you feeling?"

"Eh. Between this and the beating I'm developing a higher threshold for pain."

"You know we did it, right?"

"I figured as much."

Daniela placed her hands behind her back and stared at the scratched wooden floor.

"I'm sorry," Daniela said.

Sebastián pressed the mute button on the TV remote. He sighed.

"Where is Meche?"

"I'm not sure."

Sebastián drummed his fingers against the couch's arm and shook his head. He did not look good and Daniela could tell it was not just as a result of the accident.

"Well, she has talent," he muttered. "I could feel her hands over mine as the motorcycle swerved left and right."

"Yeah, she has loads of talent. That's probably not a good thing."

Sebastián did not say anything. He was looking at the numbers on the remote control, rubbing a thumb across the buttons.

"She scared me. When we cast that spell on you... my God, there is something dark inside her. Magic only makes that darkness stronger."

"What are you saying?"

"You know."

Sebastián put the remote on top of the box of chocolates and knitted his long fingers together, flexing them slowly.

"She's the real witch among us," he said. "Meche doesn't need a circle. At least, not for long. Whatever it is you're supposed to have, she has it."

Daniela had known it for a while. They were backup singers to the real star. Hearing Sebastián say it, however, made it tangible.

"That's it. That's what frightens me."

"You shouldn't be frightened. Meche is not mad at you."

"But you? What if—"

"I have her object of power. Besides, I don't think she would hurt me once more."

"How do you know?"

"Because it's Meche and Meche I know."

Daniela did not think that was quite enough, but what else could she say? She brushed the hair from her face. Her lips trembled a little as she spoke.

"I'm sorry, Sebastián. I really am. I helped do this to you."

"It'll be okay. I'll be fine."

She hugged him and Sebastián patted her back.

MECHE AND HER mother were sitting in the kitchen, eating in silence. Meche dipped her animal crackers in milk while her mother sipped her coffee.

"Your grandmother is going to have to go to Monterrey," her mother said, all of a sudden.

"Since when?" Meche asked.

This was the first she had heard of this. Had she missed an important family meeting or was she supposed to divine tea leaves in order to be up to date? Really, what the hell.

"I talked to your aunt about it. We had a long conversation. Your grandmother is going to need a lot of care."

"She could get better."

"She had a stroke," her mother said. "She can't walk and she can't talk. She can barely eat mush."

"I noticed," Meche said dryly.

"Your aunt is a nurse. Plus, she has more money than we do. A bigger place. Your grandmother needs more care than I can give her."

"You're just going to pack her off 'cause she's sick."

"There's nothing I can do about it."

"Don't I get a vote in this?"

Her mother did not reply. She looked at her coffee cup, long nails tapping the ceramic mug.

"Awesome," Meche said, pushing her chair back and scraping the floor in the process.

"I NEED TO talk to you," Meche said, cornering her outside the bathroom stalls.

Daniela had been evading her all day long. A clumsy effort at best because Daniela did not know the meaning of subtle. She waddled through school like a great, big goose, a panicked look on her face.

"I don't want to talk," Daniela whispered.

"Listen: I need your help."

"To do what?"

"My grandmother had a stroke. She's not well. I want to heal her. I think we might need Sebastián for this."

Daniela moved towards the sinks, slowly opening a faucet and rubbing her hands with liquid soap.

"Sebastián is at home, resting. He's in a cast. I don't think he'd be up for it and frankly I don't think he'll be talking to you until you do some serious apologizing."

"Apologize?" Meche scoffed.

"Didn't you hear me? He's in a cast. You said he'd only

get a scratch and it was awful. I feel terrible about it."

Daniela closed the faucet. The paper towel dispenser was empty, so she rubbed her hands against her skirt.

"I heard you fine. I'm not apologizing. He got what was coming to him."

"Then don't expect him to help you."

Meche was tired, nervous and more than a little irritated. She squeezed Daniela's arm and gave her a sharp, intense look.

"Convince him to help. Tell him to come by the factory and bring my Duncan Dhu record."

"No way," Daniela said. "I've done enough already. I won't goad him into it."

"I don't care what you want," Meche said. "He will be back in our circle, ready to offer his assistance or *you* will be the next one hexed."

"You wouldn't do that," Daniela said.

"Try me. I think you'll find I'm becoming very good at this sort of thing."

Daniela's eyes went round and glassy like marbles. She was really scared. Meche felt bad for a few seconds. She shoved the feeling aside. She needed Sebastián and Daniela. At the very least, she wanted her damn record back. If it took a bit of pushing around, so be it.

Daniela wriggled free of her grasp and took a couple of steps back.

"Okay. I'll talk to him."

"Today?" Meche asked.

"Today," Daniela said.

"Remind him he still has something that belongs to me. He better bring it to the factory."

*   *   *

SEBASTIÁN DID NOT reply. He was staring at the big glass full of milk and chocolate powder, observing the beads of moisture rolling down the sides, trying not to think. Trying to ignore it.

"And then?" Daniela asked.

"I won't help her."

"She'll hurt us," Daniela muttered.

Sebastián did not want to believe it. Meche was many things, but would she really force them to obey her?

She could have killed you, he thought. *She's Meche but she's also something else now.*

Sebastián sipped his milk. They sat in the darkened dining room and he listened to the clock tick, measuring the minutes.

"It's time we did something about this magic circle," he said. "But not what she expects."

"What, then?"

"Tell her I'll be at the factory Friday evening."

"You'll do what she wants?"

"No," Sebastián said, shaking his head. "I won't do anything of the sort."

This day was supposed to come, he thought. He remembered his vision of Meche heading towards an airplane. He'd *known*, long before, that he'd lose her, but he couldn't escape this melody.

THE HOSPITAL SMELLED like disinfectant. It wasn't like the smell when grandma cleaned the clothes at home or washed the floors. It was more powerful and unpleasant. Then there was the cold. Meche had to keep her sweater buttoned up, otherwise her arms would get goosebump.

She didn't like the hospital and she liked the hospital room even less. Grandma shared it with another two women and all that separated her from the next bed was a thin curtain. Meche had to sit very close to the bed in an uncomfortable, old chair.

"Do you know what I did today?" Meche asked and paused to wait for a reply even though her grandmother could not answer.

She had washed her grandmother's hair in a little basin and was carefully combing it with a plastic, wide-tooth comb.

"I made picadillo. I didn't boil the potatoes long enough so they were a little hard."

Meche set the comb down and looked at her grandmother's face.

"You're going to get better," she said, smiling. "I'm going to fix everything. That's a promise."

MECHE WAS RE-READING their grimoire, pausing to scribble little annotations on the margin of the page. She checked her watch. They were late. Were they even coming? It would be a cruel joke to leave her waiting. But this might be Sebastián's way of getting back at her.

Night was falling so she lit the candles around the room to keep herself distracted. Two dozen stubs of wax. She looked out the circular window and pressed her cheek against the glass.

With a sigh she struck another match and lit the rest of the candles on top of the coffee table.

The door opened. Daniela and Sebastián walked in, sweeping their flashlights in a wide arc. They dropped their backpacks by the door. When Sebastián moved into the light Meche felt her arrogant smile fade a bit. He had a cast on his hand, like Daniela said, and when he walked he limped a bit. There was a cut across his forehead.

He looked at her, eyes sharp and unpleasant.

She looked back, chin raised.

"Hi," he said. "I'm here. Like you wanted."

"Good." Meche knelt down to open the portable record player.

"You needn't bother, I'm not casting any spells with you."

Meche raised her head and looked at him with a frown. She brushed the top of the record player with her right hand.

"What do you mean?"

"I've come to tell you I'm done with your little circle."

"So am I," Daniela said.

Meche did not mean to laugh, but she did anyway. Their determined yet frightened expressions were just too hilarious.

"Oh come on," she said. "You don't mean that."

"Yes we do," Daniela said.

"Did he put you up to this?" Meche asked, pointing at Sebastián.

"No. I'm tired of having you boss me around. This magic... this is not fun anymore. It's nasty and I want to be done with it."

"Do you want to be done with me, too?" she asked Sebastián.

He glanced away and shook his head, smiling at her. Why, yes, of course. Now he had Isadora.

"I can't believe you," he said. "I can't believe your absolute selfishness."

"My selfishness?" she asked. "I want to heal my grandmother. Is that selfish?"

"Everything is about you, Meche. This circle was never about us. We were just your assistants, here to help get what you wanted. You did not even ask what we wanted."

"I asked what you wanted. And you have what you want, anyway," Meche said, remembering the little dance with Isadora. "So now give me what I need."

"Your circle is no more. You might as well get over it."

"Is that so?" Meche said. She glanced at Sebastián, then at Daniela. "You really want to piss me off?"

"We are not afraid of you," Sebastián said.

"Good," Meche said. "Remember that later."

She opened the record player and the needle pressed down on the record. It was Strange Days by The Doors. It had a certain kick to it, a certain pick-me-up that had electrified Meche the first time she had grabbed the record, tickling something inside her head.

She snapped her fingers and narrowed her eyes. She did not need them. A couple of losers to weigh her down. She could do this by herself. She'd show them magic.

Meche snapped her fingers again and the candle flames jumped up, grew brighter as though they were being fanned by an invisible hand.

"Bubble, bubble, hu?" she told Sebastián. "Circles are for weaklings."

She snapped her fingers again and the light of the candles grew even brighter, imbuing everything with a golden glow. Daniela and Sebastián stared at her.

She'd started by casting spells alone and it seemed she would finish casting them by herself. They could both go to hell.

The song grew and so did her magic. Meche made the candles drip rivers of wax upon the floor, long white tendrils reaching towards Daniela and Sebastián.

"My Duncan Dhu record. I want it."

"You're scaring me," Daniela said, stepping back, closer to the wall.

Meche shrugged. Always such a little baby, Daniela. The wax snaked around them, drawing secret patterns upon the floor.

"Don't!" Daniela squeaked, the flashlight trembling in her hands, the beam of light bouncing up and down.

"Stop it," Sebastián said. "She's frightened."

"Oh, come on," Meche said rolling her eyes. "I'll make it stop when you give me my record."

"Enough of this," Sebastián said.

"I'm scared!" Daniela wailed.

"Enough!"

Sebastián screamed. The scream made her jump back, staggered by the ferocity of it. Sebastián reached for his backpack and pulled out a record.

Meche could not see from where she was standing because Sebastián was half in shadows. Instead, she felt it, like a great, beating heart crouched in the corner of the room.

For a moment she smiled, feeling her object of power so close to her, almost back in her arms…

… and then he snapped the Duncan Dhu record in two. It made a sound like bones breaking .

She screamed as an invisible fissure traveled up her feet, up her legs and through her chest until it reached her heart. There came the sensation of being ripped apart. Her heart was squeezed ferociously and she could not breathe…

… and then breath returned to her in a shocked gasp.

The candles all went out at the same time, plunging the room into darkness.

Meche dropped down, crouching by the record player.

Her trembling hands touched the needle, quieting the music.

The whole factory was silent.

Sebastián stepped forward, his flashlight pointed at her. "Are you alright?"

"It's gone," she whispered. "The magic."

Meche looked at him and could not stop the tears streaming down her cheeks.

He stretched out a hand towards her. Meche slapped it away. She closed the record player and grabbed it in one hand, hurrying down the stairs and holding on to the bannister with the other.

"Meche, you can't see!" he yelled.

He was right. It was very dark. But it did not matter. Blindly she stepped down and in darkness found the way out, bursting onto the street with the record player clutched against her chest.

She ran home, her feet pounding the pavement, jumping from puddle of light to puddle of light.

When she reached the apartment she pulled her suitcase from under the bed and filled it with clothes. She latched it and hurried to the door, bumping against her mother in the living room.

"Meche," she said. "What are you doing?"

"I'm leaving," Meche said. "I'm getting out of this place and going to live with dad."

"Meche, you are not going anywhere."

She had to. She could not stay. Humiliation, rage, despair, that was the only thing which could grow between these walls, on that whole street.

"Dad will be glad to have me over."

"Your father can't take care of you," her mother said, tugging at the suitcase.

Meche pulled it back.

"Why not? He's my dad."

"Because he drinks. Because he's never able to do anything right."

"Oh, bullshit."

"Watch your mouth."

"You don't even like me! And I don't like you!"

"He stole our money!" her mother roared and tugged at the suitcase hard enough to pull it free from Meche's grasp.

Meche huffed, pressing a hand against her chest. "What do you mean?"

"Our savings, Meche. He stole our savings and spent them on that woman."

"He did not," Meche said, feeling offended. "The savings fund is for me. For university and for—"

"I barely have enough money to put food on the table. Your grandmother is going to end up in Monterrey because I can't support both of you. I am not making this up. I am—"

"You are nuts!"

Meche rushed out, carrying the record player under her arm. She heard her mother screaming after her, but she ran down the stairs fast as she could and out onto the street.

HER DAD SMILED, though his smile was a little creased at the edges.

"Meche. How's it going?" he asked. "Um... were you coming to visit today?"

"No," she said and set the record player by the entrance, looking around the apartment.

It was very small and there were lots of boxes. He had not unpacked most of his things, it seemed. Meche sat down on a little blue couch and her father took an old rattan chair across from her. There was a ratty coffee table in between them and she noticed an ashtray filled to the brim and a glass with dregs at the bottom. It smelled like whiskey. Her father grabbed the glass.

"I should take this to the sink. Do you want a soda?" he said. "I've got soda in the refrigerator. I don't have food. I'm eating out. I do have potato chips."

Meche took off her green jacket and placed it on her knees.

"It's cool. I don't really—"

"They're good chips," he said.

Her father wandered into the kitchen, pulling out glasses, filling a little bowl with chips.

"Dad, is it okay if I come stay with you?" she asked, trying to sound casual. Like it wasn't a big deal. Because it probably wasn't.

He poked his head out of the kitchen.

"For the weekend?" he asked, rubbing the stubble on his cheek. "I'm busy this weekend."

"No, for good."

"Aw, Meche... seriously?"

Meche nodded. He leaned forward, clasping his hands together. His smile wavered.

"That's probably not a great idea."

"Why not?"

"This place is very small."

"You said you were trying to get a bigger place. And next year you're moving to Puerto Vallarta, anyway. So it almost doesn't matter at all."

He placed the glasses and the soda on the coffee table. He went back to the kitchen and returned with the bowl of chips.

"Yes, but it's a bit difficult right now with the current situation," he said. "And the Puerto Vallarta thing is a little messy. I've sent my demo tape. I did. A couple of weeks ago. As soon as they play it they're going to love my voice. But, of course, these things take time. The whole hiring process is so silly these days. Human resources department this and fill that form and... it's best if you stay with your mom."

Meche felt like she had swallowed a mouthful of bleach.

"You said I could go with you one day," she said. "We'll live in Puerto Vallarta and get nice tans all year long. Grandma can come with us."

"Things are a bit weird right now, Meche. But we will absolutely go to Puerto Vallarta and I'll finish my book there. It's going to be fun. You'll see."

"Dad, I can't stay with mom."

"You can't stay here either, sweetheart."

Her father took out a cigarette and lit it, raising it to his lips.

"Did you steal money from mom?"

He smiled a jovial smile. "What?"

"Did you steal from her?"

"Stealing is an exaggeration."

"Our savings," Meche said, through gritted teeth. "Did you take them?"

Her father's smile, which was always big, folded and disappeared. He nodded and took a drag.

"Yeah. I did."

"Awesome," Meche said, standing up.

"Meche, you don't get it—"

"No dad, *you* don't get it."

She put on her jacket and zipped it up in one quick motion.

"You're a fucking disgrace," she said. "I can't believe you'd steal from us."

"Hey," Vicente said, spitting the cigarette from his mouth. "Hey, you watch that mouth!"

"I'm not watching anything! You're a lousy father."

"Yeah, too bad," he said with a sneer.

"Good thing I figured it out."

"You don't have to come back 'round here if you feel like that, Meche!"

Meche opened the door. She eyed the portable record

player sitting on the floor and gave it a good kick. After all, it didn't matter anymore. Very little did.

"Bye, dad."

WHEN SHE CAME home, her mother was waiting for her in the kitchen, looking at her cup of coffee. Meche rested her hands on the chair and sighed. Her mother stared at Meche. Neither one spoke for what seemed an aeon.

"You think it's simple, don't you," her mother said finally, "Life. It's very hard, Meche. I do what I can."

"I know."

"When you were a baby you cried a lot. Nothing could calm you down. You bawled and bawled. But when your dad put on a record and held you, you'd quiet down. It was like magic. I tried putting on records and holding you, but it wasn't the music. You knew it was him. And you knew when it was me. I can't be him."

"I don't want you to be him."

Meche found a stray crumb and rolled it between her fingers.

"Mom, I just... I want to go away. I can't stay here."

"Where would you go?"

"Monterrey. With grandma. I'd help take care of her. She needs me. I failed her and I have to help her, I've got to be with grandma."

"Your school?

"There are schools in Monterrey."

Her mother shook her head and chuckled, resting her elbows on the table. "You want to get away from me so badly?"

"No," Meche said. "But I do want to go somewhere else. This is not my place."

"We all think that when we are fifteen."

"It really isn't. And I'll phone. I'll be here during vacation."

"What kind of mother would I be if I send you to live with your aunt?"

"Mom," Meche said extending her hand. "You know I love you. But I can't live with you. You know that, don't you?"

Her mother grabbed her hand and shook her head.

VICENTE VEGA LEANED down and picked up the portable record player, setting it on the counter. He opened it, pressed a button and saw the platter was not spinning. It could be fixed. He'd work on it in the morning. For now, he needed a drink. Vicente grabbed a glass and poured himself whiskey. He was out of ice and it was warm and unpleasant, but he drank it and lit a cigarette.

He walked back to the living room and patted one of the boxes filled with records, opening it and pulling out a danzón: Como una Orquídea.

The rhythm of the danzón—music fit only for prostitutes of yesteryears, dancing in smoky salons—soothed him

He turned off the lights, sitting in the dark.

LOVE DIES IN different ways. For most, it is a slow, agonizing death. Meche, however, cut her love the same way the executioner might chop a head: with a single, accurate swing.

She never saw her father after that day.
She did not speak to Daniela and Sebastián either.

Mexico City, 2009

MECHE'S MOTHER WAS boiling hibiscus flowers for the jamaica water and the whole apartment had a sweet, pleasant smell.

"Your cousin was looking for you," her mother said, wiping her hands against her apron. "She wanted to know if you need a ride to the airport tomorrow."

"I could use a ride from Jimena. But I'm leaving early. I don't know if she wants to get up at four a.m."

"You can ask."

"Sure."

She leaned over her mother's shoulder to look at the big, boiling pot of water. The water was blooming into a nice shade of red.

"You know, jamaica water is essentially tea, but cooled down."

"I know that," Meche said.

"You should take a few bags of it and make it at home."

Meche nodded. Her mother stirred the pot with a wooden spoon.

"I'm getting rid of most of dad's records."

"Are you sure?"

"Yeah," she said firmly and paused before speaking again. "I read his book."

"Was it any good?"

"It was. A bit jumbled. It needs some editing... but it was good."

It felt odd admitting it. And it was sad. Sad to know her dad could have done something else with his life. He'd wasted away in that little apartment, with his notes and his records, so close to finishing his big project and yet so far. She supposed he'd felt safer that way, shielded from rejection.

"I salvaged something for you. Wait a second."

Meche returned to the kitchen with a small box and set it on the table. Her mother peeked inside.

"What's this?" she asked, pulling out an envelope.

"Dad was obsessive about keeping everything he wrote. These are letters he sent to you. Remember?"

"Letters?"

"Yeah. When he was trying to get you to go out with him."

"Oh, my," her mother whispered, unfolding one. "I remember. I didn't know he kept them."

"I thought you might want them."

"I do."

Her mother pulled out another letter and shook her head, chuckling.

"He could write, couldn't he? He wrote on anything. Bits of napkins and the backs of receipts. That was Vicente."

Her mother put the letters back in the box. She closed the lid and looked at Meche.

"I wish you could have talked to him before he died," her mother said.

"Whenever we talked he was drunk and sad," Meche said. "But I wish I'd talked to him."

"Well, are you going to need help packing? Do you need—"

"I could use a hug."

Meche placed a hand on her mother's shoulder. Her mother smiled.

ASSORTED EMPANADAS CONSTITUTED the dish for the last day of the novena. There were spicy tuna ones and sweet ones filled with pineapple jam.

Meche played tangos. Her father said tango was a music for mending or breaking hearts. Rhythms for close embraces and invitations to dance telegraphed with the eyes and a tilt of the head.

She saw Daniela and waved to her. The woman approached her, a broad smile painting her face.

"Hey," Meche said. "How... um... how's your day been?"

"Long. I've been up since six and have not stopped. Two kids and a full-time job," she said. "They're six and ten."

"Seriously? You have a ten-year old child? That's impossible."

"Not that impossible. It's been a while."

"No kidding. What do you do for a living?"

"I'm a cook."

"That seems strangely appropriate."

"Well, I did go crazy with that Easy-Bake oven."

"Sebos ate everything you made. Even when it sucked."

"My cooking has improved."

Meche smiled. She felt sheepish, her hands dipping into her pockets as she looked down.

"You're wondering if he's coming after all," Daniela said.

Meche opened her mouth to protest, raising her hand.

"Don't deny it."

"How do you—"

"It's all over your face."

Meche huffed. Daniela placed a hand on her shoulder, squeezing it a little.

"He's coming. He's probably delayed by traffic."

"Has he been talking to you?" Meche asked, wondering if he had spilled the beans about their tryst. Now that would be embarrassing.

"No more than a few words. But it doesn't take a genius to figure it out. I mean, I figured it out, even back then."

"What?"

"That you were head-over-heels in love with him. I told you so. But you wouldn't listen."

Meche opened her mouth and then shut up when she saw Sebastián entering the apartment. He nodded at her and waded his way through the crowded living room, evading Jimena and her tray of empanadas.

"I'll let you talk," Daniela said, moving aside.

"Hey, wait," Meche said.

"I don't think you need me to translate for you."

"Well..." Meche said, grabbing her arm. "Thanks. I don't think I ever said thanks to you."

"For what?" Daniela asked.

She thought about all the times Daniela had put up with her, showing kindness when Meche was a bundle of irritated nerves and impatience. Smiling at her when Meche made a sour face. Listening patiently when Meche ranted. Meche had just accepted all of this as fact, never questioning Daniela's devotion.

"For everything."

"I think I was a bit odd," Daniela said. "With all my crafts and sequins and little projects."

"You were amazing," Meche said and she meant it. Daniela hadn't been odd, like the other kids said, and she hadn't been corny. She'd been honest and good and fun. "I wouldn't have survived without you."

Daniela smiled, drifting towards the other end of the room.

"Hi."

Sebastián was holding his jacket under his arm and he looked very formal, though he carried a backpack on his right shoulder. She still could not quite square his current self with his former self.

"Just got off work?" she asked.

"Yep. I came right over."

Meche nodded. She wished she had a plate of empanadas, a glass of water, something to keep her hands from fluttering nervously in front of her face. She placed her hands behind her back as a last resort.

"You could have asked me to come yourself, you know," he said.

"I never do," Meche said, thinking about poor Daniela, who had served as her messenger on more than one occasion. "Bad habit of mine."

Meche glanced down, softly moving one foot to the rhythm of Carlos Gardel's "Volver." In a baritone

Carlos told her the stars mockingly look on and in their indifference observe the return of an old lover. She shuffled her feet to each word. Impatient. Annoyed. Tense. He just looked at her, which didn't help.

"I wasn't trying to insult you at the restaurant," she muttered.

"Of course you were."

"I did, but I wasn't *trying*," Meche said. "It came out all wrong. I'm not exactly a perfect orator."

"I noticed. I think the first time we ever spoke you called me 'horse-faced weirdo.'"

"It was just horse-face," she muttered. "I called you weirdo the next time we talked."

"Yeah, and I still befriended you."

"That good old masochism."

"Well, you made a very compelling case for yourself: you told me I could eat from your bag of potato chips. How's a guy going to resist a gal offering him chips?"

Meche laughed. She felt like slapping his arm, like she might have done when they were younger. Then she sobered.

Sebastián was quiet, as though he were waiting for her to say something. When she did not, he finally spoke.

"I brought you something."

Sebastián unzipped the backpack and took out a mangled, old box. Meche frowned.

"What is this?" she asked.

"Open it."

She took the lid off and saw his old sneakers with all the inked doodles.

"This is my object of power," he said. "I'm giving it to you."

The room seemed to suddenly go... muffled. As though someone had pressed a pillow against the speakers, drowning out the sound. Only that wasn't possible. The emptiness in her ears was a bizarre auditory hallucination.

She stood in that silence staring at Sebastián, not knowing what to say.

"I'm... what do you want me to do with them?" she asked, and hated the hesitation in her voice. Like she'd swallowed peanut butter and it was sticking to the roof of her mouth.

"Do what you want with them. I also have this," he said and he showed her a record sleeve.

Duncan Dhu. *El Grito del Tiempo*. Track one: En Algún Lugar.

Meche put the box down and grabbed the sleeve. She took out the record and immediately saw the cracks running down its surface.

"I glued it back together years ago."

"You can't glue it back together," she whispered. "It can't be fixed. You can't undo..."

"I know we can't undo anything. I know that," he said sternly. "I'm not asking for that."

"What are you asking, then?"

He brushed her cheek with his thumb and smiled the faintest smile.

"Don't leave me behind this time."

Meche clutched the record and frowned. She had thought about it, but it was an entry under 'idiot things that occur to me.' Only an idiot would think about starting something with someone they hadn't spoken to in years, someone who was a total stranger. Especially when she had somewhere to be. The little apartment in Oslo with her ferns, her computer... her entire life.

"Oh, whatever for... it's ridiculous," she said, shaking her head and coughing because something had lodged in her throat.

"Yeah. I'm pretty sure it is."

"I didn't... I mean, I didn't want you here for... that. I wanted to tell you something. I'm sorry. I shouldn't have cast that spell on you. I should have been kinder. I should have understood you better."

Sebastián slid his hands in his pockets and he shook his head. He looked sad and embarrassed and irritated, and it made her want to pinch him because she wasn't faring any better. And... damn it.

"You're giving me the brush off, again," he said.

"I'm apologizing."

"It still feels like a brush off."

"You don't want to be hanging out with me," she said, smiling. "I'm bad for your health."

He managed to smile back, the corners of his lips rising a little. He shook his head, a chuckle escaping his throat, though it sounded dull and forced.

"Of course you are. You are terrible for me. Not that I ever gave a damn. Not that I'd start giving a damn now."

"Please don't use that tone."

"What tone?"

That sad, defeated tone. Like she had just stabbed his hand with a fork. Like she had just run over his favourite puppy. Like she was this awful person. She wasn't. Not when you looked at it all rationally.

"I didn't want to leave without saying goodbye," she muttered, ignoring the question. "You know, like a thief."

"Maybe you should have," he said. "It's better than saying 'Let's pretend nothing happened.'"

"When did I say that?"

"Wasn't that coming next?"

Meche bit her lip. It wasn't exactly what she was thinking, but it wasn't far off. It sounded perfectly reasonable in her head. Now he made it seem like an insult. It was all very disjointed and unpleasant.

"I bet you wish you never spoke to me again."

"Not really," she muttered.

"Oh, come on. Well, don't worry. *I* wish I hadn't seen you again."

That kind of hurt. It shouldn't, but it did.

He pinched the bridge of his nose and sighed.

"No, I didn't mean that," he said. "I... um... thanks, I guess. For the honesty and all."

"I fly out tomorrow. Thanks for the record."

She thought about giving him a final hug but it was already weird enough between them. Besides, if she hugged him, she'd have to kiss him on the cheek and that was... not right.

Meche stepped back, raised her right hand, signaling 'bye.' He raised both hands as if he were surrendering.

She turned around and headed towards her bedroom. The tango was over. A new song was playing.

Mexico City, 2009

MECHE LOOKED AT the plane tickets, checking her row for the third time. The problem with flying these days was that you had to be at the airport three hours before your flight left to get through the security checkpoints. That meant you couldn't dash onto your plane, sit down in your seat and be on your way. No. You had to wait at a coffee stand and ask if they had tea. Only they did not have the tea you wanted, which only served to increase the impatience quotient.

And the music. She did not even want to mention the airport music. A banal, tiresome selection of soft rock hits which had her stuffing her earbuds into her ears as soon as the first song started playing.

Meche tapped the little circular table with her nails and wished she could board a train and be home in two hours, like in Europe. Everything was two hours away by rail there.

She looked at her iPod, pressing the arrow button. It was stuffed to the gills with songs and she couldn't find the one she was looking for. Who would have thought that in the years since she had left Mexico she had never once bothered to purchase a single album by Duncan Dhu?

Meche took out the earbuds.

*   *   *

MECHE STOPPED BEFORE the door and knocked three times in quick succession. The lock turned and Sebastián stood there, looking at her suspiciously, like she had sneaked into his building to smuggle a bomb.

"Mercedes," he said.

It was probably the first and only time in his life that he had used her real name as opposed to the nickname. Nobody, ever, called her Mercedes. Least of all him, spitting her name out like it was a kick to the gut.

She wondered if he was going to slam the door in her face and start yelling in Catalán.

"I need to give these back to you," she said, handing him the box with the shoes. "They are yours."

"I gave them—"

"They don't belong to me," she said. "I can't take them."

Sebastián cleared his throat rather loudly but did not attempt to dissuade her. He grabbed the box and set it aside, on a small table sitting by the door.

"I thought you were flying out today," he said. His gaze was not on her face but instead had fixed on a point over her shoulder.

"I was, but then the weirdest thing happened."

"What, exactly?"

"Do you know the distance between Oslo and Mexico City?" she asked him.

Sebastián frowned. He turned his face a couple of millimeters, then looked down at her fully, though with caution.

"About 9,200 kilometres. I've measured it on a map. Bad habit."

"That's quite a few kilometres."

"Yeah."

Meche looked down, nodding and shuffling a step closer to him.

"I looked it up when I was at the airport."

"And then you decided to return my shoes and tell me that factoid?"

"You are not going to make this easy on me, are you?" she said, crossing her arms.

Sebastián leaned against the door frame, all tall and smirking. He rubbed a finger against the wooden door frame, as though he were checking that the varnish was intact.

"No," he said, staring at her. "Why should I?"

"I'd appreciate the favour."

"I'd appreciate the speech, thank you."

"I'm not giving you a speech," she said. "It's not one of your books."

Besides, she was bad with words. They came out all crooked and deformed and sounded just plain wrong. Numbers and music: those she could work with.

"Mix-tapes are outdated so I decided to make a playlist for you. Kind of like you did before when you gave me that soundtrack. You know, this is a sort of... I'm afraid it's a..."

"Present?" he finished for her.

"Something like that," she said, extending the iPod towards him.

"Love letter."

Meche said nothing to that, rolling her eyes. But he waited and she recalled how he was extremely stubborn and patient. They could probably stand there, at the doorway, for an entire decade and he would not budge until she'd spelled it out.

"Take the iPod."

"I don't know. You're missing three words."

"You know I—"

Meche sputtered a word that was not a word. More like a string of consonants without a single vowel in between them.

"Just fucking take it," she said.

Meche waved the iPod and the earbuds before him. Sebastián put them on. He pushed the play button. He clicked it again, looked at the LCD display and shook his head.

"I don't hear anything."

"It's empty."

He looked at her in confusion.

"We need to make a new soundtrack. Together," Meche said with a shrug.

"Together as in I—"

"Jeg elsker deg," she said, feeling breathless when she spoke, like she'd been running for a long time. And maybe she had, just like her father had run. From responsibilities, from failure and heartache. But she'd discovered there's some truth to the ballads and she wasn't too old to learn new tunes.

"Meaning?"

"They're words, alright? It counts. I'll buy you a Norwegian dictionary."

Sebastián smiled very slowly and pulled the earbuds away, stuffing them in his pockets.

"And what will be the first song?" he asked.

"I figure Absolute Beginners, though if you don't like Bowie—"

She was going to suggest a whole swathe of songs. Somewhere Only We Know by Keane if he wanted to go recent and even Coldplay's Swallowed in the Sea and the Goo Goo Dolls with Iris if he wanted to be cliché and had never watched *Wings of Desire*, which was a much better movie than that Hollywood crap they called a remake. Though if he mentioned I Can't Fight This Feeling Anymore she was going to just stomp away. There were some things she would not accept.

Not even for him.

"Bowie will do," Sebastián said, interrupting her with a kiss.

She twined her fingers into his hair and smiled against his lips.

"Want to see the Northern Lights this weekend?" she asked.

"Sure. It's about time."

Mexico City, 1984

A GIRL SITS outside her apartment building, headphones on, listening to her music. She has a bag of potato chips, a bottle of soda and her idle thoughts. She'll do her homework later. For now, as the sun rolls down, she simply taps her foot to the rhythm of the music and listens to one of her dad's tapes. It's Boston singing More Than a Feeling. She sips her soda.

A man walks a dog. The seller of camotes pushes his cart. Kids kick a soccer ball down the street.

The girl scratches her leg. She's awkward and dressed in clothes a size too large. Her hair falls loose below her shoulders.

A boy walks on the other side of the street and glances at her. Something clicks in her brain and she thinks this is the new kid. The weirdo who lugs all those books around. She saw him with a book called *Tales of Mystery & Imagination* and she wants to ask him how it connects with Alan Parsons Project because she doesn't understand that album.

A BOY DRAGS the market bag with him trying to remember the things he's supposed to get. A kilo of tortillas. On the way back, two litres of milk and a box of detergent. He repeats them in his head as he walks—Tortillas. Milk. Detergent.

He shuffles his feet. He's a tall kid. He's skinny and dark, his long fingers curling around the plastic handle of the bag.

There's a girl his age sitting on the bottom step of an apartment building, listening to music.

The boy keeps to himself and walks with his head down, but he raises his eyes to look at her because she looks kind of funny with those big headphones on her ears.

She stares right at him. The look is like having a pin inserted into his chest. He stumbles, shifts, switches the bag from one hand to the other.

"Hey, horse-face!" she yells.

He blinks.

She takes off her headphones and points at him.

"Yeah, you. Do you like music?"

"No, sorry," he says, shrugging.

"That's too bad."

He should have said 'yes'. Maybe she would have played with him if he did. He can't make friends. He always botches it.

"Do you like potato chips?"

"I like chips," he says.

"What ya' doing over there then?"

He crosses the street and sits next to her, setting his bag on the ground. He forgets he had to run errands for his mother.

*   *   *

SHE OFFERS HIM her chips and he takes a few.

"I'm Sebastián," he says.

"I'm Meche."

"Hi."

"Hi."

He grins at her with ease even though things like this—smiling, chatting, being friendly—are never easy for him. It feels easy now.

She smiles back. It's not her usual drill. She's a scowler. Even though she's just about to hit puberty she can already tell being a teenager is going to be a load of crap. She smiles brightly for him because she feels bright, like someone lit a match.

THEY SIT TOGETHER and watch the world go by.

Deep down they know one fine morning they'll run away together to a place where the sun shines at midnight.

About the Author

Silvia Moreno-Garcia is the author of the novels *Velvet Was the Night*, *Mexican Gothic*, *Gods of Jade and Shadow*, and a bunch of other books. She has also edited several anthologies, including the World Fantasy Award-winning *She Walks in Shadows* (a.k.a. *Cthulhu's Daughters*).

silviamoreno-garcia.com
@silviamg

FIND US ONLINE!

www.rebellionpublishing.com

/rebellionpub   /rebellionpublishing   /rebellionpublishing

SIGN UP TO OUR NEWSLETTER!

rebellionpublishing.com/newsletter

YOUR REVIEWS MATTER!

Enjoy this book? Got something to say?

Leave a review on Amazon, GoodReads or with your
favourite bookseller and let the world know!